THE Captive MAIDEN

Other books by Melanie Dickerson

The Healer's Apprentice
The Merchant's Daughter
The Fairest Beauty

MELANIE DICKERSON

ZONDERVAN

The Captive Maiden

This title is also available as a Zondervan ebook.
Visit www.zondervan.com/ebooks.

Requests for information should be addressed to:
Zondervan, *3900 Sparks Dr. SE, Grand Rapids, Michigan 49546*

Library of Congress Cataloging-in-Publication Data

Dickerson, Melanie.
The captive maiden / Melanie Dickerson.
p. cm.
"This title is also available as a Zondervan ebook."
Summary: In this story loosely based on the Cinderella fairy tale, Gisela is determined to get an invitation to the ball being thrown for the duke's son, Valten, but meeting him may not lead to her happily-ever-after.
ISBN 978-0-310-72441-4 (softcover)
[1. Love—Fiction. 2. Stepfamilies—Fiction. 3. Middle Ages—Fiction. 4. Christian life—Fiction.] I. Title.
PZ7.D5575Cap 2013
[Fic]—dc23 2013034791

Published in association with the Books & Such Literary Agency, 52 Mission Circle, Suite 122, PMB 170, Santa Rosa, CA 95409-5370, *www.booksandsuch.com.*

Cover design and photography: Mike Heath/Magnus Creative
Interior design: Publication Services, Inc. and Greg Johnson/Textbook Perfect

Printed in the United States of America

14 15 16 17 18 19 20 21 /QG/ 21 20 19 18 17 16 15 14 13 12 11 10 9 8 7 6 5 4 3

Spring, 1403, Hagenheim Region

Gisela huddled by the fire in her attic chamber, clutching the miniature portrait that fit in her hand. The artist had painted it the year before, when Gisela was seven. Father had been so handsome.

Now that Gisela was eight and Father was gone, life could never be the same. If only she had stayed seven forever.

"I love you," she whispered, kissing her portrait-father's cheek as a tear dripped off her chin.

Her stepmother's unforgiving wooden pattens clicked up the steps that led to Gisela's attic room.

"Gisela!" Evfemia called.

She thrust the portrait back inside the hole in the fireplace wall and pushed in the loose brick, then kicked the ashes into the fire to smother it.

"Gisela! What are you doing?" Evfemia towered over her. "You have cinders on your hands. And your feet!"

Gisela made her face a blank as she stared at the floor.

Lighter footfalls clattered up the stairs and Gisela's two stepsisters pushed against their mother's silk skirt, staring out from behind her.

Irma was the oldest, and her long, thin face and squinty-eyed expression made Gisela wonder if the girl had a bad taste in her mouth. She had the same limp brown hair as her sister, Contzel, but that was the only trait they had in common. Contzel's cheeks were round and chapped pink, and her face was forever relaxed, her mouth open, as if she had just awakened from a nap.

Frau Evfemia raised one brow. "Go down to the stable and help the groomsman get the horses ready."

When Gisela hesitated, Evfemia screamed, "Obey me this moment or I will throw you out into the cold!"

Gisela darted forward, hoping to run past her snarling, red-faced stepmother and her two smirking stepsisters. But Evfemia reached out and snatched Gisela's hair, wrenching her head halfway to the floor before she let go.

Gisela stumbled but kept running down the stairs and to the stable, rubbing her stinging scalp.

When she arrived, Wido the groomsman was leading one of the carriage horses out of the paddocks.

"Frau Evfemia sent me to help you."

Old Wido frowned at Gisela. "She shouldn't be sending you, the young miss, to help me with the horses."

Gisela wiped her nose with the back of her hand and shook her head. "I want to help."

Gisela went in to lead the second horse out. She stood on tiptoe to rub the black horse's cheek. "Come on, boy." Gisela sniffed and took a deep breath. The big horse nudged her shoulder and let her lead him outside.

Following Wido's instructions, she positioned the horses before the carriage and kept each one steady as the harnesses were put into place. Just as both were hitched and ready to go, Gisela's stepmother, along with Irma and Contzel, came out of the house and flounced toward them.

Irma stared at Gisela with cold, contemptuous eyes as she waited for Contzel to climb in.

"Go ahead, darling," Frau Evfemia crooned, helping Irma up the step the groomsman had placed before them.

Her stepmother glanced down at Gisela with raised eyebrows, then climbed into the carriage and latched the door. They had said nothing about where they were going or when they would be back. As they left, the pain inside her chest increased until it threatened to overwhelm her.

"Why would I care where they're going? I don't care if I'm all alone. I like being alone." The pain lifted a little, so she went on. "I don't care if they hate me. I don't care about them at all." She clenched her fist. "And I don't care if they never come back."

Gisela went back inside the stable, feeling better than she had in a long time, and she concluded it was better not to care. The next time she felt the pain of her stepmother's cruelty or her stepsisters' disgust, she would remind herself that she didn't care.

She found her favorite horse, Kaeleb. The light brown destrier hung his head over the stall door and whinnied at her. Gisella stood on a stool and rubbed his cheek and pressed her forehead against his neck. "I wish they wouldn't come back."

But they would.

She began helping Wido muck out the stables and fetch hay for the horses. Another thing Gisela concluded was that horses were much more lovable than people.

"Little miss, you mustn't stay out here any longer." Wido took the pitchfork from her. "It's too cold. Go on to the house with you."

Her worn-thin dress was not very warm and she was shivering. And yet, she hesitated. Perhaps if she took the blanket off her bed, she could sleep in the stable atop a pile of straw in Kaeleb's stall. It probably wouldn't be any colder than her fireless room.

"Go on, now." Wido shooed her toward the house.

Relenting, Gisela turned and ran inside. She stirred up the dwindling fire in the great hall but dared not add any more wood.

Her stepmother did not allow her to "waste" wood. Shivering, she stepped inside the giant fireplace and knelt among the dying embers where it was warm. Her dress was already dirty from the ashes in her bedchamber fireplace, in addition to being torn and permanently stained over most of the fabric, as it was a cast-off of a former servant, having been altered to fit her eight-year-old body. Besides, she could wash it tomorrow.

She put her cold fingers under her arms and leaned her shoulder against the heat of the fireplace bricks. "I don't care what they think of me. I don't care what they do." If her father was here, he'd never let her stepmother deny her a fire in her room or treat Gisela like a servant. But she reminded herself she didn't care.

She imagined her father and mother in heaven, picturing how they would welcome her—hugging her, kissing her, their arms warming her. The thought was so comforting, she relaxed inside the fireplace, leaning her cheek against her folded hands.

Gisela woke to cackling laughter. She opened her eyes to her stepmother and stepsisters standing in front of the fireplace.

Irma pointed her skinny finger at Gisela, her face twisted in a sneer. "Lying in the cinders like an addlepate."

"She's filthy." Contzel wrinkled her nose.

Evfemia planted her fists on her hips. "Get up from there, you ridiculous girl, and go to your chamber. You shall scrub every inch of the floor from this fireplace to your door, as you couldn't possibly make a step without strewing filth everywhere. I don't know where you got such a notion, to sit in the fireplace among the cinders."

Gisela stood.

Irma clapped her hands and squealed. "I know. Instead of *Gis*ela, we'll call her *Cinders*-ela." All three of them laughed.

"Cindersela!" "Always dirty!" "The girl who smells like cinders and horses."

With the taunts and laughter ringing in her ears, Gisela walked with her head held high all the way up the stairs to her room.

Gisela changed out of her ragged work clothes, put on her nightdress, and washed her face in the cold water of her basin. Today she had washed every window on all three floors of the house, she'd helped Wido muck out the stables, and she'd mended two of Irma's dresses. She had cleaned up the mess Contzel's puppy made in the dining hall. And she cleaned the mess the puppy made on the stairs. And in the solar. And in Contzel's chamber. And then the snippy animal bit her on the ankle.

She did not like that dog.

Gisela wrapped herself in a blanket and sat on the bench in front of her window. Across the hills, over the city wall to the north, stood Hagenheim Castle, barely visible through the deepening night except for its five towers interrupting the horizon. The castle towers' lit windows seemed to carry her back to a year ago.

When she was still seven, and before her father died, the Duke of Hagenheim and his oldest son, Valten, had come to buy a horse from her father, because, as Father said, he bred and raised the best horses in the region. Valten wanted a war horse, a destrier that would serve him as he practiced jousting and other war games.

The two of them, Duke Wilhelm and his son, rode up the lane to her house. Duke Wilhelm and her father greeted each other like old friends. The duke's son was fourteen, and Gisela had been seven. Valten was already quite as tall as her father and broad-shouldered. She remembered his hair was blond, and he'd looked at her with keen eyes and a sober expression.

Within the first moments, she decided she did not like him. He had come to take one of her horses away, and worst of all, this boy meant to ride her horse in the lists. She didn't want one of her horses competing in the dangerous joust, risking serious injuries with each charge.

But the boy and his father treated the horses gently and respectfully. From several feet away she had watched as they examined all the youngest destriers. By the time the duke's son made his choice, Gisela realized he would love the horse, would take care of him. The horse would have many adventures with the duke's son, more than Gisela could give him.

As their fathers settled their price, Gisela watched Valten—she was supposed to call him Lord Hamlin, as he was the Earl of Hamlin, but she thought his given name suited him better—as the young earl rubbed the horse's nose and cheek and talked softly to him.

"He likes carrots."

Valten turned and looked at her. "Then I shall make sure he gets some."

Valten displayed compassion, where her new stepmother and stepsisters showed none. And even though he was taking away one of her horses, she could not hate him. In her mind, she had believed he would treat the destrier well.

Tonight as it grew dark, she wondered what Valten and the horse were doing. Was the horse well? What had Valten named him? Did the horse like training for the jousting tournaments? Were they both happy? Her thoughts, as they often did, gradually focused on Valten alone, the handsome young heir to the duchy of Hagenheim. Did his mother kiss him good night the way her father used to kiss her? Valten was probably too old for that. Was he still handsome? Who would he marry? His bride would be pretty and certainly would not smell like cinders and horses.

Gisela imagined herself grown up, wearing beautiful clothes, and Valten coming to find her and asking her to be his bride. Valten would want to marry someone kind, wouldn't he? Someone who believed in goodness and mercy and love.

And in spite of the fact that her father was dead and her stepmother and stepsisters hated her, she did believe in goodness, mercy, and love.

Valten would never be cruel. He would be kind and good. At least, she liked to think so.

Gisela turned away from the window and the sight of the castle towers in the distance. She climbed into bed, clutching her blanket to her chin, and closed her eyes. "*Guten nacht*, Valten."

Chapter 1

Nine Years Later . . . Spring, 1412, a few miles west of Hagenheim.

Gisela rode Kaeleb over the hilly meadows near her home, letting the horse run as fast as he liked. The morning air clung to her eyelashes, as a fog had created a misty canopy over the green, rolling hills. The wall surrounding the town of Hagenheim stood at her far right, with the forest to her left and her home behind. Hagenheim Castle hovered in the distance, its upper towers lost in the haze.

If her stepmother found out she'd been riding one of the horses without permission, as Gisela often did, she would find some way to punish her. But Gisela didn't care. She could leave any time she wanted to, as she had hidden away the money her father had given her just before he died. She chose to stay, at least for now, because of her love for the horses.

Gisela would probably be forced to leave soon. Her stepmother would end up selling all the horses, or would marry someone despicable, or would create some other type of intolerable situation. When that happened, Gisela planned to go into the town and find paying work, perhaps tending a shop or serving as a kitchen maid at Hagenheim Castle.

Evfemia thought she controlled Gisela. But some day her stepdaughter-slave would be gone.

She didn't want to think about her stepmother anymore. Instead, Gisela focused on the wind in her hair as she flew over the meadow on Kaeleb's back. The cool air filled her lungs almost to bursting. For this moment, she was free.

Kaeleb loved these rides as much as she did. She could sense it in the tightness of his shoulders, in the way he fairly danced in anticipation before she even tightened his saddle in place.

Movement to her left made her turn her head slightly. A horse and rider emerged from the trees and stood watching her from the edge of the meadow.

Gradually, Gisela slowed Kaeleb. She could tell even from this distance the horse and rider were both taller than average. The bare-headed man had short, dark blond hair and wore a green thigh-length tunic that buttoned down the front. His horse was the same size and color as Kaeleb.

The man reminded her of Valten—more appropriately known as Lord Hamlin.

The duke's oldest son had been away for two years, but she'd heard of his return. Gisela figured he would be about twenty-four years old now, as it had been ten years since he and his father had come to buy a horse.

She turned Kaeleb back the way they had come. But instead of riding away, she stared at the man. He seemed comfortable in the saddle, and he held his head high and his back straight. No doubt Valten was proud and self-possessed, but was he also still the kind, gentle boy she had dreamed about as a child?

Probably not. But why should she care? She had ceased daydreaming about him years ago, when she realized she was but a servant now and no longer the wealthy land owner's daughter whose father had been so friendly with Duke Wilhelm.

She glanced down at her coarse woolen overdress. She'd tucked her skirt into her waistband, exposing the leather stockings she wore to cover her legs while she rode, since she hated riding sidesaddle. Her feet were bare and dirty, and her hair was completely unfettered, as she liked to feel the wind lifting and tossing the long strands.

She wouldn't want the duke's son to see her looking this way, if this was indeed Valten. He would mistake her for a peasant, which, when she thought on it, she might as well be, given her position in her stepmother's household.

Gisela urged Kaeleb forward, and soon they were flying back over the hills again. She wasn't running away from the duke's son; she had to go home, for her stepmother and stepsisters would be demanding their breakfast soon, and she still had to give Kaeleb a good brushing after their ride. Besides, Valten, the tournament champion and future leader of Hagenheim, would hardly care to get acquainted with her, the stable hand, cook, and all-around servant for a spoiled, selfish trio of women.

As a little girl she had imagined marrying Lord Hamlin. Now, she knew it was a silly dream. Though she had once cared very much about Valten—following the reports from town of his accomplishments as a tournament champion—it was getting easier to tell herself he couldn't be as noble and good as she had imagined. Her usual trick to keep from feeling bad—to tell herself that she didn't care—worked nearly as well with Valten as with everything else.

Valten strolled through the *Marktplatz* for the first time since leaving Hagenheim two years ago. Very little had changed. The vendors were the same. Same old wares—copper pots and leather goods—carrots, beets, leeks, onions, and cabbages laid out in rows of tidy little bunches. People talked loud to be heard over the bustle of market day. They stepped around the horse dung on the cobblestones while brushing shoulders with the other townspeople. Everyone had somewhere to go, a purpose.

What was his purpose?

A restlessness possessed him, the same restlessness that had haunted his wandering all over the Continent. Entering all the grandest tournaments for two years had not eased that restless feeling. He'd succeeded at winning all of them in at least one category—jousting, sword fighting, hand-to-hand combat—but often in all categories. He still wasn't a champion at archery, which rankled. But he couldn't be perfect at everything.

Perhaps God had given him archery to keep him humble. Archery, and his little brother Gabe.

He couldn't truly blame his brother. Gabe had seen an opportunity to make a name for himself and he had taken it. Valten would have done the same. And Gabe probably hadn't *intended* to steal his betrothed.

He didn't like to relive those memories. He'd forgiven his brother, and truthfully, Valten had not been in love with Sophie. He hadn't even known her. Now he couldn't imagine being married to her. She was Gabe's wife, and he didn't begrudge them their happiness or doubt that it was God's will that the two of them were together. But he had been made to look foolish when everyone wondered why Gabehart, Valten's younger, irresponsible brother, was marrying Valten's betrothed.

Why was he even dwelling on this?

He shoved the thoughts away and instead dwelt on the last tournament, where he'd defeated Friedric Ruexner, the man who seemed determined to be his nemesis. Ruexner had tried to trick the judges in Saillenay by substituting a metal-tipped lance for a wooden one when tilting with Valten. But in spite of his lack of chivalry, or perhaps because of it, Ruexner seemed to take special offense every time Valten bested him.

Valten had defeated Ruexner in many tourneys over the years, although the man had defeated him a few times as well, usually under suspicious circumstances. And now Valten was always watching his back, for Friedric Ruexner had muttered a vow of vengeance at their last meeting. But that only meant Valten would relish defeating him all the more in the next tournament, which was to be held here in Hagenheim, hosted by his own father, Duke Wilhelm.

Valten wandered past a vender selling colorful veils and scarves from the Orient, which reminded him of all his travels. Truth be told, he was beginning to weary of the tournaments. He had hardly admitted the fact to himself, and certainly hadn't told anyone else. His dream, his goal all his life, had been to distinguish himself in each competition, to be the best at all modes of war, to be known far and wide as the champion of … everything. And now people far and wide knew his name, troubadours sang about him, wealthy and titled men's daughters in every town wanted him to wear their colors, and their fathers offered him money and jewels to make their daughters his wife.

He liked the acclaim. All the fame and attention had assuaged his hurt pride after his betrothed chose to marry his brother, but he was tired of that life. What was he accomplishing? What good did it do anyone for him to win another tournament? What good did it do him?

He continued through the marketplace. Most people stayed out of his way and didn't make eye contact. He was used to that; men of his size were often hired soldiers or guards, and sometimes bullies. Valten had been away so long that his people—the people he would lead upon his father's death—didn't recognize him. He wore his hair shorter, he had new scars on his face from his many battles, and today he was wearing nondescript clothing—a knee-length cotehardie of brown leather that laced up the sides and made him look like a farmer just come to town to buy and sell. A few people did stare, as though trying to remember him, but Valten kept walking.

As he wandered, a girl of perhaps seventeen or eighteen years caught his eye. Truthfully, it was her hair that fixed his attention—long and blonde, and somehow it reminded him of his sister Margaretha's hair, even though his sister's was reddish brown. It must have been the thick wildness of it, and that, instead of being covered or braided, it was tied at the end, at her waist, with a piece of rough twine. It also reminded him of someone else, someone he'd seen recently ... Yes. The girl he'd seen riding at great speed across the meadow just outside the town wall.

The girl's coarse gray overgown was covered with patches and odd seams where someone had mended it.

She was arguing with a man over something he was selling.

"You told me it cost three marks and now you say five." Her speech sounded strangely cultured, not like an ignorant country girl.

Also at odds with her dress was the horse whose bridle she was holding. He was magnificent, a horse worthy of carrying a king. Had the girl stolen him?

"I never told you three," the man yelled back. "You're daft."

"I'm not daft, but you are a liar."

"You dare call me a liar?" The man leaned toward her menacingly.

The horse reared, striking the man's flimsy, makeshift counter with his front hoof. The man threw his arms up in front of his face as the rough beam of wood crashed down. The side of his awning gave way, and a rope hung with leather goods fell to the ground, the collapsed fabric on top of it.

"Give me my money back," the girl said, unruffled by

the chaos her horse had caused, "and I'll give you back your saddlebag."

"Get your crazy horse out of here!" The man slung his arm wide, cursing under his breath as he stared at the mess at his feet. "Be gone, and take the saddlebag with you." He shook his head, muttering and stooping to pick up his goods, then struggling to push the wooden beam back into place in order to set his booth to rights again.

The girl, whose face Valten still couldn't see, walked away, a leather saddlebag in her hand and her now-calm horse beside her.

Valten followed, almost certain she and her horse were the same horse and rider he'd seen two mornings ago. He continued to admire both her hair and her horse. In fact, the animal looked almost exactly like Valten's own horse, Sieger, the faithful destrier he'd ridden in every tournament. This horse could be his twin.

The girl bought a sweet roll from a plump old woman, then pulled a piece of carrot from her pocket and gave it to the horse, who deftly plucked it from her palm. She gave him a second carrot, then ate her bun as she made her way between the rows of vendors.

Valten admired the way she walked: confident, flowing, graceful, but with a hint of boyishness, as if her horse was more important to her than her hair or clothing. Yes, she was the type to ride astride, instead of sidesaddle, especially if no one was looking. He recalled how she'd given that remarkable beast a free rein when they'd galloped across the open meadow. Her hair had looked like liquid gold in the sun, streaming behind her. But he still hadn't gotten a good look at her face.

Her horse was limping slightly. Had she noticed? The girl was leaving the Marktplatz now and heading toward a side street. He wanted to see where she was going, but more than that, he was curious to see her face.

Just before she entered the side street, Friedric Ruexner appeared around a half-timbered building from the opposite direction, laughing and walking toward them with his squire and two other bearded, unkempt men.

Valten stopped and waited beside a bakery doorway. His nemesis approached the girl. Friedric Ruexner sneered, which drew his lips back and showed his yellow teeth.

The girl planted her feet on the cobblestones in a defiant stance as she stared Ruexner in the eye. Her horse snorted and shook his head restlessly.

Valten was close enough to catch most of their words. "... Too much horse for a girl like you. Where are you going with that fine beast?" Ruexner asked her.

"I have business, and it isn't with you," the girl retorted. "Move out of my way."

"A feisty one." Ruexner looked around at his companions, and all three laughed, continuing to block her way to the side street. He looked her up and down, then muttered something to his companions.

Valten stepped out and strode toward them. "We do not allow anyone to accost maidens in Hagenheim, Ruexner."

The smile left Friedric's dark, brutish face. "Valten Gerstenberg."

"The girl isn't interested in whatever you're offering."

From the corner of his eye, he could see her looking from himself to Ruexner and back again.

Ruexner focused on the girl. "I will fight you for this one."

"No. You will leave her alone, or you'll pay the consequences."

Indecision played over Ruexner's wide brow; he was obviously trying to decide his next move. Finally, he chuckled. "Too bad you came along when you did. The good knight and his good deeds." He turned his head slightly toward his companions. "Valten keeps a close eye on his townspeople—when he happens to be here."

Valten crossed his arms while he waited for their scoffing laughter to die down. "For once you are right."

Friedric Ruexner leaned toward Valten, his upper lip curled in menace. "I will be here for the tournament, and there I shall defeat you, once and for all."

Valten gave him stare for stare. "We shall see who defeats whom."

Ruexner turned to the girl and ran his hand down her cheek. Her hand flew up and slapped him, the sound echoing off the buildings on either side of the street. He raised his fist. Her horse reared.

Valten stepped forward and caught Ruexner's forearm and wrenched it behind his back. The horse's hooves pawed the air mere inches from Ruexner's face, causing his eyes to go wide and his friends to jump back. Valten let go of his arm, and Ruexner and his lackeys edged away. When they were twenty feet down the street, Ruexner called, "This will be your last tournament, Valten. For every blow you've ever given me, you'll get double. I swear it."

Valten made sure Ruexner and his friends kept walking, and waited to move until they were out of earshot.

When he turned around, the girl was staring at him.

No wonder Ruexner had noticed her. Her eyes were a clear blue, without a hint of gray or green. Her features were bold and generous—long, thick eyelashes, a straight, proud nose, a full brow, a gently squared chin, and high, prominent cheekbones. Her skin fairly glowed, and he had to remind himself to breathe.

She seemed to be studying his face too. "Thank you." She abruptly turned away and continued on her way as if nothing had happened.

He stood stunned. Should he call after her? He only knew he couldn't let her walk away, so he followed her.

As she turned down the narrow street to the blacksmith's,

she looked over her shoulder. "Do you want something, my lord?" She added the last phrase with a bit of slyness in her voice, it seemed. She must realize who he was.

Never good at making conversation with maidens, he ransacked his brain for something appropriate to say. Another way Gabe had been better than him — talking with women. His brother always knew what to say, and it was always something charming or clever. Valten's experience was much different. He'd had little time for women due to his travels and training, and most of the ones he'd met he'd only spoken to briefly. Their fathers had paraded them before him at balls given for the tournament knights, but he'd never known them long enough to feel comfortable. He had not been ready to marry, and therefore he had no interest in showing them how lacking he was in the art of conversation.

He hoped he didn't sound like Ruexner as he said, "A fine destrier you have. He looks very much like my horse, Sieger."

She turned and gave him her full attention. He marveled at her self-reliant expression, a unique trait in a woman, especially one who was less than twenty years old and obviously poor. Or maybe she was only eccentric, wearing ragged clothes to disguise herself, as he was doing.

"Thank you. He is a great horse." Then she turned and continued walking.

He still wasn't ready to let her go.

Chapter 2

He should look like your horse, Gisela almost said. *The two are brothers.* But it was best she didn't tell him. He wouldn't remember her, wouldn't recall that it was her father who had sold him the horse ten years ago — and had been dead almost that many years.

Valten — Lord Hamlin — followed her. But Gisela pretended not to notice, hoping to disguise how seeing him thrilled her and made her heart pound.

It was evident she was a stranger to him, though she would have recognized him even if that disgusting foreign knight hadn't called him "Valten Gerstenberg." His hair was shorter than she remembered and was more of a dark blond. He bore numerous small scars on his face, and his nose was crooked, no doubt from being broken in one of his many jousting tournaments. But his ruggedness, his height and breadth and confident swagger — even his scars — only added to his appeal. And the way he had come to her aid, the kindness and respect that shone from his eyes when he looked at her, made him the most handsome man she had ever seen.

And he'd not been the least afraid of that bully he called Ruexner.

She, on the other hand, had been terrified when the man blocked her way, though she knew better than to show fear.

Spitting fire and giving a man the evil eye usually intimidated him enough that he kept his distance. But this man had two large friends to embolden him.

When Valten appeared by her side, she was so relieved—and thrilled just seeing him—that her knees went weak. But she was also unnerved by her reaction. The response made her feel vulnerable, and she hated feeling vulnerable. So she kept walking, never turning back, when all she really wanted to do was look at him and ask him what his life had been like the past nine years—what he had been doing while she'd been dreaming about him in her desolate room, staring out her cold window and wondering where he was.

She could hear and sense him behind her as she approached the blacksmith's. Did he want to talk to her? What could he possibly want to say? Even if he remembered her as that little girl from so long ago, he certainly hadn't thought about her the way she'd thought about him. Besides that, she was a nobody now, disowned by her stepmother and stepsisters and without family of any kind.

The blacksmith, a burly man covered in soot, turned from his forge as she walked up.

Gisela forced any sign of emotion from her face and focused on her task. "My horse has thrown a shoe. How long to get him fitted with another?"

"One hour. This one's ahead of you." He pointed to a palfrey standing patiently on the tether.

After haggling a price with him, she lifted her arm to take the money from her moneybag, which she kept close to her side. She placed the sum in the blacksmith's sooty palm. Gisela removed Kaeleb's old, ragged saddlebag and stuffed it into the new one hanging over her shoulder, then whispered soft words in the horse's ear while she attached a tether to his bridle.

She turned to leave and found herself face-to-face with

Valten, who was still standing behind her. He was so close she could see the flecks of brown in his green eyes.

"I will escort you … until your horse is ready."

Gisela stared at him a moment before saying, "I thank you."

She was unsure what to do next. Did he want her to take his arm? She walked toward him, trying not to look nervous, and together they started down the street.

Gisela suppressed the smile that tugged at her lips. She was walking beside Valten, future Duke of Hagenheim. She was considered slightly tall for a female, but even so had to look up to see Valten's face.

He looked down and met her eye. "Where would you like to go?"

"I have no more business, except to wait for my horse."

They meandered along a main street in the general direction of the Marktplatz, encountering people leaving the market with their purchases.

Where could they go? She and Valten needed a destination, something to do. Abruptly, Gisela said, "I would like to see your horse."

She couldn't tell if he was surprised, but he looked at her askance from his gray-green eyes. "You like horses?"

"More than people sometimes." She sensed, by the way he was looking at her, that he felt the same way.

Their arms brushed as they passed through a tight crowd.

"We can go to the stable. Sieger expects me to visit him at least once a day."

"I'd like to see him."

Did Valten often meet women in the street and then offer to take them anywhere they wanted to go? She was determined to be on her guard. Could it be that he simply wanted to watch over her until she could return to the blacksmith's shop for her horse? There was something in his eyes, such a look of chivalry.

Though the rest of him had transformed and matured since that day when he was fourteen, his eyes had not changed. Even then, he'd had trustworthy eyes.

"How long have you been away from Hagenheim?" She already knew, but she wanted to hear him speak.

"Two years."

"Your family must have missed you."

"So they told me." Valten rubbed his chin, wincing. "I got scolded quite a bit. All three of my sisters are good at scolding."

She tried to imagine what it must be like to have sisters who cared so much. His younger brother Gabehart, the one who had married Valten's betrothed, had also been away for two years, living in Hohendorf. Did Valten miss him? She thought it best not to ask.

They continued on their way, forced to pass through the Marktplatz to reach the castle stable.

"Are you wearing those clothes to disguise yourself? No one seems to recognize you."

"And yet you knew who I was."

"I heard that coarse fellow say your name."

"Ah." He nodded. "But I am inconspicuous in these clothes, don't you think?"

Gisela allowed herself a brief laugh. "You could hardly be inconspicuous no matter what you wore." Her heart nearly stopped as she realized he could construe her words two different ways. Either she meant he looked so good that it didn't matter what he wore—which was certainly true—or her real meaning, which was that he was so tall and broad and intimidating that he could hardly be missed.

They entered the most crowded part of the town square and were no longer able to converse. She couldn't help but feel pleased at how he kept glancing behind to make sure she was there. When a particularly dirty, burly man stood in their way,

Valten waited for him to pass before leading her forward. A few minutes later, she got distracted by some leather feed bags at one booth and bumped into Valten's back. She felt herself blush, but he pretended not to notice.

They emerged from the packed marketplace, and Hagenheim Castle stood before them as they approached the gatehouse. Valten nodded at the guard, who waved them through while glancing curiously at Gisela.

Once they were inside the castle wall and walking across the quiet yard toward the stable, she asked, "How many horses do you have?"

"Our family owns about thirty, but my father's knights' horses board here too."

Excitement welled inside her as she anticipated seeing so many horses. At one time her father had owned twice that many, but her stepmother had sold them off one by one over the years—often for less than they were worth, since she was ignorant of their value—to satisfy her desire for extravagant clothing and carriages for herself and her daughters. Now her father's stable housed fewer than ten.

As they made their way across the yard toward the stable, Gisela grew impatient with Valten's slow stride, wanting to walk ahead of him as they drew near the dark building, where a horse was whinnying and two men were talking.

The men bowed respectfully when Valten entered, then went back to cleaning stalls.

Valten walked straight to the third stall on the right. A horse that looked almost identical to Kaeleb came and bobbed his head up and down over his stall door. He snuffled as Valten rubbed his cheek.

"This is Sieger."

Gisela held her breath, wondering if the horse would remember her. She let him smell her hand. He held still as she rubbed his forehead. "*Guten morgen*, Sieger."

The big animal stretched his neck and sniffed her hair, then nickered. When he rubbed his head against her shoulder as if he had seen her only yesterday, her heart swelled inside her chest. She rubbed him behind his ear and he nickered again, wiggling his nose and searching her hand, no doubt looking for a carrot. He was remembering how she always fed him his favorite treat.

Valten gazed at her out of the corner of his eye before patting his horse. Sieger ignored him and nudged Gisela's shoulder again.

"I've never seen him act this way with a stranger."

Gisela remembered the last day she'd seen this beautiful creature—a day when life was still happy, when she felt safe and loved, and she still had a father to protect her. Seeing Sieger made her remember all the other horses she'd said good-bye to over the years.

"Perhaps he does know me." She rubbed the destrier's nose affectionately, breathing into his nostrils.

She could feel Valten's eyes on her. With a final pat, she reluctantly moved away from Sieger and turned to Valten. "Can you show me your other horses?"

Valten stared a moment, then said, "Have you seen Sieger before?"

Gisela smiled innocently. "How could I?"

He frowned at her, then led her to the next stall, introducing her first to his courser, then to several other mounts, including the ponies and palfreys preferred by his three sisters. She got an idea about each sister's personality as she got to know that girl's horse, and as she listened to the small but pertinent information Valten gave about each one.

"Margaretha's favorite horse is this palfrey." Valten led her to a horse with friendly eyes and a white blaze on her forehead. "Her horse loves to run, but she's gentle and obedient."

They moved to the next stall. "Kirstyn's horse is calm and easy to manage, but she doesn't like crowds."

Gisela stopped to let the mare get a good look at her and sniff her hand before she rubbed the horse's head.

"And this is Adela's pony. We call her Dizzy because she dances around a lot."

The pony was gray with white spots, a shaggy mane, and shy eyes. Gisela rubbed the pony and talked to him softly.

As much as she enjoyed meeting his sisters' favorite horses, she found herself wishing she could meet his sisters and also see Valten with them. She imagined the youngest one asking him to play. He would pretend to be impatient with her—at first. When she begged, she imagined him eventually giving in, patiently playing a game with them. He would give her a piggyback ride and let them bring out a playful side he didn't show anyone else. Yes, she would very much enjoy seeing him with his family.

But how was that ever to be? She would enjoy this hour with him, then savor it in her memory, tucking it beside the memory of him when he was fourteen. It would comfort her when she felt alone, along with the few memories she was still able to retain about her father.

A groom, upon Valten's request, returned with a few carrots. Valten handed half of them to Gisela. "Sieger likes carrots. They're his favorite."

Gisela bit back a smile as she fed her carrots to Sieger while Valten distributed his carrots to the others.

She watched Valten out of the corner of her eye, trying to burn his every feature in her memory. She took note of his clean-shaven jawline, the small hollow above the middle of his top lip … Staring at his lips made her heart skip a beat, so she shifted her gaze to his eyes. His lashes and brows were thick and darker than his hair.

Afraid he might notice her staring, she ducked behind Sieger and gave the horse a final rub, pressing her cheek against his.

She hated to spoil the moment with thoughts of her stepmother, but Evfemia would be finishing her shopping and would want Gisela to hitch Kaeleb back up to the carriage. She should hurry, since Evfemia wouldn't hesitate to cause an embarrassing scene if she couldn't find her stepdaughter. And if she knew Gisela had spent the last hour with the duke's oldest son, it would be even worse. For years, the woman had been scheming a way for her daughter, Irma, to marry the future duke of Hagenheim, or to at least meet him and talk to him. She'd be jealous fit to die if she knew Gisela had done by accident something all her scheming had failed to do.

"I should be getting back to the blacksmith's."

"Let us go, then."

"You don't have to escort me." It was best for both of them if no one saw them together. Her stepmother and stepsisters would humiliate her in front of him.

"With Ruexner prowling around, yes, I do."

She thought it better not to argue with a man who looked as determined and grim as Valten. His face was like chiseled stone. Best to just say, "Thank you" and pray they didn't encounter her stepfamily.

They walked along, discussing the horses and their different characteristics. But once they reached the Marktplatz, she remained alert, hoping they could get to the blacksmith's shop before she saw her stepmother.

Her eyes darted in every direction, Valten noted, as they made their way through the Marktplatz, as though she was looking for someone. And Valten didn't think that person was Ruexner. She'd been confident when she'd encountered that rogue — now she seemed nervous.

He couldn't look at her without thinking how beautiful she was. Where did she come from? When would he see her again? He couldn't let her go without finding out who she was. But the noise of the crowd made it momentarily impossible to ask her anything.

A woman suddenly grabbed her by her arm and yanked, making her stumble. "Where have you been?" the woman screeched.

Valten stepped up, getting between the extravagantly dressed woman and the girl. Startled, the woman took a step back but didn't let go of her arm.

"It's all right." The girl looked at him with pleading, desperate eyes. "Just let me go with her."

"Who is she?" he demanded, this woman who was dressed like a queen and would dare hurt her.

"My stepmother." She turned and walked away with the woman.

The woman squawked, "Who is that man? What are you about?"

They walked away and were quickly swallowed by the throng.

Chapter 3

Gisela walked as quickly as possible as they squeezed their way through the crowded town square. Her stepmother's grip was painful, but Gisela didn't pull away, in case Valten was following. She didn't want to cause a scene or slow her stepmother down, as then Valten would see how she was treated. Not that he would ever see her again.

Her stepmother was still asking questions. "Who was that man?"

"One of the duke's knights." It wasn't a lie exactly. He was a knight, and he did belong to the duke.

"What were you doing with him?"

"He asked to escort me while my horse was at the blacksmith's." Gisela stumbled. She caught herself before she fell on her knees in the street, then she yanked loose from her stepmother's grip.

On the other side of the Marktplatz, they were joined by Irma and Contzel, who turned their haughty noses up at Gisela and began piling their packages and bags in her arms. Sir Edgar's daughter, Rainhilda, stood beside Irma. Rainhilda closed her eyes and turned away, as if looking at Gisela upset her delicate constitution. She wore an elaborate headdress, complete with a gauzy veil and exotic plumage, which made her as out of place at the Hagenheim Marktplatz as a peacock in a dovecote, and even more conspicuous.

The townspeople gaped at Rainhilda, but not just because of her headdress. Her beauty was unrivaled, except perhaps by the duke's daughters, and they were still a bit young. Her father had been rewarded by the king for service rendered, and next to Duke Wilhelm, Sir Edgar's was one of the wealthiest and most powerful families in the region. A popular speculation of the people was that Rainhilda was hoping—expecting—Valten to designate her the Queen of Beauty and Love at the Hagenheim tournament in two weeks. The tournament champion, whom everyone believed would be Valten, would be allowed to choose one young maiden to sit on the throne for the final display of arms.

Rainhilda looked coifed and pampered. From underneath her headdress her golden hair hung in perfect ringlets, like shavings from a woodworker's planing blade. The precise folds of her veil and the vibrant pink of her flat, rolled turban accented her pale skin to great advantage.

Irma had managed to endear herself to Rainhilda with gifts and flattery and gossip. Gisela had overheard her stepmother's whispered counsel to her daughters to ingratiate themselves to Rainhilda in order to get closer to the duke's family, and most particularly his oldest son. But how on earth Evfemia could think Valten would ever look twice at homely, sticklike Irma, Gisela couldn't imagine.

She hoped she never had to see Valten with Rainhilda, to witness her triumphant smirk as she flirted with confident abandon. It would only make it painfully clear how impossible it would be for someone like him to care for someone like Gisela. With her wild hair and ragged clothes, Gisela was certainly no Rainhilda.

She walked to the carriage and dumped her stepmother's and stepsisters' purchases inside. She continued on to the blacksmith's shop. Once there, she quickly thanked him and took Kaeleb's reins.

When she turned, Valten was striding toward her. She drew in a quick breath at the fierce protectiveness in his eyes.

"Will you be at the tournament?" His question was almost a demand.

"I . . . I will try." She wanted to touch his arm, his hand, to feel a connection with him before she said good-bye. But that was foolish. He was the duke's son and she was little more than a servant in her stepmother's house.

"I don't even know your name."

Gisela glanced over his shoulder. Irma, Contzel, and Evfemia were standing at the carriage, staring suspiciously at her. But at least Rainhilda wasn't with them.

"I can't talk now." She tried to walk past him.

"Come to the tournament." He touched her elbow. "Please."

The intensity in his eyes made it impossible to look away.

"Cinders-ela!" Irma screeched, then laughed.

"We are waiting for you, Cinders-ela!" Contzel added.

Gisela's cheeks burned. She brushed past Valten with Kaeleb, but Valten touched her arm again.

"Gisela," she said, looking into his eyes one last time. "My name is Gisela." Then she turned and continued walking away from Valten.

Chapter 4

Evfemia leveled a steely, dark glare at Gisela. No doubt she was thinking of some punishment for her. For what? For speaking to a man? Or for taking too long to get the horse hitched back up to the carriage? Likely both. But Gisela didn't care. Not even her stepmother could ruin this day for her. She would remember it forever as the best day of her life.

Gisela, as usual, drove them home sitting on the coachman's box. Evfemia probably considered it another method of humiliation, but Gisela loved the arrangement. She could see everything, and she loved the bustling atmosphere of town. Besides, in the driver's seat she was closer to the horses.

When they arrived home, Gisela helped brush the animals down and get them fed. As she walked toward the house, thoughts of Valten paraded through her head. She wanted to hold on to everything he had said, envision every detail of his face, and recall the way he paid attention to his horses, which somehow reminded her of how she'd felt about her father. Valten had even noticed Sieger's special reaction to her, how he had remembered her. Perhaps he—

"Gisela!" Evfemia yelled through the open window.

She saved the memories for later and went inside the house.

Evfemia met her in the great room. "I suppose you're going

to turn out like most serving girls—lewd and brazen and offering yourself to men."

"You suppose wrong." Gisela crossed her arms, facing her stepmother.

"I don't like your tone." Evfemia infused her words with an icy chill. "In fact, I don't like the way you're looking at me, as if this was *your* house." Her voice went from low and icy to loud and screechy. "I am mistress of this house. Everything here belongs to me. *You* belong to me." She strode toward Gisela and didn't stop until she was able to reach out and grab her.

Evfemia pinched Gisela's chin between her thumb and forefinger, her thumb digging into her flesh.

Gisela wrenched away from her.

"If you are consorting with men," Evfemia hissed out between clenched teeth, "I'll throw you out. You'll never be welcome here again."

"Good. I can go wherever I want. You don't control me."

"I'll tell everyone what you have become.

Gisela raised her eyebrows. "I don't care."

Evfemia's eyes flashed and her jaw hardened as she appeared to grind her teeth together. "I never loved your father. I only married him for his money."

Gisela looked up at the ceiling, as though infinitely bored. "So you've told me before." Why did her stepmother still try to hurt her with that information? It no longer worked.

"Who is that man you were with today?"

"I told you, he is a knight."

"What is his name?"

"He didn't tell me his name."

Evfemia eyed her with suspicion. "Until you tell me who he is, you will scrub the entire house. You'll start with the floors, then you'll scrub the walls, then the ceilings. Then you'll— "

"I cannot help it if he did not want to be introduced to you."

She relished the fury on Evfemia's face. How much more furious she would be if she knew it had been Valten, Lord Hamlin, paying special attention to her?

Evfemia's face turned red.

"He's kind and noble, so you wouldn't like him."

Evfemia's voice was raspy. "You are never to see him again."

Gisela shrugged, turned around, and started for the stairs.

Evfemia sputtered, as though she couldn't decide what to say, "You—go help Miep in the kitchen! And you are not to—go back to town with us ever again! Do you hear me?"

"Yes, Frau Evfemia." Gisela started for the kitchen, laughing inside at Evfemia's impotent rage.

"Wait! Come here."

Gisela stopped and braced herself for whatever poisonous words Evfemia was about to spew.

"You don't care about anything, do you?" Evfemia studied her from narrowed eyes. "No, that's not true, is it?"

Would she truly take away the one thing Gisela couldn't pretend she didn't love? The dread was like a hollowness inside.

"I intend to sell every one of those horses, do you hear me? I'll sell them to the butcher, the tanner ... and your favorite horse will be the first to go. I believe Kaeleb will make a fine meal for the duke's falcons, and the leather workers will be able to use his hide to make quite a few bags and harnesses, and several pairs of boots ..."

Heat rose up the back of Gisela's neck and into her head. *She's bluffing.*

"But if you stay away from this man ... I might let you keep your precious horses." Evfemia clicked her tongue against her teeth. "Although it is so hard to believe a knight would ever be caught talking to you." She cackled, an ugly but gleeful sound that echoed off the walls.

Irma came running into the room to see what was going on,

and Gisela hurried away before Evfemia could control herself enough to call her back.

Gisela's blood was still boiling as she joined Miep, their cook, in the kitchen and helped her prepare the bread. She pounded the dough Miep had started, kneading it blindly as anger blurred her vision. If only she could think of some way to stop Evfemia from threatening to sell the horses every time she wanted to force Gisela to do something. Her stepmother was certainly capable of making good on her threat. And although Kaeleb still had many good years before him, Evfemia was right that no one but the butcher, the falconer, or the tanner would want the older horses, to kill them for their meat and their hides. She couldn't let that happen. But how could she stop her stepmother?

Valten went into the library after breakfast. Duke Wilhelm walked in a few minutes later with Valten's mother. Valten hugged her and gave her a peck on the cheek because he knew his mother liked that, and his father would scowl at him if he didn't.

"You wanted to speak to me?" He didn't truly want to know what this was about and hoped it didn't take long. He was a bit old for scoldings and lectures.

His mother smiled, but it was a sad smile. His parents stood together and exchanged a brief glance. "We've been so happy to have you home, and were wondering what your plans are after the tournament next week."

Valten took his time as he thought about what to say.

"I was hoping you would settle down here in Hagenheim," his mother said, with a lift of her brows, "instead of leaving us again."

She seemed to try to sound nonchalant, but there was a glisten in her eyes that signaled she might be about to cry. Valten shifted his feet uncomfortably. He wasn't afraid of much, but a crying woman made the hair stand up on the back of his neck.

"I don't know, Mother." Valten crossed his arms and turned to face the window to the courtyard. "I haven't decided."

"We want you to be happy." His father stepped forward. "Are you happy competing in the tournaments? You are very good at it, but you can't do it forever, and you will be needed here in Hagenheim someday. It would be good to have you at my side, son. There is always something that needs our attention."

"To confess the truth," Valten said, turning to face them, "I don't get much satisfaction from the tournaments anymore."

They were looking at him as if waiting for him to go on.

"I feel restless." Valten started pacing, talking to the floor. "I want to do something but I don't know what it is. If there was a war going on I could go fight, to offer myself as a knight in the king's service." A tightness in his chest signaled the familiar frustration.

"Perhaps it is time you thought about taking a wife." His father's voice was firm but quiet, confidential. "You are twenty-four, the same age I was when I married your mother. It is a good time to settle here at the castle, with a wife. Your people will need you here, and I could use your help. You have an obligation to them to provide an heir, which will also provide stability. You've proven yourself on the tournament fields, and now it's time to learn about governing and leading."

Valten's jaw clenched. His father was probably right. He wasn't against finding a wife, but it was awkward to have his father tell him it was time. Just how did a man go about deciding on a wife anyway? How much easier to have your betrothed picked for you, brought to you, without having to court her. Or, as Gabe had done, to rescue your betrothed from some evil fate. That appealed to him. But he'd yet to find a damsel in distress, oppressed by evil and in need of rescue.

A few unkind thoughts about Gabe came to his mind.

He'd thought he might accept Rainhilda, Sir Edgar's daughter. She was beautiful, after all, and seemed to get along well with his mother and sisters. But he hadn't at all liked the way she looked at Gisela in the street a few days ago. It showed a haughtiness and meanspiritedness that she'd hidden from him. He was glad she hadn't noticed him as he watched Gisela being treated badly by her family.

Gisela. She was beautiful, and easy to talk to. And unlike Rainhilda, she didn't prattle on and on about things Valten didn't care or know anything about. She talked about horses—a subject he was quite comfortable with. And he had always thought a love of horses was a sign of gentleness and good character. The way she had bonded with Sieger had quite awed him.

But ... he didn't understand why those people, her family, treated her so badly. She had stood up to Friedric Ruexner and practically spit in his eye. So why were those girls not afraid to laugh at her? She said the woman was her stepmother. Why was her stepmother dressed like a nobleman's wife, and yet Gisela was dressed like a peasant? Something was wrong with that situation, and Valten hoped to find out what it was when he saw her at the tournament. Perhaps he would find her in the crowd and then send his squire to spy on her.

"You're right, Father. Maybe it is time I think about getting married."

His father cleared his throat. He was surprised, no doubt, at Valten's easy acquiescence.

"That's very mature of you, son."

"We will have a banquet after the tournament." Already his mother's voice sounded happier—almost giddy, in fact. "And we can have a ball and invite eligible maidens of the region. Unless you wish me to invite the titled men of the Empire and their eligible daughters. But that will take more time ..."

"The girls of Hagenheim will be sufficient, I believe."

His father clapped him on the shoulder. "Don't worry, son. The restless feeling will go away in time. You are young, but you've seen and done more than most men twice your age." He added softly, "God will give you a new purpose, if you ask him."

Valten wished he had the confidence that his father always seemed to have when it came to the idea of God-given purpose. But Valten did believe that God had been with him many times in the lists and in his travels. Often he'd been saved from danger or injury by the thinnest of margins. He'd gathered quite a lot of followers as well—other knights who'd allied themselves with him, traveled with him, said that God's favor rested on him and that God was watching over him. But Valten figured it was mostly superstition.

Most men who claimed allegiance to God were more afraid of the devil than they were of God, and were careful to do what they thought would appease evil spirits. They put money in the poor box and carried a splinter of the supposed holy cross of Jesus around in their saddlebag to ward off bad luck, but they would carry a witch's charm or utter an old Druid spell just as readily. Many never set foot in a church, but they were quick to enter into debauchery.

The thought of God giving him a purpose, other than winning tournaments, was appealing, but asking God for something did not mean he would get it. Still, he should pray, and perhaps he would also ask the priest to ask God what his purpose was.

There must be more to life than tournaments.

He couldn't believe he was saying this, but … "A ball is a good idea, Mother."

"I will go make a list of who to invite." His mother's smile was as bright as the sun and almost as wide. "I'll get Margaretha and Rainhilda to help."

"Will you invite *all* the marriageable girls in the region?" It was important that she invited Gisela, but he still didn't know who she was. After all, Gisela was a common name. There could be a hundred Giselas in Hagenheim.

"I can't invite *all* the marriageable girls." Mother raised her brows as she smiled at him. "They wouldn't fit in the Great Hall." She squeezed his arm. "I'll invite as many as I can."

He might need to enlist Rainhilda's help in order to make sure Gisela attended this ball. She obviously knew Gisela's family, though he didn't think she would be happy to help him find her.

Otherwise, he would have to find Gisela at the tournament and invite her himself. Surely she would be there.

He was counting on it.

Chapter 5

"You can't go to the tournament. You have too much work to do." Evfemia looked down her long nose at Gisela. She was even taller than bean pole Irma, who stood at the foot of the stairs, smirking with Contzel.

Today the tournament would take place in Hagenheim. Although it was unlikely Gisela would get a chance to speak with Valten at the tournament, she desperately wanted to see him again, even if it was only from afar. It would be worth going just to see him defeat that nasty Friedric Ruexner. She hoped Valten knocked him out of the saddle and onto his pompous derriere. And she didn't want to just hear about it; she wanted to see it.

But she didn't argue with her stepmother. She simply continued scouring the walls. The soot from the fires that burned all winter did build up on the walls, but Gisela had just cleaned them a few weeks ago. While her stepmother watched her, Gisela scrubbed diligently.

"Besides, you don't have any clothes fit to be seated in the gallery," Evfemia went on. "You'd have to stand below with the yeoman farmers and peasants."

Irma and Contzel snorted and whispered from the other side of the room.

Gisela pretended not to hear. She wouldn't be goaded into saying what she was thinking — that her stepmother was a mean, selfish, petty-minded she-devil. If she bad-mouthed Evfemia, it would be an excuse to lock Gisela in her room. Then she'd have no chance at all of getting to the tournament.

Gisela continued cleaning, planning how she would arrange her hair. Irma and Contzel had already dressed, with Gisela's help. They were wearing elaborate gowns made from the finest materials. Irma's was a dark red silk with enormous bag sleeves and a jeweled belt that almost succeeded in hiding how emaciated she looked. But the color didn't become her at all. The red heightened her sallow complexion. And Contzel's emerald green dress was fitted with a lace-up bodice that was low-cut enough to show her ample cleavage. Though the green was a beautiful shade, it gave her the distinct look of a bullfrog. Gisela was sorry to think such ugly thoughts, but every time she glanced at Contzel, she imagined the girl sitting on a lily pad, catching a fly with her tongue.

Evfemia's new dress was a gaudy gold, embroidered with a pattern of large red leaves. The bodice and hem were trimmed with ermine. All three of them had matching headdresses in the popular two-horned style, with flowing headrails hanging down around the sides and back to disguise the limpness of their dull brown hair. A jeweled pin adorned the front.

Gisela planned to wear her mother's wedding dress, which she had kept carefully packed away in a trunk in her attic chamber, hidden in the corner. The dress was a lovely sapphire blue. Though plain compared with the current fashion, Gisela knew the color made her eyes look even bluer, and was a good match for her skin color and blonde hair.

"Look after the horses while we're gone — not that you would forget your darlings." Evfemia rolled her eyes.

"Yes, my lady." Gisela tried to keep the sarcasm out of her voice. She would pretend submission, pretend she wasn't planning to do anything that day except what her stepmother told her to do, and accept the consequences later if she was caught.

"Irma! Contzel!" Evfemia called out in her imperiously shrill voice.

"We're right here, Mother. You don't have to shout."

Evfemia gave Irma a withering look. "It is time to leave."

"You're stepping on my hem!" Contzel elbowed her sister.

"If your hem wasn't as big as a tent, I might not step on it. You're too slow!"

"Stop pushing me! Ow!"

A scuffling noise, then screams, but Gisela didn't turn to look. She hoped they would hurry on out the door so she could go get ready.

"Stop that!" Evfemia screamed. "Stop this moment! If you make a mess of your headdresses, I will—"

The two sisters stopped squealing, and the only sound was the swishing of their many layers of clothing and the scuff of their slippers on the floor.

Gisela glanced up as they reached the door. Her stepmother stood staring coldly at her. Irma and Contzel stopped and followed suit.

"Gisela," Evfemia began in her calmest voice, "if you get anywhere near the tournament lists, I shall sell every horse. Every. Single. One. Do you understand?"

"Yes, my lady." Gisela gave her an equally cold stare.

"Good." She turned and swept out the door, holding up the hem of her ermine-trimmed cape.

Gisela's teeth began to ache as she realized she'd been clenching her jaw. Evfemia would eventually empty the stables, continuing to sell everything off, whether Gisela obeyed her or not. But her stepmother's threat still had its desired effect.

But with God's favor, her stepmother might not see her at the lists. They wouldn't be expecting to see her, after all, especially not wearing her mother's blue gown. Evfemia did not even know the gown existed.

Gisela waited until her stepmother's carriage had started down the long lane that led away from the house to the main road, where it would no doubt join the crowds on their way to the tournament. She threw her cloth in the bucket of water and ran up the stairs. Quickly, she took off her ragged work clothes, pulled on a clean white chemise, and dressed in her mother's silk gown, with its long, detached angel sleeves and plain belt.

Even though Evfemia had worn an ermine-trimmed cloak, the late spring weather was blessedly too warm to actually need one. It was a good thing, since Gisela didn't own a decent one.

Hurriedly, she brushed out her hair and braided a small section on either side, wrapping the braids around her head and pinning a plain veil to them. She studied her reflection in the cracked, cloudy looking glass. Her hair wasn't hanging in perfect ringlets like Rainhilda's would be, but she liked the effect of her long hair flowing over her shoulders and down her back, the contrast of the blonde and the dark blue gown.

She ran out and saddled Kaeleb, then mounted sidesaddle. She rode slowly, reining her horse in so he didn't kick up mud onto her skirt or make a mess of her hair as she traveled to her neighbor, Ava von Setenstete's house. Ava had insisted she let her take her to the tournament. "That old Evfemia"—Ava had wrinkled up her nose with distaste at the woman's name—"will find an excuse not to let you go. Promise me you will come here and let me take you in my carriage." But that had been two months ago, when they'd first heard about the tournament. Now Ava was heavy with child and probably wouldn't be able to go.

Ava's husband was a wool merchant who was often away from home for months at a time, which had led to Gisela visiting as often as possible to keep her friend company. Gisela arrived at the impressive house, which, as a wealthy merchant, von Setenstete was well able to afford. It was even larger and grander than Gisela's stone and half-timber home.

Gisela knocked at the door. A servant let her in and led her to Ava's chamber.

"I'm so sorry to disturb you." Gisela saw that Ava was still in bed.

"Nonsense. You are not disturbing me. I should get up. It's just easier to lie here." Ava laughed — a delicate sound, like little bells. She pulled herself into a sitting position, her large, pregnant belly protruding under the bedclothes.

"Are you not coming to the tournament?"

"No, my dear." She reached out and squeezed Gisela's hand. "I am too close to my time. But you may still use my carriage."

"I can ride Kaeleb."

"I insist you ride in my carriage." She gave Gisela her sternest look, which wasn't very stern. "I don't want you mussing your beautiful hair or that dress."

Ava was only a few years older than Gisela, but she had such a motherly way about her. She'd had a child already, but the baby had died shortly after birth.

"How did you ever get that dress past that old witch, Evfemia?"

Gisela laughed. "I put it on after she left."

"That color … it looks beautiful on you." She smiled, and in that moment Gisela thought there was no one more beautiful than Ava, with her kind gray eyes, flawless face, and pouty lips. Then her eyes flew wide. "Wait! I have a scarf that very color. You must take it with you, in case you find a knight who wishes to wear your color."

"That's silly, Ava." Gisela shook her head at the thought. Ava the Hopeful.

"Go to that trunk over there." She pointed in the corner. "Open it up. Look on the right side. See it?"

Gisela lifted out a handful of gauzy blue material that indeed matched her dress perfectly.

"Now wrap it around your neck. Come here. Let me do it."

Gisela, feeling a bit foolish, leaned down to allow Ava to wrap the scarf and drape it over her shoulders and down her back so that it didn't detract from her dress.

"Now you must go. The knights will be inspired to fight ever more valiantly with you watching them." She winked.

"Do you want me to help you get up and get dressed?" Her friend looked so uncomfortable, though she also looked ... content.

"No, no. Gudda will do that. You go now. I've already had the coachman get the carriage ready. He will drive you." She flicked her hand at her.

Gisela leaned down and kissed her cheek. "Thank you."

On arriving at the tournament grounds—a natural amphitheater with gently sloping sides, grassy and green in the late spring sunshine—Gisela alighted from the carriage with the help of Otto, Ava's coachman, and felt almost as if she was someone special. She could still remember how it felt to be cared about, to have a father who would bring her to a tournament in a carriage like this one. But it had been so long ago that it seemed like another life, another person.

Otto drove away, leaving her before the flat expanse outside the south side of the walled town of Hagenheim. Teeming with people, the profusion of color was dazzling, with bright hues of red, yellow, green, and blue, more extensive than the rainbow. Knights appeared here and there. Over their heavy breastplates and mail they wore a surcoat with their coat of arms in bright colors. Their horses were decked in similar mantles called caparisons, each in various patterns matching their rider.

Her eyes were drawn to blue and red checks on one caparison, red and black stripes on another, and on yet another, a bright yellow background with the repeating pattern of a white lion on a shield of black. Banners waved in the breeze from atop brightly striped or checked pavilions that dotted the field outside the lists. Ladies' scarves flew from some of the knights' helmets or from around their arms, displaying the colors of the knight's lady-love.

Joy swelled inside her. She was here, actually here, at the Hagenheim tournament. All she had to do was avoid being seen and get home before her stepmother and stepsisters. But for the moment, she hardly cared if she got caught. Being here and seeing this spectacle was worth it.

She couldn't help searching the grounds for Valten. He would no doubt be wearing his family's coat of arms and the Gerstenberg colors of green, black, and gold. Perhaps she might even sneak away and see Sieger, when he wasn't needed in the competition. But she didn't see Valten or his steed in the crowd of people.

She made her way toward the tournament lists, along with everyone else around her. There was standing room around the perimeter of the field, with a light wooden barrier between the spectators and the combatants' field of play. Many men, wearing the garb of farmer and peasant, stood and mingled there. Behind them, on the longer north and south sides of the large rectangle, great galleries had been built, the middle part shaded by large awnings that were graced with cushioned benches and wooden steps for the nobles, their ladies, and the wealthier citizens of Hagenheim.

As she neared the lists, she saw that several attendants and the younger Gerstenberg children—Valten's brothers and sisters—were already seated in the north side gallery. As she watched, a flourish of trumpets announced Wilhelm Gerstenberg, Duke of Hagenheim, and his wife, Lady Rose, as they rode two beautiful black horses toward the stands. The duke dismounted then helped his wife dismount, and they climbed the steps to the seats of honor.

Many people, dressed in their vibrant finery, made their way toward the choice seats surrounding the duke and his family. Similarly, on the opposite side of the field, the more well-dressed people hurried to find seats in the south gallery.

A few dirty, raggedly dressed children tried to sit on the benches meant for the upper classes but were shooed away by the guards patrolling the perimeter. In the center of the gallery was a seat of honor, a throne-like chair placed there for the lady who would be crowned the Queen of Beauty and Love. Every tournament had to have its queen, and this one would be no different. Duke Wilhelm, as the sponsor of the tournament, would be expected to choose a queen, but rumor said that he would confer that right on the tournament champion. The queen would have the honor of bestowing on the winner his prize, and, in turn, receiving from him ... a kiss. Then she would be led by the champion knight to the banquet, which was by invitation only, at Hagenheim Castle.

Gisela was sure the day's winner would be Valten, but who would he pick to be his lady? The prospects made her feel slightly ill.

Her most pertinent question for the moment was where she was to sit. A man stared at her as she made her way toward the gallery. More than one man was staring, actually. One well-dressed burgher stepped toward her. "Beautiful maiden, I would be honored if you would sit with me."

"The pretty girl doesn't want to sit with you, Hugh. She wants to sit with me." This from a man equally well-dressed but with a belly as huge as a sow.

"Excuse me, good sirs, but I am sitting elsewhere." She pretended to see her place farther down at the other end of the gallery, but a guard approached her.

"Fraulein, I am charged with seating the fairest young maidens in the center section of the gallery, from whom the champion will choose a queen." He held out his arm to assist her up the steps.

The other men moved away, grumbling under their breath, for which Gisela was thankful. She looked the guard in the eyes. He had a kind face and was old enough to be her father.

"Are you sure you want me to sit here?" she asked. Perhaps he had only meant to scare away those men.

"Of course. And"—he lowered his voice—"you are too beautiful to be wandering around without an escort."

She placed her hand on his gauntleted wrist and let him lead her up the wooden steps. As they climbed higher, her eye caught sight of Rainhilda sitting near the top of the gallery to the left, on the other side of the empty throne. Her nose was stuck high in the air, but Gisela had to admit she looked gorgeous. Her dress was made of panels of pale pink and pale violet silk that brought out the flawlessness of her skin. Instead of the big horned turban on the heads of many of the ladies, she wore a simple veil attached to a jeweled circlet, which better displayed her honey-gold hair, styled as always in ringlets that cascaded over her shoulders.

Gisela tried not to stare, hoping Rainhilda wouldn't notice her. Were Irma and Contzel nearby?

She sat in the empty space the guard led her to. "Thank you." The guard nodded and made his way back down the steps. Gisela was left to wait, alone, for the tournament to start.

"Isn't this exciting? It is my first tournament."

"It is my first tournament too." Gisela liked the girl immediately. "Do you know any of the knights?"

"I know one, Sir Ulrich von Rechberg, as he grew up near me." She leaned close to Gisela and whispered, "Even though he is a childhood friend, and I must cheer for him, he is a dim-witted sort of fellow, and I never liked him much. But his mother is kind and used to give me gingerbread. And you? Do you have a favorite?"

It was probably best not to tell her new friend about her childhood dreams about marrying Valen, or that she had talked with him several days before. Gisela cast about for something appropriate to say. "I am surely not the only girl here who will be cheering for Valten, the duke's son."

"True, he is quite the favorite, and the most accomplished. I wonder who he'll pick to be the Queen of Beauty and Love if he wins. Do you think he is in love with anyone? Maybe he has a childhood sweetheart."

Reluctantly, Gisela admitted, "It is said that he will marry Sir Edgar's daughter, Rainhilda."

Cristyne wrinkled her small nose, which was sprinkled with tiny freckles. "I certainly hope not. I met her earlier, and she seems an arrogant, spiteful girl."

Gisela glanced over at Rainhilda, who was at that moment smirking at something the girl to her left was saying. Did Valten love Rainhilda? She couldn't imagine that he did, although Ava had once told her that men rarely saw past a woman's outward appearance—until they were married, and then it was too late. Would that happen to Valten? Would he marry Rainhilda and be stuck with a conceited, spiteful wife?

She frowned. "I don't know her, but she certainly looks arrogant." Gisela glanced again in Rainhilda's direction and caught her staring. Gisela ducked behind Cristyne, hoping Rainhilda hadn't recognized her. If she had, she would tell Irma, and then Evfemia would learn that Gisela had managed to come to the tournament.

Then instead of cowering, she sat up straight. If Evfemia tried to force her to go home, she'd pretend she didn't know the woman, or she would find that kindly guard. Perhaps he would help her. Though if she hoped to attend the second day of the tournament, she probably shouldn't go home at all tonight. Perhaps she would sneak into Ava's stable and sleep in the hay.

The knights began to enter the lists, mounted on their war horses, which were draped in the most spectacular colors. The knights themselves shone brightly, their highly polished armor glinting in the sun. Many helmets were decorated with bright scarves, streamers, or feathers. They carried their lances pointed to the sky as they paraded onto the grassy field and lined up, facing Gisela's side.

Each knight was introduced, his parentage and ancestry were declared, and the crowd applauded and called out approval for the local knights. But for the foreign knights, only a smattering of clapping could be heard, and even a few cries of derision arose for some.

Valten wore only his stripes of green, gold, and black. He wore no scarves or any other adornment on either his helmet or his arm. Gisela looked down at the scarf Ava had made her wear around her neck and imagined it tied to Valten's arm as he competed in the joust today. But it was a silly thought.

When it was Valten's turn to be announced, he nudged Sieger, and his horse made a graceful bow, bending one knee and lowering his head as Valten in turn bowed his head and dipped his lance toward the crowd. A roaring cheer arose.

When Friedric Ruexner was introduced, a few hisses spread through the crowd, as his reputation as Valten's chief nemesis had preceded him. The visor of his helmet was open, and he seemed to be staring at her as he raised his fist defiantly.

After they'd all been introduced, many of the knights walked their horses over and banged on another knight's shield. Gisela watched as Friedric Ruexner made his way to Valten's shield and banged it forcefully with the end of his lance. At least he had struck Valten's shield of peace and not the shield of war. A few more tapped their lances on Valten's shield of peace. As far as Gisela and Cristyne could tell, and according to the spectators around them, none of the knights had touched a shield of war, all choosing to fight with wooden-tipped lances rather than the sharp metal tips of war. They were probably saving those for the second day of the tournament.

After the challenges were made, the knights dispersed to their pavilions to await their turn at tilting with their opponents.

Ulrich von Rechberg, a local knight and Cristyne's childhood acquaintance, readied himself to meet his challenger, Count Adolf Burgkmair of Thuringia. Cristyne exchanged a look of excitement with Gisela and said, "For his mother's sake, I hope Ulrich doesn't break his head."

The two waited for the signal from the marshal at the middle of the south end. At last, the man held aloft a white flag. As he let the flag fall, the two knights spurred their horses forward, lances aimed at the shield of their opponent. They struck their marks, and both lances splintered, with pieces of the wooden spears flying in every direction. But the knights kept their saddles.

They returned to their places at the east and west ends of the list, where their squires brought them each a new lance. When the marshal's flag dipped, they charged each other once again at terrible speed. This time both lances held firm, and once again both men kept their seats. For their third and final tilt, they once again came toward each other at full speed. Count Burgkmair's lance glanced off Ulrich's shield, while Ulrich aimed for the count's helmet instead of his shield. The count ended up on the ground, unhelmed, with a bloody gash on his forehead.

Several ladies gasped, while Ulrich, the victor, pumped his hand in the air. The crowd cheered for the Hagenheim youth. Cristyne shouted over the noisy crowd, "He trains with Lord Hamlin."

The count was helped up by his squire and attendants and was able to walk off the field. The crowd clapped for him. As the loser of the encounter, he would have to forfeit his horse and armor to the conqueror. However, it was customary for the victor to allow the loser to ransom either or both for an agreed-upon sum. That must have been how Valten had been able to hold onto Sieger while competing in so many jousts.

Cristyne leaned closer to Gisela. "Do you think anyone will get killed today?"

"I hope not. My friend Ava says men crave danger, or at least adventure. They like to think they are strong and powerful." Gisela supposed Ava must know what she was talking about, since she had seven brothers.

"My mother says the same." Cristyne nodded. "I have three brothers. Sometimes I think they care naught for life or limb."

Valten entered the lists mounted on Sieger, and Gisela's heart jumped into her throat. He sat so straight in the saddle, the picture of manly grace and strength. His armor was bright silver with intricate carvings and decoration, and his helmet was a pleasing shape, high and rounded at the top.

Ruexner's helmet was like an enormous beak, the way the visor jutted forward. On the top was a spike, to which was attached a profusion of gray and white feathers. His armor was black. A skull marked his shield and his surcoat.

Valten and Ruexner took their places, and Gisela placed her hand over her heart in a vain effort to keep it from beating so hard. Sieger stood perfectly still as Valten lifted his lance parallel to the ground. Ruexner's beast stamped his hooves impatiently, and the marshal seemed to be waiting for the challenger to get his horse under control. When the destrier stilled, the marshal dropped the flag.

Valten and his mount leaped forward, and the two opponents charged each other.

Gisela's heart seemed to stop beating altogether as each knight's lance crashed into the other's shield. Ruexner's weapon shattered and he was thrown backward. He teetered sideways. The crowd seemed to hold their breath until he righted himself.

Valten's lance held firm, and he sat facing his adversary.

Ruexner roared some unintelligible words from inside his closed helmet. Throughout the tirade, Valten remained still.

Gisela watched Ruexner as he rode back to his place. His squire handed him a new lance, but he shook his head and barked something Gisela didn't understand. Then he spurred his horse toward the side of the lists where Valten's shields were hanging and struck Valten's shield of war so hard it fell to the ground.

When Friedric Ruexner returned to his starting position, Gisela could more clearly see the new lance he was holding. The point was sharp, with a metal tip from which multiple wicked points splayed.

Valten received a similarly tipped lance from his own squire.

The crowd voiced their awe in hushed tones, then waited for the marshal to drop his flag. Gisela leaned forward, her hands clasped together as she held her breath. *O God, please help Valten emerge victorious. Don't let him die.*

The flag fell and the two horses sprang forward. Ruexner seemed to be aiming for Valten's neck, while Valten shifted his lance's aim at the last second from Ruexner's shield to his helmet.

Each lance struck the other rider. Ruexner's glanced off Valten's helmet, and the duke's son kept his seat, but Valten's lance had apparently struck Ruexner's visor and wedged itself between the air slits. Valten kept hold of the lance, the other end stuck in Ruexner's visor, and Valten's surefooted horse moved to follow the foe.

Loud curses could be heard from Friedric Ruexner as he threw down his lance and, with both hands, tried to pull Valten's lance out of his helmet, but to no avail. His squire and two attendants ran to help him, but they still could not release him. Instead, they ended up taking off his helmet.

Friedric Ruexner's face was red, his hair and beard wet with perspiration. He cursed Valten in French—at least, she thought he did, as he was using words Gisela had never heard before.

Valten sat mute, holding his lance with Ruexner's helmet still attached.

They each went back to their end of the field. Ruexner's attendants placed a new helmet on his head, then gave him a new lance, again with a metal tip. Valten replaced his lance as well.

The two once again faced each other, waiting for the marshal to drop the flag. For their third and final encounter, Gisela could feel the rage emanating from Ruexner. When the flag fell, Ruexner shouted as he spurred his horse toward Valten.

There was a great crash as Valten's lance struck Ruexner's helmet and splintered, and Ruexner was knocked off his saddle onto his back. At the same time, Valten's helmet was knocked off with such force, it hit the ground thirty feet behind him.

Gisela was desperate to see Valten's face, to see if he'd been injured. But his back was to her as he gazed down at his challenger.

Ruexner jumped to his feet, snarling like a wild animal, and drew his sword. The marshals urged their horses forward but weren't able to reach the two before Ruexner swung his sword at Valten and missed. Sieger let out a wild scream and reared, his hoofs flailing in Ruexner's face.

One marshal on horseback placed himself between Valten and Ruexner, while another dismounted and wrenched Ruexner's sword out of his hand from behind.

Ruexner spun around and yelled something indistinct, then stalked off the field toward his pavilion, leaving his squire and attendants to bring his horse.

The field marshal declared Valten the victor, taking his right hand and lifting it in the air.

As Valten's squire brought him his helmet, Gisela finally got a glimpse of his face. A bright red line ran across his forehead just over his left eye, from which a trickle of blood dribbled over his eyebrow and down his cheek.

The marshals conversed with Valten for a moment, and then Valten took his place at the end of the lists while his squire helped him put his helmet back on. Another opponent emerged.

Cristyne took her fingernails out of her mouth long enough to ask, "Is he fighting again?"

Gisela swallowed. "I think he must. He has more challengers."

Valten exchanged his lance of war for a blunted one and prepared to face a foreign knight with a French-sounding name. After the flag fell, the two met in the center of the lists with a loud crash. Valten splintered his lance on his opponent's shield, while his opponent struck Valten's shield with only a glancing blow.

The two lined up again. The flag fell and the two horses charged forward, but the challenger's horse reared, then shied to one side. Valten could have taken advantage of the situation and struck his opponent while he was unable to strike his own blow, but Valten halted his horse and did not strike. It was a display of courtesy, according to the rules of chivalry. The crowd shouted their approval.

The marshals allowed them to return to their places. The challenger's horse whinnied, but then seemed to calm down. He stood still until the marshal once again flung down his flag.

Valten and the challenger met in the center again, and once again, Valten's lance broke apart upon impact on the other knight's shield. The challenger was unhorsed, landing on the ground with a crash and rolling helplessly to a stop. He didn't move as they led his horse away. His squire and attendants used a wooden litter to carry him off the field.

Valten waited at the end of the lists, accepting a new blunted lance.

Feeling reasonably assured that he wasn't badly injured from the bleeding wound over his eye, Gisela sighed in delight at his two decisive victories. She didn't know how many more challengers he would have to face.

A knight in shiny silver and gold armor with a bright yellow scarf around his arm entered the lists. The two waited for the flag to fall, then charged at one another. They both splintered their lances on each other's shields. A maiden seated about twenty feet away in a dress the same shade of yellow as the scarf on the new knight's arm started to clap and cheer. Then she and her companions giggled as the two knights made ready for their next encounter.

Hoping with all her heart that Valten would conquer the yellow lady's knight, Gisela held her breath as they met each other again in the center of the lists. Valten aimed for the knight's helmet and struck a good blow, while the other knight struck Valten's shield. Neither lance broke, and though the other knight tottered a bit in the saddle, they both stayed on their horses.

For the final tilt, Valten appeared to be aiming for the other knight's helmet again, while that knight's lance was aimed too low and would surely strike Sieger in the shoulder. Gisela gasped. Sieger would be killed! But just before they could collide, Valten pulled the horse aside, avoiding the other knight's lance, and missing the other knight's shield as he passed.

Normally, Valten would have been penalized for dodging the strike, but since the other knight's lance was aiming for Valten's horse, which was against the rules of the tournament, Valten was proclaimed the victor of that round.

Gisela shouted with the rest of the crowd, applauding for Valten as he paraded slowly around the field and waved a gauntleted hand at the crowd. He seemed to pause just in front of Gisela, then make a bow as Sieger also bowed one knee toward the crowd of beautiful maidens in the gallery. Gisela gave him her happiest smile, just in case he was looking.

Valten was allowed to leave the field for a short rest before he would be expected to face the rest of his challengers.

She watched two more rounds of jousts, but quickly lost interest in the rest of the knights or how they might fare and turned to Cristyne. "I think I will go look around. I'm tired of sitting."

"I'll come with you."

Gisela was hoping she would say that, especially given the guard's warning about walking around alone.

She and Cristyne made their way down the scaffold to the ground below and circled around the tournament grounds, having to skirt the edge of a wood as they walked.

In their conversation, Gisela learned that Cristyne was the youngest of nine children, and a couple of her sisters were considered great beauties and had married well. Cristyne was expected to do the same, but she rather fancied a poor yeoman farmer she'd grown up with.

"My mother says I will forget about him soon enough." Cristyne looked sad. "Do you have anyone you hope to marry?"

"Me? No, I have no one like that." She hoped her face didn't display the truth about her feelings. And it wasn't as if she hoped to marry Valten. At least, not since she'd grown up and realized how unreasonable that was.

They encountered an older woman with a large cloth-covered

basket. Gisela and Cristyne each bought one of her buns with gooseberries and honey inside.

While eating, they wandered toward the area where the knights' pavilions were set up and where some of their horses were tethered, resting until they were required for the remainder of their jousts. Gisela wanted to see Sieger to reassure herself he was unhurt. The steel shaffron protected his head, but the rest of his body was only protected by the cloth caparison that displayed Valten's coat of arms.

She also hoped Valten's injury had not been serious. Perhaps she might overhear one of his attendants talking about his condition.

"Oh, my cousin and her family!" Cristyne waved at a girl who was waving back. "Do you mind if I go talk with them?"

"Go on. I will see you in a little while." Gisela continued on as Cristyne hurried off to join her relatives.

Gisela looked all around, trying to add the scene to her favorite memories—the beautiful colors of the pavilions, the banners and coats of arms of the knights, the lavishness of the decorations. And then there were the dresses of the wealthy women and maidens... Gisela had never seen anything like this tournament. She longed to store up every detail, even though she probably looked like a country bumpkin who had never been in the wider world before.

As she wandered along, she spied Valten's striped pavilion. She was drawn toward it but continued to look around as she wandered nearer. She could even see Sieger, as he was tethered under a small wooden shelter behind Valten's tent.

A familiar laugh, shrill and annoying, rang out behind her. It was Irma, she was sure of it. She ducked behind a large barrel before looking behind her. Her stepmother and stepsisters stood a mere thirty feet away.

Chapter 7

*Evfemia and Irma stood talking with Rain*hilda, their heads together as if they were trying to make sure no one else heard what they were saying.

While they were not looking her way, Gisela turned her back on them and hurried to get out of sight.

Sieger stood near other knights' horses lined up on the other side of several large tented pavilions. Her stepmother and stepsisters would never go near such an area, so she headed toward him.

As she drew near, a boy who looked about twelve years old approached Sieger's makeshift stall with a bag in his hand. He was glancing around nervously, holding the bag protectively against his body.

The boy's odd behavior made Gisela stop and hide behind the first horse. What was he doing lurking near Valten's destrier? Then, with a deliberate step, he approached Sieger, drew out some green leaves from his bag, and stuffed them into Sieger's bucket. The boy turned and broke into a run, disappearing behind the horses' stalls.

Sieger stuck his nose into the bucket, then pulled it out again, snuffling discontentedly.

Gisela hurried forward, holding up her hem so it didn't get soiled. Once she reached Sieger, she spoke softly to him, rubbing his nose. He nickered, nodding his head, and nudged her neck. "Hey, boy. Let me see what's in your feed."

She bent down and pulled out the green leaves from inside his bucket of oats, and her blood went cold. They were the leaves of a water hemlock plant.

Another young boy, who appeared about the same age as the one who'd placed the water hemlock in Sieger's bucket, walked toward her from Valten's tent. "May I help you, fraulein?"

Gisela caught the boy by the arm. "Someone tried to poison Valt—your master's horse. You must tell him with all haste." She held up the offending leaves, her hands starting to shake. If Sieger had eaten them, he might have been dead in half an hour.

Without a word, the boy turned and ran to the tent. Valten came out moments later without his heavy armor, wearing only his shirt of mail, the white under-tunic, and leather breeches.

He saw her and stopped in midstride.

"Someone tried to poison Sieger." Gisela held out the water hemlock.

Valten strode forward, his gaze seeming to move reluctantly from Gisela's face to the green substance in her hand.

"Hugo!" he barked. The boy came running. "Take this and bury it in the ground. Bury it deep, understand?" There was a cold, dangerous look on his face that sent a chill through Gisela, but was somehow comforting at the same time. Valten would not let anyone get away with harming a horse—or a person—he loved.

The boy took the leaves carefully into his hands. She bent and made sure there was no more in Sieger's bucket while Valten looked into the horse's mouth.

After the boy hurried away, Valten said quietly, his voice so deep it rumbled, "Do you think he ate any of it?"

Her heart skipped a beat at his nearness. "I don't think so."

The dangerous glint vanished from his eyes. "I'm glad you came when you did."

She nodded.

"And not just because you saved Sieger's life." He stopped rubbing his horse and turned his body toward her. Now she could see the cut over his eye. Someone had stitched it closed, but there was still a light smear of dried blood on his skin. His hair was damp — no doubt he'd had to wash the blood out of it — making it look brown instead of blond. Up close in his shirt of mail, his shoulders seemed even broader, his chest thicker, and he looked like a warrior — a very handsome warrior.

"Did you see the person who did this?"

She nodded. "A boy, about twelve years old."

"Could you recognize him if you saw him again?"

"I think so."

Valten motioned to his squire. "Guard Sieger and don't let anyone near him."

"Yes, my lord," the boy said.

Valten looked at Gisela. "Come." He strode behind the horse's stall, taking such long strides that Gisela had to hurry to keep up. He stopped in front of Ruexner's tent. A boy was lounging outside on the grass near the front.

"That's him," she whispered. "That's the person who put the water hemlock in Sieger's food."

"You're sure?" The fierce look was back on his face, his jawline looking like it was carved from stone.

"I'm sure."

Valten took a step toward the tent and stopped. He turned back to Gisela, and the look in his gray-green eyes gentled instantly. His jaw relaxed, and her breath hitched in her throat at the sudden transformation. "Go back to Sieger's stall and wait for me there."

She nodded. *Be careful.* She wanted to say the words but was sure a man like Valten wouldn't appreciate, or heed, them. She made her way back. What would Valten do?

While Gisela waited, she rubbed Sieger's side and talked with Valten's squire. He was a polite boy from the north near the sea, the third son of a wealthy earl. She asked him about his winters there and if he wanted to be a knight. The boy was rather talkative and answered her questions well, until his eyes grew big as he seemed to be staring over her shoulder. Before Gisela could turn around, she felt a tug at her neck as someone jerked her scarf.

"Well, if it isn't the pretty little peasant from the streets."

Gisela turned and glared into the ugly sneer of Friedric Ruexner.

He brought the blue scarf up to his face and held it against his cheek, an unpleasant smile on his bearded face.

As the scarf slipped away from her neck, Gisela grabbed the end of it. "Give it to me." She pulled as hard as she could but could not break his hold.

Ruexner yanked as well. Gisela lost her balance and stumbled into him. She immediately jumped back but kept hold of the fabric.

"You want me to wear your colors, don't you?" He grinned down at her.

"Not if I live to be a hundred years old."

Ruexner laughed raucously. "I might not want to wear it if you were a hundred years old."

"Give her the scarf." Valten's voice came from behind Ruexner.

Ruexner visibly stiffened, but he let go of the scarf. Gisela snatched it up before it fell to the ground.

Ruexner spun around and made a wild swing at Valten's head

with his fist. Valten sidestepped the blow, then landed one of his own on Ruexner's chin. Ruexner bent over, clutching his face.

Ruexner's hand slipped into his boot while Valten was looking at Gisela.

"Valten!" Gisela cried.

At her warning he jumped back. Ruexner's hand flew up, and something shot across the three feet between him and Valten. A dagger, which struck a glancing blow across Valten's chest but couldn't penetrate his shirt of mail. It missed his chin by only a couple of inches and fell harmlessly to the ground.

Valten leaped forward and knocked Ruexner to the ground, wrapping his hands around the man's neck. Ruexner tried to push Valten's hands away.

"I should kill you now," Valten growled. "Swear you will never bother this maiden again." A moment's silence, then he yelled, "Swear it!"

Ruexner made a strangled sound as his face grew red.

Valten seemed to loosen his hold on the man's throat a fraction.

"I swear!"

"And if you ever send your servants to harm my horse— "

Valten tightened his hold again, making Ruexner's eyes bulge and his mouth open and close like a fish on dry land.

His knee pressing against Ruexner's chest, Valten let go of his strangle hold on Ruexner's neck and pushed himself to his feet in one swift movement.

Ruexner gasped and rolled onto his side, clutching at his neck as he coughed and panted.

Valten motioned to Gisela to come to him. She hurried forward, and he pushed her behind him as he continued to watch Ruexner warily, his hands by his sides but extended slightly, as though readying for another attack.

"You almost killed me," Ruexner rasped, still clutching his throat.

"You tried to kill me with your dagger," Valten said calmly. "I can get you disqualified from this tournament."

"Are you threatening me?"

"Yes."

Slowly, Ruexner pulled himself to his feet. Gisela watched over Valten's shoulder as Ruexner glared dangerously at him. "I'll see you in the lists."

"Just remember. One word from me and you will be thrown in the dungeon for trying to poison my horse and then threatening my life."

Ruexner's face was unreadable. Then he sneered. "Are you afraid I will defeat you the way I did at Arcy? For this time, I will take that horse of yours instead of taking your coin."

Valten didn't say anything for a moment. Then he answered, "If I don't report your evil deeds, it will be because I shall enjoy defeating you so much more."

Ruexner snorted, then walked silently back to his own tent. Gisela watched him go and shuddered.

She focused instead on Valten. Even sweaty, with the dust of his tussle with Ruexner still clinging to his damp hair, he made her breathing shallow at being the object of his attention. His expression gradually relaxed.

"Did he hurt you?"

"No." Gisela realized she was still clutching her scarf. Valten too seemed to notice it.

He gave her a questioning lift of his eyebrows and held out his right arm. "May I? Wear your colors?"

She nodded and stepped forward. She hoped he didn't notice the way her hands shook as she tied the blue scarf around his arm.

He looked into her eyes for a long moment, and neither of them spoke. Clearing his throat, he said, "I must go."

Gisela wanted to say something. "Of course. Be careful." *Dumb. Of course he won't be careful. He's jousting.*

One corner of his mouth went up. "Say a prayer for me."

"I will."

And he walked away, the ends of her scarf dancing around his forearm.

Chapter 8

Once back in the stands with Cristyne, Gisela fidgeted nervously, waiting for Valten to return to the field. She talked with her new friend as much as her attention would allow, and when Valten's turn came, he rode out looking tall and powerful on Sieger's back.

Her hands grew sweaty as the blue scarf seemed to wave at her from around Valten's arm. Her face heated and her heart pounded faster.

"Is that your scarf the duke's son is wearing?" Cristyne stared at Gisela with wide eyes.

Gisela forced herself to breathe. "It is."

Cristyne said her name in a slow, awed whisper. "Gisela."

Gisela shrugged, trying to pretend nonchalance. "He is very kind. I met him accidentally in the Marktplatz two weeks ago."

"Lord Hamlin, the duke's son, was wandering around in the Marktplatz?"

She shrugged again. "He was there."

"And he talked to you?"

"He admired my horse, then he took me to see his at the castle stables. We talked about horses."

"What will Rainhilda say?" Cristyne asked breathlessly. They both chanced a discreet glance in that lady's direction. Her gaze was fixed on Valten as he paraded around the lists, and she looked a shade paler than usual. Her jaw looked set and tight, her lips a firm line.

Cristyne turned her gaze on Gisela, a questioning glint in her eye.

She shook her head slightly and smiled. "He is very kind." She'd already said that, but it was true. It was a lame explanation for why Valten had wanted her, Gisela Mueller, to tie her scarf around his arm. The fact was, she wasn't sure why he'd done it, and his kindness seemed the likeliest reason.

Perhaps he thought she was pretty. Many people had told her she was, and perhaps he liked talking about horses with her. He also seemed grateful that she had found the water hemlock in Sieger's food. He'd said she saved his horse's life. When he found out she was little more than a servant, however, he would realize his mistake in wearing her colors.

The voice in her head taunted, "Perhaps he is only grateful to you for saving his horse. He feels sorry for you because he saw how badly your stepmother and stepsisters treat you. He's being kind to you out of gratitude ... and pity."

She wanted so much to believe that he had felt the same thing she felt when she was with him. His eyes softened when he looked at her. There was something in their interactions, a camaraderie that Gisela only felt with a few of her friends. But there was also an attraction, like a magnet drawing metal, creating a spark that she could feel in the air between them when he was near.

Cristyne was looking back and forth, from Valten out on the lists to Gisela beside her. "Ohhh," she sighed. "I am sitting beside the lady-love of Valten, Lord Hamlin, the next Duke of Hagenheim."

Gisela snorted—an unladylike sound—before she could stop herself. "He never called me his lady-love. I barely know him."

"We shall see." Cristyne winked.

Valten jousted with another young local who had been

knighted only recently. In their first encounter, the other knight dropped his lance. Valten, in the spirit of chivalry, didn't strike him, but held his lance aloft. In the second encounter, he missed Valten's shield altogether, while Valten struck the young knight's shield so solid a blow, he fell to the ground with a mighty crash.

The crowd cheered both Valten's skill and his gallantry.

As Valten waited for his next opponent, Gisela heard the two maidens seated just below her talking in low voices. The curly haired brunette said, "Whose scarf do you think Lord Hamlin is wearing? Is it anyone we know?"

"I've no notion who it could be," the one with the horned headdress answered. She looked behind her friend and up at where Rainhilda was seated. "Sir Edgar's daughter isn't wearing blue." They both began looking around, searching the section around the Queen of Beauty and Love's throne. No doubt they were searching for someone dressed in the same sapphire shade.

Many girls around Gisela and Cristyne were talking intently with their heads together, and a few were staring wonderingly at her. Gisela's face heated again. She faced forward, keeping her gaze on Valten. Though she couldn't see any part of his face, not even his eyes because of his helmet, his head was turned toward her as he sat on his horse.

His final opponent came out, Sir John de Lacy from England. His armor was golden and etched with black designs. Sir John was renowned throughout the world as a great tournament champion. Even Gisela had heard of him. She clasped her hands in her lap, praying Valten would defeat him.

The Englishman's black horse snorted and stamped his feet from his place at the other end of the lists. Valten and Sieger waited in perfect stillness until the marshal dropped his flag. Both horses charged forward, and both lances struck the shield of the other knight and shattered into pieces. The black and gold knight didn't waver in the saddle, but seemed to withstand the blow as if it were nothing.

The knights' squires brought them new blunt-tipped lances. Gisela clamped her hands over her mouth as she watched them ready themselves for their second encounter.

When the two destriers charged forward, both knights aimed their lances at the other's helmet. They both hit their mark. Valten's head was knocked sharply to the side by the English knight's lance, and Valten's lance knocked Sir John backward, almost unhorsing him, but he kept his seat.

The two knights went back to their places. The black and gold knight kept moving his head side to side, as if trying to shake something off. He called one of the marshals over, apparently to ask for some time. He spoke to his squire, who ran off and then came back with a new helmet. It took him several minutes to remove the earl's helm and replace it with the new, identical one. Meanwhile, Valten and Sieger stood still and waited.

Gisela's fingers began to go numb from being clasped too tightly. She let go and pressed them hard against her lips as the marshal raised his flag. Squinting so she couldn't see the marshal, she focused instead on Valten, praying fervently that he would emerge unscathed from the final encounter.

He'd already faced so many knights. How could he win against them all? He was only human. Valten was surely tired by this time from the many jousts he'd fought, while this knight had only faced one other opponent all day.

They all wanted to face Valten, looking to distinguish themselves by defeating the mighty Earl of Hamlin, the knight who had won more tournaments than any other.

Finally, Valten and his horse—as if they were one being instead of two—leaped forward across the tournament field toward their opponent. Gisela forced herself to watch as they once again aimed their lances at the other's helmet.

The impact was ferocious. But Valten kept both his helmet and his saddle, and splintered his lance on Sir John's helm. But that knight did not fare so well. He ended up on the ground, and he lay perfectly still.

The crowd cheered. Valten's victory was indisputable, as the black and gold knight's attendants had to come and assist him off the field. Valten was undeniably the winner of the tournament and would be awarded the prize, as well as the honor of choosing the Queen of Beauty and Love, who would subsequently reign over tonight's banquet and tomorrow's tournament activities.

The thought of watching Valten fighting hand to hand the next day with these other knights made her stomach churn. But this was what men did; they enjoyed the sport of pounding each other. And as long as they used blunted weapons and full body armor, it was less likely they would kill each other. Fighting a war would have been much more dangerous.

There was a flourish of trumpets as the day's tournament activities came to an end. Many of the other knights came back out on the field in full armor to wave their banners and be recognized. But Friedric Ruexner was conspicuously absent.

After the parade of knights, Duke Wilhelm called for his son to come forth. Valten rode over to the opposite side of the lists from Gisela, where the duke and his family were seated in the north gallery.

Duke Wilhelm stood and declared, "The victor of today's jousting event is . . . Valten Gerstenberg, Earl of Hamlin."

Valten opened both his visor and bevor so that his face was visible as he listened to his father.

"He has conducted himself with honor and valor, and succeeded in defeating all opponents," Duke Wilhelm declared in a loud voice, his words clear and precise. "It is now time for the victor to exercise his rightful privilege of choosing for us our

Queen of Beauty and Love, whom, for the duration of this tournament, we are duty bound to honor and obey."

With those words, he placed a circlet of vines and flowers on the end of Valten's lance.

Gisela's stomach tied itself into a knot as Valten slowly walked his horse to the south gallery, where the fair maidens were sitting. A hush fell over the crowd, and Cristyne sat stiff and straight by her side, her mouth open slightly as she seemed to be holding her breath. Gisela concentrated on looking as calm and dignified as possible.

Instead of pacing to and fro in front of the section of fair maidens, as he might have done, Valten guided his horse straight toward Gisela. Did he really mean to pick her? It felt like a dream, not real at all, as Valten made his way to her, lifted his lance over the barrier, and laid the circlet at Gisela's feet.

Every eye was on her, including her stepmother's and stepsisters', she thought absently. But Gisela only had eyes for Valten.

Valten's squire ran forward and took off his helmet, then took his lance. Valten dismounted—very nimbly for a man clad in so much armor—and made his way up the gallery steps. The crowd parted for him like the Red Sea. He fell to one knee before Gisela, and it was as if they were the only two people at the tournament.

Valten picked up the circlet and placed it on her head.

Beads of sweat had tracked lines through the dust on his face. A new trickle of blood was seeping down his cheek from his left eye again, as his cut had reopened. But even in his disheveled state, she was sure she had never seen anyone more masculine and handsome. His gray-green eyes fixed her with a gaze that was for her alone.

Her heart pounded. The tournament champion was supposed to give the Queen of Beauty and Love a kiss. Surely he wouldn't truly kiss her, not on the lips. But the way he was looking at her, she was not sure at all.

"My queen." He bowed his head and took her hand. He lifted it to his lips and kissed her knuckles.

He rose from his knee and held out his arm to her. She placed her hand on his forearm, on top of her own scarf, which was still tied there. Their eyes remained locked on each other.

The crowd erupted in cheers and shouts, a roar that filled Gisela's ears but didn't make the moment feel any more real. She felt as if she was floating, as if the world around her was misty and indistinct. This moment was a dream, and though she stood, her feet didn't touch the ground.

Valten started down the steps, and somehow Gisela managed to walk down beside him. The next thing she knew, there was a horse in front of her, a beautiful white mare with flowers braided into her mane and a sidesaddle on her back. Valten placed his hands around Gisela's waist and lifted her onto the horse as easily as if she were a child. He mounted his own horse, and they made their way toward the castle.

The cheering crowds made way for them, parting and throwing flowers onto the road in front of them.

She spent most of her time looking at Valten, and he didn't seem to mind, since he was mostly looking at her, especially as they left the crowd behind and descended the gentle hill to the Hagenheim entry gate. But for one moment, maybe two, she wondered what her stepmother would think, and pictured the look on her face at seeing Valten crown Gisela the Queen of Beauty and Love.

Chapter 9

Valten's mother and sisters took her into their care once they arrived at the castle, while Valten went to take a bath, or "to make himself more presentable," as Lady Rose explained it.

Valten's sisters, Margaretha and Kirstyn, were Irma and Contzel's opposites. They were warm and friendly, smiling and kind from the moment they greeted her when she arrived in the Great Hall, which was still empty except for the duke and his family and the servants who were busy running to and fro.

Margaretha took her arm and led her to a prominent seat at the duke's own table on the raised dais. "You must be tired and thirsty." Margaretha was a lovely girl, and Gisela secretly hoped they would become friends, as Margaretha appeared to be only a little younger than Gisela.

Immediately, a servant stood at her elbow offering her a tankard.

"Thank you." Gisela took a sip of something fruity and slightly sweet. She rarely drank anything except water, and the occasional water-and-wine at her neighbor Ava's home. This was something different, but she liked it, and took a long drink.

She looked up from the rim of her cup to see Margaretha smiling at her. "Do you know that everyone is talking about you, saying how beautiful you are? And everyone is wondering who you are. No one seems to know your name. Does Valten know you? Are you and Valten sweethearts?"

"You shouldn't ask so many questions." Kirstyn frowned at Margaretha and moved closer. Valten's second sister looked to be about fourteen years old, not as tall as Margaretha, and with lighter hair.

Kirstyn looked sympathetically at Gisela. "If you let her, Margaretha will talk you to death. But we love her anyway."

Margaretha smiled. "I do talk too much. It's my worst fault. At least, I hope it is, because I know sometimes we never realize our faults, while they're glaringly obvious to everyone else." She raised her eyebrows at Kirstyn, then turned back to Gisela. "Do you know what I mean?"

Gisela smiled back at her. "I do."

"Shall we try to guess your name?" Margaretha went on. "Perhaps it is Gertrude. Or Elsa?"

"Close. It is Gisela."

"That is a lovely name, and it suits you perfectly. I'm surprised I didn't guess it." Margaretha clasped her hands over her heart.

"Very lovely," Kirstyn agreed.

After speaking to a couple of servants at the other end of the Great Hall, Lady Rose joined them. She laid a gentle hand on Gisela's arm. "We are so pleased to have you join us tonight for the banquet. If there is anything you wish, anything at all, you have only to tell us. And tomorrow it will be the same."

"Thank you."

Valten's mother smiled so kindly, Gisela felt a strange yearning in her heart, and a sudden panic that these people would not treat her so well if they knew who she truly was—a girl without family, and certainly not a wealthy noble, which was the only kind of bride Valten, as a future duke, would take. Perhaps she should go ahead and tell them to avoid any future disappointment.

The banquet guests began to enter the Great Hall. The room became noisy as the people took their seats.

Gisela saw the moment Evfemia, Irma, and Contzel entered through the door. Evfemia fixed her gaze on Gisela, her expression as sly and calculating as any fox. She and her two daughters sat where they'd have a clear view of Gisela, but at a lower table too far away for them to speak to her.

Gisela tried to ignore them. What might they do or say to try to destroy her night? She tried to believe they couldn't do anything, but she'd made the mistake of underestimating them before. They had ruined friendships in the past, out of jealousy, and there was no knowing what they might do to ruin her in the eyes of Valten and his family.

Even worse than the cold anger and scheming looks of her stepmother and stepsisters was Rainhilda's amused derision. The resplendently dressed knight's daughter sat at the upper dais with her mother and a younger cousin, across the table, not far from Gisela. Rainhilda smirked until Gisela met her gaze. Then Rainhilda whispered in her cousin's ear. They broke into raucous giggles, shooting glances first at Gisela, then turning around and catching Irma's eye.

Gisela gritted her teeth and pretended not to notice them. She certainly wasn't dressed as extravagantly as Rainhilda, but their treatment of her only made her lift her head higher and determine not to behave as though she was any less than any other maiden in the room. *We shall see what is more important to Valten and his family, whether it be fine clothes and social status, or* . . . what Gisela had. She wasn't sure what that was, but if Valten valued sincerity over pride and malice, then Gisela wouldn't have to behave haughtily to win Valten's heart.

She refused to compare herself to Rainhilda. Gisela would enjoy this night, this banquet, sitting with Valten's sisters, and being chosen by Valten. She would squeeze every bit of joy out of this banquet, because her stepmother would make her pay dearly for every moment of it as soon as she got her home.

Margaretha asked, "Have you and Valten met before today?"

Gisela didn't mind telling Margaretha the story of Valten coming to her rescue in the street when Friedric Ruexner was harassing her. While Lady Rose and Kirstyn leaned in to listen, she told how they had gone to the stables and how much Gisela had enjoyed seeing the horses.

The subject of horses sent Margaretha on a long discourse on the animal. "Horses are very loyal, I have found, and they seem to have a sense about them, an understanding that tells them if a person is good or bad. They will shy away from an angry person, and yet they are drawn to a kind person. They never forget someone they love, and they will recognize people even after not seeing them for years. Did you know that?"

"Horses are intelligent creatures."

"My youngest sister, Adela, is afraid of horses and won't go near them, but I love my mare."

Gisela and Margaretha continued talking about horses as the servants began bringing out the first course of the meal and filling all the guests' goblets with wine, including an extra goblet beside Gisela.

Lady Rose seemed to notice her looking at the goblet. "That is for Valten. He will sit next to you and should be here soon. Actually, there he is." Her face lit up as she focused on someone behind Gisela.

Gisela looked over her shoulder. Valten strode toward her, now dressed in a green doublet, white shirt, and black hose. He looked clean and a bit pale, making the black stitches over his eye more noticeable. He had not shaved, and the light brown stubble made him look even more rugged than usual.

She tried to appear regal and relaxed while refusing to look at Rainhilda. *God, help me not to disgrace the one who has chosen me.*

Valten stepped over the bench and sat down beside Gisela. He looked at her and almost smiled—that softening of his expression. Gisela smiled back.

Just then, Duke Wilhelm stood where he had been sitting at the head of the table. The room gradually grew quiet.

"Thank you all for accepting our invitation to this banquet. Lady Rose and I are happy to honor our brave knights who have taken part in the competition of this, our first Hagenheim tournament."

The guests cheered almost as tumultuously as they had at the lists earlier in the day. At that moment, Gisela's eye caught Friedric Ruexner's, who was sitting at a lower table with several other knights. He was scowling at Valten in a way that sent a shiver down her back. His gaze then shifted to Gisela, and he gave her a lecherous leer, kissed his two fingers, then raised them in a sort of salute to her. She shuddered and quickly looked at Valten, not realizing she was leaning toward him until her shoulder touched his. He looked from his father to Gisela. She felt instantly safer.

Duke Wilhelm raised his hand to quiet the crowd. "Lift your cup in deference to our tournament sovereign, Gisela"—Duke Wilhelm lifted his goblet high in the air—"the Queen of Beauty and Love." He reached out to her.

Gisela took his hand and stood.

She looked around at all the people raising their goblets to her. She tried not to appear as terrified as she felt, and forced herself to smile and nod, thankful she had the presence of mind to pick up her own goblet. A cheer arose, then they all took a drink.

Perhaps not all. From the corner of her eye she noticed her stepmother and Irma did not partake.

Gisela sank back down on her bench.

"And let us drink to our day's champion and victor, my son, Valten Gerstenberg, Earl of Hamlin."

Another clamor of cheering went up, seeming to fill the high ceilinged hall and Gisela's ears.

Valten stood and gave a small bow. He looked completely at ease, as if this was an ordinary moment for him. The crowd drank. Someone cried out, "To Lord Hamlin's health!"

"Hear, hear!" they all shouted. Another man cried out, "To his prosperity!" And another cried, "To his future wife. May they have many children!"

Valten lifted his cup at the man. "I thank you." And drank the entire goblet of wine.

The crowd shouted yet louder, and did not begin to quiet down until Valten had taken his seat again.

While it was still quite noisy, Valten did not speak to her, but began to eat, and Gisela did the same. She ate slowly, imagining who might be staring at her, but she was determined not to look. She was grateful to have Margaretha's constant chatter on one side to distract her, and Valten on the other, like a rampart of safety.

Margaretha said she had never had a suitor and often wondered who her father would find for her to marry. "But I'm in no hurry to leave home. Factually speaking, I haven't decided yet if I *will* marry, which is why Father still has not made any effort to find someone suitable for me. The idea of marriage isn't altogether appealing. Do you know what I mean, Gisela?"

Gisela nodded thoughtfully. "I do. But I think I should like to marry someone who loved me."

For nearly the first time since she had sat down, Margaretha was silent. Her brow furrowed and she pursed her lips and stared down at the table with clouded eyes, as if unseeing. Gisela took a bite of roast pheasant as she waited for Margaretha to speak.

"My parents love me so much, it's hard for me to imagine a man loving me as much as they do."

Gisela couldn't help the slight frown that tugged at her

mouth. Margaretha's life had been so different from Gisela's. How similar might their lives have been if her parents had lived?

Gisela ate while glancing at Valten out of the corner of her eye. He systematically devoured his food and spoke briefly to his father or mother when they asked him a question about the joust. When he had eaten four courses, he stopped and told the servant he was finished. The servant cleared his place of his trencher and all traces of food, and refilled his goblet. Then he turned to Gisela.

"Are you enjoying the banquet?"

"Yes, I thank you."

"I hope you don't need to return home, because my mother plans for you to stay the night here at the castle, with Margaretha."

"Oh." Stay at the castle? That would solve her problem of how to avoid whatever dastardly punishment her stepmother had in mind for her if she were to go home tonight. "I-I don't need to go home. That is, I believe I can stay."

"You will need to be here tomorrow, to preside over the tournament as its queen." His eyebrow twitched, as if his words were slightly amusing to him.

"And to watch you defeat all challengers again." She lifted her brows at him now.

"If God wills."

"You were impressive today." She tried to sound matter of fact. "Your skill is evident, and no one was able to best you."

He gave her a small bow. "God was with me." He looked at her more intently and said, "Ruexner shouldn't be bothering you anymore. As soon as the tournament is over, I will make sure he leaves town."

"Thank you. I was happy you defeated him today."

"And I was happy you stopped him from poisoning Sieger."

Her heart skipped a few beats at the way he was looking at her. "Me too."

"What will happen tomorrow?" She already had a good idea of what would take place, but she wanted to hear him speak.

"Tomorrow the challengers will make their choice of weapons, either sword, battle-ax, or mace, and we shall fight on horseback until someone is unhorsed. We shall then continue to battle on the ground until someone gives up or the marshals stop the fight."

She hesitated, then asked, "Do you enjoy fighting? Is it thrilling for you?" She wanted to understand him, to understand why he had dedicated his life to jousting and tournaments and combat.

He was quiet, looking down at the table. Had she offended him with her question?

"I used to find it thrilling." One corner of his mouth went down. "It seems pointless now, so much so that I wonder why I do it." He looked her in the eye for a long moment before continuing. "There used to be something driving me, making me strive to be the best at everything. I wanted to prove myself. But now it sometimes seems like a waste of time."

Gisela nodded. "I understand. Sometimes I feel like I should be doing something different. Sometimes I feel as if I will die if I don't get away—from home." She almost said, "from my stepmother."

He tilted his head to the side as he stared at her. " Do you know what it is you want to do? Where would you go?"

"That is the problem. I can't leave. I don't want to leave my horses."

She was afraid he would laugh at her, but he nodded gravely. At that moment, she was certain he understood, as no one else had, why she couldn't leave her horses.

"But at the same time, I feel connected to my father's home, to the place where I was born. I don't want to give it up to anyone." *Especially Evfemia and her evil offspring.*

"Do you have an older brother to inherit your home?"

"No, my stepmother is the heir. It isn't my home at all."

He stared into her eyes until she could no longer meet his gaze. He was feeling sorry for her, she was sure. In her experience men didn't want to feel sorry for anyone, and she didn't want him to pity her. She had to turn the conversation back toward him.

"So what will you do when you stop competing in tournaments?"

He smiled and shook his head almost imperceptibly. "I don't know. But I feel like I'm getting closer."

In fact, he was getting closer. His head was bent toward her, in order for them to hear each other in the noisy Great Hall. But his undivided attention was doing strange things to her heartbeat, making it trip and stumble inside her. Perhaps she should keep talking, to distract herself from his beautiful eyes.

"Your sisters and parents are so kind. I like them very much."

A lock of her hair had fallen across her cheek. It brought to mind the fact that her hair didn't look like the other maidens around her. Their locks were either arranged in perfect stiff curls, or were covered by their elaborate headdresses. She must look like a poor peasant in comparison.

His hand came up and his fingers brushed the strand of hair from her cheek. "I don't like your stepmother treating you badly." His voice was brusque, as if he were talking about a battle maneuver.

His unexpected words caught her off her guard. "I ... I take care of myself." Unable to meet his eye, she found herself staring at his big, brawny hand, which rested on the table.

The minstrels, who had been playing softly while they ate, began to play a much louder, much livelier tune.

"Come. Dance with me." Valten swiftly turned around, lifting his legs over the bench, and he grabbed her hand. She turned around too, pulling her skirt over the bench with her legs. Then he stood and pulled her up.

Gisela let him lead her to an empty space at one side of the Great Hall, away from the tables. The entire hall of people was watching them.

A terrifying thought overcame her. "Wait! Please." Gisela pulled on his hand to get his attention.

He lowered his brows in question.

Her cheeks started to heat, but she had to tell him the truth. She couldn't look like a fool in front of all these people. "I-I only know the country dances that the servants and farmers dance. I don't know any others." Now he would surely think her completely unsuitable and would forget about her.

His hard, masculine features softened even more. His eyelids lowered as he bent his head near hers. His lips were so close, his breath brushed her cheek when he spoke. "Don't worry. I know those dances too." Giving her that intense, almost-smile of his, he started dancing the ***reigen***.

Gisela nearly laughed in relief, as she knew the dance well.

They danced, and though a whole crowd followed their every move, she felt as if she and Valten were the only two people in the world. The music carried them over the floor. She was mesmerized at being the object of this man's attention—this very tall, very powerful tournament champion. He was looking at *her*. He was dancing with *her*. He was giving his almost-smile to *her*. It was an even headier feeling than racing Kaeleb over the countryside, his powerful legs pumping beneath her and the wind whipping her hair out behind her.

She felt free on Kaeleb's back, free from her stepmother's and stepsisters' spite. Just as at this moment. They couldn't hurt her now, not while she was dancing with Valten. She wished he would dance with her forever.

But she had a strange feeling that her stepmother would still haunt her somehow, as if she had some strange hold over her that wouldn't be broken no matter what.

She pushed the unwelcome thought away as she gazed up at Valten's chiseled face. He should have been frightening with the scars, the stitches over his eye, and the day's growth of stubble darkening the lower half of his face.

But he wasn't. At all.

When the dance was over, the musicians immediately began another lively tune, an *estampie*, and the two of them were joined by several guests, who linked hands with them and lifted them high, stamping in time to the music, shouting at regular intervals as they released hands to spin around, then clasped hands again to sway and stamp in their human, breathing circle of life.

Gisela had never felt so alive, so pretty, and so accepted.

Even when Rainhilda joined the dance, it didn't dampen Gisela's spirits, as Valten never seemed to look at her once. Even Irma and Contzel eventually joined a few dances as well. Every time Gisela glanced their way, Contzel was staring at her as if in amazement, and Irma looked at her with contempt to rival even Rainhilda.

Valten danced every song with her. She sighed inwardly with joy every time his hand held hers, or they brushed shoulders, or they stepped so near their faces were only inches apart. Valten never seemed to grow tired, and though Gisela still wished the night wouldn't end, she was becoming so exhausted she was afraid she would stumble.

Standing and getting everyone's attention, Duke Wilhelm called a halt to the festivities by thanking everyone for coming and dismissing the guests.

While his father was speaking, Valten took her by the arm and turned her to face him. His hands wrapped around her upper arms, holding her gently. "You are even more beautiful when you dance."

"Thank you." She sounded breathless.

"I will look for you tomorrow."

"Oh."

"But I may not be able to talk to you at the tournament. You will come to the ball?"

He meant the ball the duke was giving on the third night of the tournament—the ball which would end the festivities. "I will try."

He leaned down and pressed his lips to her hand.

When he lifted his head, Margaretha was walking toward her.

"I will leave you with my sister. Good night." He released her and walked away.

Gisela's knees went weak but she forced herself to stand upright and look at Margaretha, who was smiling from one ear to the other. "Did you enjoy yourself? What am I talking about? Of course you did. Your joy was all over your face. And with my brother! My serious brother, Valten, who hardly even looks at girls, and never asks one to dance—at a banquet, no less."

Before Gisela had time to ask her what she meant, Margaretha took Gisela's arm and steered her toward the staircase, where several other people were ascending.

"So, do you like Valten?"

Gisela laughed at the directness of the question.

"Kirstyn would be embarrassed at me asking you that. Forgive me, but I am always saying too much and asking too many questions." Margaretha clasped her hands and her eyes rolled as if in ecstatic joy. "We will not speak of anything too embarrassing," she went on, lowering her voice. "But I must say that I've never seen him look at anyone the way he looked at you tonight. And he was once betrothed—but that was a strange situation, and I don't have time to tell you about that. It was only for a short time. At least, she was only here for about two days before we found out that she was in love with my other brother—but you don't want to hear about that. Anyway, you must be completely exhausted. I confess I'm quite tired myself, and I didn't dance for two hours! You will sleep in my chamber with me. Kirstyn and Adela will probably already be asleep when we get there, so we should be quiet. I have a nightdress for you to sleep in."

Gisela did her best to keep up with what Margaretha was saying as they climbed the steps and made their way to Margaretha's chamber. She got ready for bed and gratefully slipped in beside Valten's sister, who was soon breathing evenly.

Gisela lay awake reliving the banquet. She closed her eyes, seeing Valten's face hovering above her, the way he'd looked at her when they danced, and the way his lips felt on her hand. She let out a long breath, a tear of happiness squeezing from the corner of her eye. What a wonderful night. To think that Valten would choose *her* as the Queen of Beauty and Love. It was all too wonderful: the dancing, the looks, and the kiss. And tomorrow she would see him again, even if it was only from afar.

His words echoed in her memory, the way he had talked to her at the banquet, asking her where she would go and whether she had a brother, telling her he didn't like the way Evfemia treated her. His face was etched on her eyelids as she drifted to sleep.

Chapter 10

Valten had never enjoyed a banquet so much in his life. As he readied himself the next morning, instead of meditating on the day's tournament battles, his mind kept going back to Gisela.

He had surprised himself again at how much he liked talking with her. He may not be as smooth-tongued as his brother Gabe, but Gisela also seemed to like talking to him. The night was full of surprises, as he had not expected to ask her to dance, or, when it was time to say good night, to kiss her hand.

Her skin was so soft and her smile so sweet. Even surrounded by such a great crowd of people, he'd considered giving her a real kiss.

Strange that he could be thinking such a thing when he had only spoken to her once before yesterday. Either he was going daft, or there was something special about her. She seemed to understand how he felt about wanting to do something that mattered.

He wished he had made her promise to come to the ball and be his partner, even if he lost today.

He was no good with women. He never knew what was proper. If he was able to talk to her at the tournament, and if she talked to him at the ball tomorrow night, would it be too soon to kiss her on the cheek? At the banquet, had he exhausted her too much with all that dancing? Would she rather have sat and talked? He was so inexperienced it made him unsure of himself, which was irritating. He was never unsure of himself.

Valten was desperate enough to wish Gabe was here so he could ask his advice.

He grunted, making his squire hurry over. "What do you need, my lord?"

"Fetch me some fresh water."

Hugo left quickly, closing the chamber door behind him.

Valten didn't need more water, but he wanted to be alone for a few minutes. He sat down and began eating the breakfast that had been brought up to him. In spite of his unwelcome shyness toward Gisela, he felt oddly energized this morning after getting less rest than he liked before a day of combat. But Gisela had been worth losing sleep over. She danced as if nothing had ever made her so happy. She smiled as if it was only for him. He hoped those smiles meant she liked him, because he hoped to dance only with her at the ball tomorrow night.

But for today, he would ready himself for his battles. Above all, he must not injure himself too badly to dance. The time he had broken his leg had proved disastrous, as far as getting a wife.

Gisela made him not care about that, made him think it was for the best. But breaking his leg today would certainly *not* be something he'd be thankful for.

Friedric Ruexner would likely be his most dangerous opponent. That fiend would do anything to defeat Valten. He'd already tried to poison his horse, forcing Valten to post a guard to watch over Sieger day and night. But what else would Ruexner try? He had been eyeing Gisela during the banquet last night. Would he bother her today? Ruexner would despise her if he knew she had been the one to discover the water hemlock in Sieger's food. But just the fact that she was the one Valten chose to be his Queen of Beauty and Love made her a target for Ruexner's jealous wrath.

He would post a guard to watch over Gisela as well.

Hugo helped Valten dress, putting on his mail, then his armor. Soon he was ready for the day's tournament activities. Valten closed his eyes and said his usual prayer at the beginning of a tournament day. He asked God to help him focus his mind on his task, to give him strength and skill, and to bless him with victory.

Valten crossed himself, then kissed the small iron cross around his neck. He stood and pulled his sword from its scabbard to hear the metallic *zing*, but it didn't send the usual vibration of suppressed-but-eager energy through his limbs. He had been thinking for some weeks that this might be his final tournament. Was he ready to quit tourneying because he'd met Gisela and decided to pay court to her? Or had he decided to pay court to Gisela because he was quitting his tourneying?

He had no time to ponder it. He had a long string of knights to defeat, knights who would love nothing better than to beat him into the ground and make names for themselves by defeating the seldom-defeated Valten Gerstenberg.

Valten resheathed his sword. His whole body felt as taut as a bowstring. He was ready.

Gisela awoke wondering what she would wear. She had only the blue dress she'd worn the day before. Would she disgrace herself by wearing the same dress again?

The sun was peeking through the narrow window in Margaretha's chamber as Gisela slipped out of bed, careful not to wake Valten's sister. But as she stood, Margaretha rolled over and opened her eyes.

"Good morning, Gisela." She stretched her arms over her head. "Oh, I'm so excited about today." She pushed the blanket away and sprang out of bed. "Tournaments are wonderful, don't you think? The servant should be bringing us some breakfast soon." A maid entered through a side door. "There she is now! It was as if my speaking about it made our breakfast appear." Margaretha's cheerfulness was so unique in Gisela's limited experience of people, she found herself raptly anticipating her next exclamation of delight.

Adela and Kirstyn, who were sharing the chamber, awakened and sat up. When they saw the servants with the food, they climbed out of bed, rubbing their faces.

"Come, Gisela." Margaretha motioned her toward the small table where their repast was being laid out. "Let us eat so we can be ready when the tournament begins. We mustn't be late."

While the three sisters chattered happily, Gisela tried to comply. But the buttery bread stuck in her throat. Must she wear her mother's blue dress? What would people think of the Queen of Beauty and Love having only one suitable gown?

She let the girls draw her into their conversation as they ate the delicious pastries, stewed fruit, and cold meat.

Two maids entered the room and began helping Kirstyn and Adela with their dresses. Gisela glanced around but did not see her own dress.

"Your hair is so beautiful." Margaretha stood up from the table. "May I brush it for you?" Gisela sat on a stool while Margaretha did just that—and talked.

The maids finished readying the two younger girls, then one said, "Miss Margaretha, are you ready to dress?"

"Oh! I almost forgot. Gisela, I can't wait for Valten to see you wearing this dress."

She hurried over to a corner of the room and gathered up a crimson dress that was draped over a trunk. "This color is perfect for you. The blue you wore yesterday was perfect too, but this red"—she held the gown up to Gisela's chin—"goes wonderfully with your skin and hair."

Still holding it up, Margaretha looked as satisfied as a mama cat with her kittens. "Do you like it?"

The dress was a deep red with intricate embroidery around the square neckline and the hem. "I can't tell you how thankful I am." Tears filled Gisela's eyes.

Margaretha didn't seem to notice. "We had a servant girl once who was in love with a cobbler's son, but he never paid her any notice. So I dressed her up and taught her to dance, and at the next Midsummer's Eve festival in the Marktplatz, he couldn't take his eyes off her." Margaretha smiled smugly. "They're married now and expecting their first child in a few months."

Gisela stared openmouthed at Margaretha, then laughed. "Margaretha the Matchmaker." Would Margaretha be able to work her matchmaking influence on Gisela and Valten? But that was too much to hope for.

Though this red dress was a hope builder. The enormous sleeves flared at the elbows and hung down in a point. The belt was of the same material and embroidery as the border, and the bodice looked like it might be too small.

"What if it doesn't fit?"

"We'll put it on you and see."

Margaretha and the servant helped pull the elaborate dress over Gisela's long white chemise, then adjusted it into place and laced it up in the back. "It fits perfectly!" she crowed. "I thought it would. I hope you don't mind that it was made for my mother, but she declared that red wasn't her color and gave it to me. Red is not my color any more than it is hers, but it looks as if it was made just for you, Gisela." Margaretha beamed as she threw open the window shutters.

The light streamed in and made the beautiful fabric shimmer. Gisela smoothed her hands over her waist, amazed at how well the gown fit. It was by far the most beautiful and extravagant dress she'd ever worn. Mentally comparing this dress to the ones she wore every day at home made Gisela feel she had exchanged her servant rags for a princess's ball gown.

"I shall be sure and return it to you."

"Oh, no, it is my gift to you." Margaretha looked her over from head to foot. "It has found its rightful owner."

Gisela threw her arms around Valten's sister. "Thank you."

Margaretha hugged her tight. "But we must hurry and get ready. You are our tournament queen and you mustn't be late. I'm not sure they can start the day's bouts without you."

Gisela submitted to the ministrations of a servant, who prepared her hair in loose curls and dressed it with small braids, ribbons, and a circlet and veil. She did the same for Margaretha, who dressed in a lovely pale green dress. As soon as the servants were finished with them, she grabbed Gisela's arm and ran out of the chamber.

"Oh, I forgot something." Margaretha ran back inside her chamber and came back out with a long red scarf the same color as Gisela's dress. "Valten will want to wear this today." She grinned at Gisela and together they ran down the steps.

What other delights would this day hold? Or would the next twenty-four hours be quite different from the last?

Valten and Sieger waited for their first challenger. Gisela's red scarf dangled from where Margaretha had tied it around his arm. He liked it there.

And he liked looking up into the center of the south gallery and seeing Gisela sitting in her special place as the queen. She was there because he chose her, and every person at the tournament knew it.

He let his gaze stray to her again and again. The red of her dress seemed to emphasize her beauty. She was the most beautiful woman in Hagenheim.

Hagenheim? She was the most beautiful woman he'd seen anywhere. He looked forward to being able to talk to her again.

His first opponent came out onto the lists, a young knight from Burgundy who had distinguished himself in a few tournaments. He had chosen the sword as the weapon they would use. They waited until the marshal dropped his flag, then ambled their horses toward the middle of the empty field, holding their swords at the ready.

Both horses held steady as they neared each other. Valten nudged Sieger forward, closing the gap between them, then struck at the young knight, clashing blades with him.

The man fought well as Valten tested him, biding his time and hoping to wear him down. Valten would miss fighting—a little—but by stepping away from tournament life, he could do other things, and his mother and father would be happy.

Just then, the Burgundian knight landed two quick blows; the second one Valten wasn't quite prepared for, and he was only able to block it partially. The tip of the blade struck Valten's shoulder.

He'd let his mind wander, and he never did that.

Valten began to attack, careful to stay solidly in the saddle and turn his horse instead of his body. If he got off balance he could easily fall, and falling off one's horse placed a man at a decided disadvantage. Armor was heavy and made it difficult to get up quickly, and a knight's opponent could dismount, stand over him, and be declared the winner before he was even able to get to his feet.

Sieger nimbly maneuvered exactly where Valten needed him to go, and soon Valten had the upper hand, forcing his opponent to parry his every strike. The Burgundian knight was barely able to keep his blade between Valten's sword and his own body armor. Soon, the young knight was leaning back in the saddle and his horse was backing up. Valten pressed harder until he had his opponent twisted at an odd angle in his saddle. Quickly, Valten flipped his sword around the other knight's blade, and though the Burgundian knight hung on to his weapon, he lost his balance and fell, landing on his side in the dirt and churned-up grass of the field.

This was a familiar position for Valten. He dismounted and stood over the young knight, crossing his sword with the downed knight's before he could stand up. He didn't have a chance and shouted his surrender, as the marshals were running toward them to halt the fight and declare Valten the victor.

Valten immediately backed off.

One bout finished, several more to go. And Gisela was smiling and clapping her hands and looking as lovely as she had the night before when he'd danced with her.

Gisela heaved a sigh of relief when Valten knocked his opponent off his horse. When he stood over him in triumph, she allowed herself to cheer and applaud with the rest of the crowd. The sight of him, looking valiant in his armor, his feet planted solidly, and her red scarf flying on his arm, made her heart soar, and she couldn't have repressed her smile if she'd wanted to.

Sitting on her "throne" in the gallery, Gisela felt honored, and also a little ridiculous. To be looked upon as the Queen of Beauty and Love was both enjoyable and awkward, but knowing she'd been chosen by Valten ... that was by far the best part. And he was wearing the red scarf Margaretha had given him. She remembered how he had looked at her when she tied her blue scarf to his arm. She wished she could have tied this one on too, but she'd had to hurry to her place. The duke's own guard had escorted her there, and he stood nearby, as though keeping watch over her.

Gisela felt a bit lonely by herself, but she soon saw Cristyne and motioned for her to come sit with her. She wished Margaretha could be with her too, but she was with her family on the opposite side of the lists. Cristyne and her cousin, who came with her, kept up a friendly chatter that soothed the uncomfortable feeling that the entire crowd was watching her. The children in the crowd had continued to stare and make comments about her, as if she couldn't hear them.

Out of the corner of her eye she couldn't help but see the jealous glares of Rainhilda and her friends, and she'd made note of where Evfemia, Irma, and Contzel were sitting. She felt, rather than saw, their eyes on her but refused to allow them to ruin the day.

She instead focused on Valten while he was before her, and once or twice she fancied that he was looking at her too. But he kept his visor down and she couldn't see inside the dark helm.

Dear Lord God, I know this day can't last, but I will remember it forever. She caught her breath at the fervency of her own feelings. But she couldn't expect Valten to feel as much for her as she did for him. And though everyone might expect Valten to marry the lady he chose to be the Queen of Beauty and Love—hadn't everyone expected him to choose Rainhilda, and to marry her?—no one would expect him to marry an orphaned servant.

But he felt something for her, at least. No matter what might happen in the future, he at least thought of her now. And she had never dared dream of being noticed by him.

No, that wasn't true. She had dreamed.

Valten's second challenger rode onto the field. Friedric Ruexner was easily distinguishable by his black armor and the ugly gray skull on his surcoat and his horse's caparison. The spike on his helmet was not crowned by feathers this time. There was no extra decoration besides the gray skull on a black background. It made the red scarf on Valten's arm seem to stand out even more.

Her heart beat faster. She had to swallow the nervous lump in her throat as she thought about the malice in Ruexner's eyes when he'd looked at Valten, and the fact that the man would do anything to defeat Valten, even poison his horse.

O God, please protect Valten from any malicious tricks. Ruexner would take any unfair advantage he could, as he did not adhere to the rules of honorable conduct that knights swore to uphold. But Valten would never violate the codes of chivalry, putting him at a disadvantage.

Knowing people might be watching for her reaction, Gisela strove to keep herself from looking anxious. She would convey complete confidence in her champion. Making an effort to keep her hands unclenched, she stared as impassively as possible at the scene before her. She had always been good at concealing her true feelings from her stepmother and stepsisters, laughing in their faces when she wanted to cry, hiding her anger and contempt to avoid punishment, and refusing to let them see how much their cruel words hurt her. So surely she could conceal, from this rough crowd, her anxiety for Valten's safety.

She concentrated on breathing evenly as they all anticipated the moment the marshal would lower his flag. Valten and Sieger waited, still and quiet, while Ruexner and his mount fidgeted, his horse pawing the ground a bit and lifting his head and pricking his ears forward. Ruexner pulled on the reins with one hand and flexed his other hand around his sword hilt, while his mount whinnied nervously.

The flag dropped, and both horses sprang forward at the same time.

Instead of slowing when he approached, Ruexner continued to charge his horse forward. With an enraged roar, he slashed his sword downward as he reached Valten, slamming the blade onto Valten's head and shoulder as he thundered past. Valten, unable to turn Sieger out of the way without forcing him into Ruexner's horse, took the full force of Ruexner's blow, but he dealt a blow of his own to Ruexner's helmet.

Valten, as far as Gisela could tell, was unfazed, but Ruexner's head hung low. After a moment, he straightened and turned his horse around. As soon as he did, Valten was upon him. Ruexner raised his sword just in time to block the blow.

The two crossed swords again and again, the sound of clanging blades ringing through the open air as they parried each the other's strike. *Please don't let him make a mistake*, Gisela prayed, clutching the arms of her chair. The fight was punctuated by Ruexner's roars and growls as he seemed to fight out of an evil fury, a special hatred for Valten. But Valten's experience and skill were legendary. He would defeat this foe as he had defeated many others. *Please, God, let it be so.*

Valten seemed to get the upper hand, and forced Ruexner to lean away from him and turn in his saddle. If he could throw Ruexner off balance ... Suddenly Ruexner slashed downward, farther than necessary. Valten pulled on Sieger's reins to move him aside, but it was too late to prevent Ruexner from deliberately striking Valten's horse. Sieger screamed.

Valten took advantage of Ruexner's lowered sword and awkward angle to thrust his blade into the small space under Ruexner's arm that was unprotected, between his plates of armor.

Sieger, still reacting to being struck, reared, unseating Valten as Ruexner roared with pain and rage, and both Valten and Ruexner went down.

The crowd gasped as the two warriors landed on the ground at the same time, their horses sidestepping out of the way.

Gisela prayed under her breath, hardly knowing what she was saying. She clasped her hands over her mouth as Valten and Ruexner scrambled to be the first to get to their feet.

Chapter 11

Valten braced himself as he hit the ground, barely feeling the impact as he focused on keeping a hold on his sword, getting to his feet before Ruexner, and trying to land the first blow. He was unable to see where Ruexner had struck Sieger, but he hoped the blow had been a glancing one, and that the saddle and the fabric of his horse's caparison had saved him from significant injury.

Ruexner was still struggling, moving slow as he rolled over. Valten got himself to one knee and was pushing himself up with his sword when he was hit in the eyes with stinging sand.

The dirt came through the eye slit in his visor and the air holes in his bevor, choking him and obstructing his vision. He clawed at his helmet with his free hand but it was futile; he couldn't do anything to wipe the dirt from his eyes. He blinked, and the sand seemed to cut his eyelids.

Forcing his eyes open, he stared through the dust, holding his sword in a defensive position. He could barely see and couldn't find Ruexner at all. Where had the devil gone? Or was he there in front of him, still trying to get to his feet, and Valten just couldn't see him through all the grit in his eyes?

This sort of behavior would not win over the crowd. And striking Valten's horse was a violation of the tournament rules.

He couldn't tell Ruexner that, even if he'd wanted to, because his throat was too clogged with dust.

He fought the urge to close his eyes, ignoring the burning and the tears streaming down his face.

Ruexner roared, then Valten saw him running toward him, his sword high over his head.

Valten stood still, waiting; then, just before Ruexner's sword landed its blow, Valten lunged to the side, slashing Ruexner under his other arm.

The man must be bleeding from under both arms. But Ruexner spun around and came after Valten again, still roaring his fury, as he struck over and over. Valten parried and landed a few blows that forced Ruexner back. Then Ruexner surprised him and struck at his left side, landing a blow on Valten's unprotected left hand, as he wore a gauntlet only on his right. Valten ignored the pain, and while Ruexner was stretching for Valten's left side, Valten used his foot to cut Ruexner's feet out from under him. As the man fell, Valten's sword wrapped around his opponent's blade and sent Ruexner's weapon flying. It landed in the dirt some thirty feet away.

Valten stood over his foe, his foot on Ruexner's chest and his sword tip under Ruexner's chin, pushing his head back.

"Surrender to me! And swear you'll never challenge me again." Valten said the last part quietly, for only Ruexner's ears. He was sick of this man's grudge. "Or should I dispatch you to your maker?" He deserved it, the dishonorable cur.

"I'll never surrender to you," Ruexner ground out between clenched teeth.

Just then, the marshals tried to get between them, declaring that the match was over and Valten was the victor. They urged Valten to back off, but he wasn't willing to let Ruexner up just yet. He pressed his sword point to Ruexner's neck, between his helmet and his mail, pricking his skin. How dare he play his dirty tricks—striking Sieger and throwing dirt in Valten's eyes.

The marshals pulled Valten off Ruexner by force.

As Ruexner slowly got to his feet, one of the marshals stood between them, but Valten could see Ruexner's bloodshot eyes fixed on him.

"It is finished." Valten meant to warn the man.

"It is not finished," Ruexner shot back. "I am not finished with you, Valten. Not until I defeat you. *You* will surrender to *me*. I swear it."

Don't make me kill you. Valten kept the words to himself. It had been his good fortune to have never caused the death of any of his opponents. But he was at peace with it if he was forced to kill in self-defense.

Ruexner just might be the first.

Gisela's breath caught at the sight of Valten's limp left hand and the way he was holding it.

Blood oozed down Ruexner's sides, showing bright red against his armor. He was hurt too. *Good.*

The marshals forced Ruexner to walk away from Valten and off the field. The crowd shouted insults and hissed, and the ignoble knight yelled curses and shook his fist at them. The crowds laughed from the safety of the perimeter and shouted back at him.

While Ruexner was leaving, Valten's squire helped him take off his helmet, and Gisela noticed he didn't use his left hand. Though his face was sweaty and dirty, he didn't appear to be seriously hurt. Valten raised his sword at the crowds, facing one side, then the other, while the people cheered wildly and yelled praise and cheers. Gisela forced herself to swallow down her anxiety for him before he faced her side of the lists. He lowered his sword and bowed to her.

Her heart lurched inside her.

He bowed low, going down on one knee, and the crowd went even wilder with their cheers. She acknowledged him with a shaky smile and a slow nod.

As Valten stood, he put his sword hilt to his lips, then opened his arm in a wide gesture to his queen. He stood there until the crowd gradually stopped cheering.

When the people were quiet, he said in a loud voice, "Long life to Queen Gisela, the Queen of Beauty and Love."

Gisela felt all eyes on her, but she only saw one person. "And to you, Valten, Earl of Hamlin, the bravest and most noble knight of them all."

"Hear, hear!" the crowd cheered, yelling and stomping and clapping.

He seemed to raise his chin at her in approval. She tried to look demure. All those years as a child when she had dreamed about him, she could not have imagined how it would feel to be here now, the object of his homage and his smile.

Valten walked off the field, and his squire led Sieger away. Gisela was happy to see that his caparison wasn't even torn and the horse didn't appear to be injured.

How she longed to go to Valten, to find him as she had the day before. She would love to know how badly his hand was injured, if he had other injuries. But she could hardly wander around unnoticed today. Yesterday she had been nobody. Today she was the Queen of Beauty and Love.

Gisela could hear people discussing whether Valten would come back to fight the rest of his opponents. Was he finished for the day? How many more challengers were waiting to fight him?

"Gisela?"

She turned to Cristyne, who was standing at Gisela's left side. "Emeludt and I want to walk around. Will you come with us?"

Was she allowed to leave her place while the tournament was still going on? "I think I should stay here."

"Valten was wonderful, wasn't he?" Cristyne squeezed Gisela's arm, her eyes wide.

"Oh yes," her cousin Emeludt agreed. "He is the bravest knight of all. I hope we will see him fight again."

Cristyne must have understood Gisela's lack of excitement, for she said sympathetically, "I don't think he is seriously injured, but if we find out anything, we will come back and tell you."

"I would be grateful."

"He looked very well when he smiled at his queen." Cristyne winked.

"Yes he did," Gisela admitted. She clasped her new friend's hand for a moment before watching Cristyne and her cousin go down the steps of the gallery and disappear into the crowd.

Two more knights came out onto the field to fight, but Gisela felt little interest in it.

Once, when she looked to her right, Evfemia and Irma were looking at her. They waved. Irma punched Contzel, who looked startled, and then she turned toward Gisela and smiled and waved too.

A chill went down Gisela's spine, but she gave them a stiff wave in return. Why were they pretending they were happy to see her? She was sure it did not bode well. But perhaps they wanted to be nice to her, hoping she would do something for them. Perhaps they would treat her kindly now that she had been singled out by Valten. Maybe they were even sorry for the way they'd treated her in the past.

Such thinking was pure folly.

After watching three more bouts of fighting, Gisela could hardly sit still. In the third one, they took off the defeated knight's helmet as he lay on the ground. He was unconscious and bleeding from the nose, and he had to be carried off the field on a litter.

Two more knights took the field. Cristyne came into view through the crowd and began climbing the steps toward Gisela.

When Cristyne reached her, she said, "I saw a boy who knows Valten's squire." Cristyne paused to catch her breath. "He says the healer told Valten his left hand was broken and he shouldn't fight any more today."

Poor Valten. He must be disappointed not to be able to finish the day. She hoped he wasn't in too much pain.

Cristyne swallowed, still trying to catch her breath. They clasped each other's hands, and Gisela was thankful for the comfort of her friend's small fingers.

"But Valten says he will keep fighting."

"Oh no." Gisela noticed people leaning toward them, trying to hear. So she leaned closer to Cristyne and lowered her voice. "How many more? What will he do about his hand?"

"He is to fight two more challengers," Cristyne whispered. "The healer will bind up his hand. He says he only needs that hand to hold the reins."

Gisela looked into Cristyne's eyes and pretended her stomach wasn't churning dangerously at the thought of how painful it would be to hold the reins with a broken hand.

"Don't worry." Cristyne squeezed her hand. "He will be all right. He wouldn't fight if he didn't think he could win."

"I'm sure he'll be all right." Her voice sounded raspy as she tried to reassure herself. "Thank you, Cristyne. You are a true friend."

Cristyne smiled in that understanding way of hers, the tiny freckles wrinkling around her nose. "All will be well." She leaned forward and whispered in Gisela's ear. "And tomorrow night at the ball, you can see for yourself how well he is."

Gisela would love to dance with Valten again, but at the moment she only wanted him to be taken care of. If only he could survive these next two encounters without another serious injury.

Chapter 12

When Valten came out to fight again, the crowd cheered for him as if he'd already won the tournament and been declared the day's victor. And when his challenger came out, Gisela watched anxiously. Valten's hand looked twice its normal size, at least partially due to the bandage covering it. He was once again mounted on Sieger.

The marshal's flag fell and the fight began. Valten and his opponent crossed swords several times. Then Valten forced the sword out of his opponent's hand. Rather than dismounting to continue fighting, the other knight seemed to realize that he was severely outmatched, and also perhaps realized that by fighting an injured man he would not win the crowd over, and surrendered to Valten.

Only one more battle.

His last opponent came out—and Gisela almost groaned out loud. She'd hoped it would be someone inexperienced, an easy opponent, but Sir John, the Englishman whom everyone called the black and gold knight, would not be easily defeated.

Still, Valten had surely fought with injuries before, had fought long and hard and been victorious. He could do it again.

Valten and Sir John waited for the flag to drop. When it did, they moved their horses forward and met in the middle of the lists, both thrusting at the same time, clanging their blades together, maneuvering so that their horses were side by side and there was nothing between them except their own swords. The battle was fierce, and Valten was forced to sit slightly angled in his saddle.

God, don't let him lose his balance. He could injure his broken hand even worse if he fell. Sir John held on to the pommel with his left hand to help himself stay in the saddle, but Valten did not do the same.

They continued to cross swords, parrying each strike. How much longer could they both go on? Sometimes one seemed to be getting the better of the other, then it was the opposite. They were quite evenly matched. Perhaps the black and gold knight's horse would make a wrong step and throw him off balance, or he would grow tired and make a mistake.

The longer they fought, the more the crowd yelled encouragement to the combatants. Sir John unleashed a flurry of fast thrusts and strikes, forcing Valten to make Sieger sidestep away, but the black knight kept striking, faster and faster, until Valten was hard-pressed to parry his blows. He had Valten's sword pinned against his breastplate.

Gisela could hear them talking to each other as they were locked in this position, but she could not make out the words. "Please help him, God," Gisela whispered, not caring if anyone heard her or saw her concern. She pressed her clasped hands against her chin and prayed, never taking her eyes off Valten, trying not even to blink.

Valten pushed, moving Sir John off of him until they were in the opposite position, with Valten's sword holding his opponent's sword down on his chest, and Valten leaning his weight against the black and gold knight.

Sir John began to slide backward off his saddle, and he wrapped his free hand around Valten's neck. The black knight fell on his back and took Valten with him, with Valten falling on top of him.

They both struggled to get up. Then Valten pushed himself onto his feet. He fought the black and gold knight with his left hand out to his side, while the black knight was on his back, fighting with both hands on his sword hilt. But he was at a great disadvantage lying on his back, and soon Valten sent his sword flying beyond his reach. Sir John was defeated, and he surrendered.

The crowd cheered like hysterical children, throwing their arms around each other and jumping up and down. Gisela's arms went limp with exhaustion and relief. *He did it!* She pressed her lips together so no one would see them tremble.

Cristyne was jumping up and down and screaming. First she hugged her cousin, then she turned to Gisela and squealed, raising her hands over her head.

Gisela embraced her new friend, but she didn't think a queen was supposed to jump up and down. Besides, she wasn't sure her legs would hold her.

When Valten reached his tent, Frau Lena, the healer, was waiting for him. The pain in his hand was so bad, his head was spinning. He thanked God he'd made it through the last battle without disgracing himself by fainting.

A tub of water had been brought into his tent, and the entrance was secured behind him. He allowed the attendants and his squire to take off his armor and undress him and help him into the tub. Frau Lena gave him some herbal drink. He didn't ask her what it was; he didn't care. He drank it all, then relaxed in the warm water. He began drifting away. But pain brought him fully awake again. Someone was unwrapping his bandage. He opened his eyes enough to see Frau Lena leaning over him.

"Just rest," she said. "I need to make sure the swelling isn't getting worse and making the binding too tight."

His hand throbbed. He knew she was trying to be careful, but every movement, no matter how slight, sent sharp pains shooting through his hand.

"I shall bind it with a splint I made from pieces of wood."

He wanted to tell her he didn't care, just hurry and finish, but he was so weary he decided not to talk. He tried to think about how good the water felt. A servant was bathing his face, and he kept his eyes closed, imagining it was Gisela's gentle, soft hands bathing his face.

If only he could fall asleep and remain so until he awoke in his bed tomorrow. His hand would feel better by then. And he could bask in his victory—of this, his last tournament.

Though she stayed for the rest of the tournament battles, Gisela didn't pay attention to who defeated whom. She was thinking of Valten, wondering when she would see him again. Of course, she was invited to the ball, but that wasn't until tomorrow evening. Would she be able to spend the night with Margaretha again? She didn't dare go home. Perhaps Ava would let her sleep in one of her spare rooms. It was at least an hour's walk away, which Gisela could easily do, but in this dress? And alone?

Perhaps she could stay with Cristyne. Gisela had almost made up her mind to ask her when Margaretha started up the steps toward her.

"Did you see Valten win?" Margaretha squealed.

"He was magnificent," Gisela gushed, almost laughing with joy. He must be well if his sister was smiling.

"He will be tired and hurting, but happy because he won."

"Have you seen him?"

"No, but I'm sure he is well. It is only a broken bone in his hand. He has had worse. Nothing to worry about. He will be quite ready to see you tomorrow, you can be sure." Margaretha grinned.

The tournament ended and Duke Wilhelm stood and proclaimed Valten the victor of the second day's battles as well. The crowd cheered, but not quite as enthusiastically as before, as Valten did not come out on the field to take his victory ride around the lists. Duke Wilhelm spoke a blessing over the crowd and bid them a good night, as it was late and soon would be dark.

Gisela looked around and saw Margaretha was still beside her, but her back was turned as she was speaking to a young woman on her other side. Cristyne was starting to leave with her cousin. She turned and waved at Gisela. Gisela waved back, deciding not to ask her new friend if she could go home with her after all.

Margaretha turned back to Gisela and took her arm. "I can hardly wait to see you and Valten dancing together tomorrow night. It will be—"

"Gisela!"

Her heart froze as an icy chill raced across her shoulders.

"Gisela!" Her stepmother's unmistakable voice.

Margaretha stopped and turned around, and Gisela was forced to do the same.

"Gisela, dear." Evfemia was smiling, actually smiling at her. The friendly look chilled her blood worse than the darkest scowl. What could she be scheming?

Margaretha smiled back, completely unsuspecting.

"Gisela, my dear, aren't you coming with your family?" Irma was flashing a sinister grin, and Contzel's mouth was hanging open, her eyes wide and bulging.

Gisela almost said, *What family?* She looked at Margaretha, silently begging for help. But Margaretha only seemed to be waiting for an introduction.

"Lady Margaretha, please allow me to present my stepmother, Evfemia Mueller, and her two daughters, Irma and Contzel."

"My lady." Evfemia bowed low. Irma and Contzel curtsied.

Margaretha clasped her hands in front of her chest. "How lovely to meet Gisela's family. You all must come to the ball tomorrow night."

"You are too kind," Evfemia purred. "Please do give your mother and father our greetings and well wishes. You must be so proud of your brother Valten. He has fought well."

"And you must be so proud of Gisela, our Queen of Beauty and Love."

Evfemia's smile faltered.

"I am so delighted with her," Margaretha went on. "I do hope to call her my sister some day. But I suppose I shouldn't be saying such things. I will embarrass poor Gisela."

Yes, and cause Evfemia a fit of fury.

Evfemia recovered well, only turning a slight shade of green, and she seemed to have difficulty swallowing. When she was able to speak again, she said, "We must go home now. Come, Gisela." Evfemia held out her hand to Gisela.

Gisela turned desperate eyes on Margaretha.

Margaretha said, "I was about to ask if Gisela could sleep in my chamber again tonight, but if you need her to go home ..."

"I'm sure my stepmother can spare me," Gisela said quickly.

"No, in fact I can't spare you, Gisela." Evfemia's eyes glinted. "I need you home with me. Come, come, we will be back tomorrow," she sang out cheerfully, a cheer that no one except Gisela would suspect held a cartload of malice.

"Very well, then," Margaretha said. "I shall see you tomorrow, my queen." She gave Gisela a quick curtsy, then hugged her.

Don't leave me! The words were on Gisela's lips, but she didn't want Valten's sister to think she was crazed. She held on to her composure. Besides, what could she say? How could she avoid going home with her stepmother without causing a disturbance and embarrassing herself and Margaretha—and enraging her stepmother?

As Valten's sister pulled away, Gisela stared at her, pleading with her to read her thoughts, but Margaretha only turned to speak to the guard who had been watching over Gisela all day.

The guard nodded, took one last long look at Gisela and her stepmother, then followed behind Margaretha through the crowd toward Hagenheim Castle.

"Let us be on our way, Gisela." Evfemia's voice was almost normal, almost friendly, almost the voice she used with her own two daughters.

Slowly, Gisela faced her. Her expression looked downright pleasant. It was terrifying.

"Come." She motioned at Gisela with her hand and started down the steps, but when Gisela didn't follow her, she said, "You aren't afraid of your own stepmother, are you? Come, we must go home. The roads will be crowded and you must get your sleep so you can be ready for the ball tomorrow night. We must all be ready, as we were all invited. Didn't you hear?"

Chapter 13

Was Evfemia sincere? Did she now want to show respect to Valten's "Queen of Beauty and Love"? Had she decided to truly be kind, at least on the outside? Gisela didn't dare believe it. Nevertheless, she followed her stepmother and stepsisters across the grassy slope toward their carriage.

Surely Evfemia wouldn't harm her with the duke's family all expecting her to come to the ball tomorrow night. She was the tournament queen, after all. Even Evfemia wouldn't dare keep her away.

Was she foolish to think that?

She walked slightly behind the three as they made their way down the steps and across the lists. Irma and Contzel kept taking peeks over their shoulders at Gisela, like skittish horses spying something moving in the grass. Were they only biding their time until they got her into the carriage? Would they make her walk home after all? They'd never let her ride in the carriage before.

Soon they found Wido with the horses, waiting patiently. Gisela and Wido exchanged glances. His eyes were wide and curious, and darted briefly at her stepmother waiting by the door.

"After you, my dear." She graciously allowed Gisela to enter the carriage ahead of her.

Gisela hesitated, but afraid of angering Evfemia, she stepped onto the first step, then the second, and entered the carriage and sat down on the seat cushion.

Her stepmother came in next, then Irma, both of them sitting across from Gisela. Contzel took the only remaining seat next to Gisela.

She studied their faces, trying not to stare. What was their plan? She suspected by the look on Contzel's face that she was wondering the same thing, while Evfemia and Irma wore smug expressions. Wido's weight made the carriage sway as he climbed onto his perch and started the horses forward.

The silence was like a fifth person inside the carriage, taking up all the breathable air. Gisela stared out the tiny window, but she couldn't seem to focus on anything, and out of the corner of her eye she watched for any sign of violence from her stepmother.

"My dear." Evfemia broke the silence, still sounding as she had in front of Margaretha. "We are so proud of you. It is quite an honor to be chosen by the duke's own son to be the tournament queen."

Since when had she ever been proud of Gisela? When had she ever said a kind word to her? If Evfemia thought Gisela would forget all her cruelty and injustice since her father died, she was mistaken.

Gisela gave her a blank stare, the one she used when she didn't want Evfemia knowing what she was thinking.

"I know I haven't always been as kind to you as I could have, but you didn't make it easy for me, either." Evfemia raised her eyebrows, as though the truth of her statement were indisputable. "You were always so hostile to me and my girls, from the first day we entered your father's house."

It was a lie. The truth was that Evfemia had hated Gisela from the moment she set eyes on her.

"But we won't quarrel about that. What's past is past." There was something sinister hiding behind those thin lips—probably adder venom, or some other deadly poison.

Irma squirmed a bit in her seat, her gaze flicking all around the inside of the carriage, anywhere except at Gisela or her mother. And Contzel was as still as a statue, but there was a wariness behind her eyes, a watchfulness that was a rarity in the girl who seldom stirred from her bed or her most comfortable chair unless forced to.

Perhaps Gisela could sneak out tonight, after they were all asleep, and spend the night at Ava's house. For now, it was probably best to let them think they were fooling her. They would reveal their intentions sooner if she pretended to believe they were sincere. But she also wouldn't make it too easy for them. It might be fun to see them squirm.

"Valten would not like to see you mistreating me."

"Mistreating you? Why, foolish girl, when have I ever mistreated you? But as I said, we won't quarrel about it. You are our own dear Gisela and we wouldn't want it any other way."

With those words, Irma fidgeted even more, and Contzel's eyes darted around like frightened chickadees. *Oh yes. She's scheming something, and her girls know it.*

"Of course." Gisela gave her stepmother a fake smile. "Perhaps, if Valten marries me, you and Lady Rose could become bosom friends."

Evfemia's face turned red as she stared hard at Gisela. *Trying to tell if I'm lying. Or despising me, and despising the thought of me marrying Valten.* But even now, if her stepmother could put her cruel ways behind her, Gisela would not retaliate against her. She would not want revenge against Evfemia, if only Evfemia could lay aside her own malice.

But that was a big "if."

"Has the duke's son asked you to marry him?" Evfemia ran her hand over the material of her skirt, as if trying to smooth out a wrinkle, finally glancing back up at Gisela with low-hanging eyelids.

"Not yet."

"Who knows whether he will." Evfemia shrugged. "Rich men like the Earl of Hamlin can be fickle, especially about a mere orphan girl with no title and no wealth." The corners of her mouth turned down, as if to say, "Such a pity."

"Very true, stepmother."

"But we shall hope for better things, shan't we?" Evfemia brightened, sitting up straighter in the carriage. "After all, it would benefit all of us if you should marry the duke's son. However unlikely that might be."

Yes. However unlikely. Margaretha had said Valten behaved differently toward her, and that she hoped Gisela would be her sister someday. Perhaps he was ready to get married. That was the rumor that had circulated before the tournament. And he could marry anyone he wanted to. But would he want to marry her badly enough to give up marrying a titled lady, with wealth and connections to the king?

She couldn't think about that now. She had to keep up her guard while in her stepmother's presence.

"Irma," Evfemia said, "don't you think that dress looks beautiful on your sister Gisela?"

Irma's eyes got big. Her mouth opened, and then closed, as if she'd just swallowed a fly. "Oh-oh, yes, Mother. She looks … very … beautiful." She looked as if the fly she'd swallowed was coming back up.

"Is that Lady Margaretha's dress? I saw that she was talking with you."

"As a matter of fact, it is. I shall return it to her tomorrow."

"What shall you wear to the ball then?" Evfemia's evil smile was back on her face.

"I'm sure I have something suitable. Don't worry, stepmother."

Gisela grinned to hide her own panic. She hadn't thought about what she would wear to the all-important event tomorrow night. She knew every dress in her mother's trunk, and there was nothing that looked as good as the blue one . . . which she had left at the castle, in Margaretha's chamber.

The carriage was nearing their home. It was already dark, with the last vestige of sunlight glowing in the sky. Wido stopped the horses, and Irma threw the carriage door open, flouncing out before anyone else. Contzel got out next, moving faster than normal, then Evfemia motioned for Gisela to go next. Once they were all out, Gisela started to help Wido unhitch the horses.

"There's no need for you to do that." Evfemia seemed amused. "Come inside, Gisela, and we shall eat something and go to bed. You must not concern yourself with the horses." She laughed, as if the idea were absurd.

It had never been absurd before. Evfemia had always expected her to take care of their animals. One of the many things her stepmother expected her to do. But she would play along. She was curious to see how far Evfemia would take this farce of Gisela being part of the family.

Gisela went inside, where their middle-aged, white-haired servant, Miep, was setting out the cold meat, cheese, and bread on the large wooden table in the dining hall. Gisela wasn't even allowed in the room except to clean, and she never ate with Evfemia and her daughters. All her meals since her father's death had been taken in the kitchen with the other servants. She watched her stepmother and stepsisters from the doorway until Evfemia seemed to notice her there.

"Come." She motioned Gisela in, as if there was nothing strange about it.

Gisela cautiously stepped inside. She pulled up a simple stool beside Contzel, cut herself some bread, expecting every minute that her stepmother would snatch it away from her. She then helped herself to some cold roast pork and some cheese. She ate, silently watching her stepsisters and stepmother. Irma and Evfemia seemed to make an effort to smile at her every so often, but Contzel just stared.

When Gisela had eaten, she poured herself some water from the pitcher into a small cup while Evfemia poured from a wine cask.

"Would you like some wine, Gisela?" Evfemia raised her eyebrows.

"No, thank you."

Gisela drank her water, watching over the rim of the cup. When she finished, she took her cup to the kitchen. Miep gave her a questioning look but said nothing.

Gisela hurried up to her chamber at the top of the stairs. Her stepmother had trapped her inside before. Standing outside her door, she looked behind her down the long staircase. Nobody was in sight. She took the crossbar that was resting beside her door and carried it into her chamber, hiding it in her oldest trunk.

She left her door ajar so no one could sneak up on her. Gisela lifted the old blanket that hid her mother's trunk. Inside it were all her mother's possessions that had not been lost, sold, or taken over by her stepmother. She picked up one of her mother's old dresses, a lovely pink silk, but a bad stain marred the front. Gisela couldn't wear that. The next was emerald green, but it had a tear in the bodice. She could mend it, but it would show, and the bodice seam would be noticeably crooked. She looked through the rest of the dresses. One by one she reluctantly rejected them for some serious flaw. Lastly, she went back to the green dress with the tear. She would simply have to make it do.

She searched for her needle and thread. Sitting by her little window with the shutter open, she began to mend the gash.

Footsteps on the stairs, coming closer to her room, made

Gisela put the dress down and stand. What if her stepmother had another crossbar?

Miep came in carrying a pitcher of water.

"Frau Evfemia bid me bring this to you." Miep set the pitcher on the scarred table that was actually nothing more than a plank of wood propped up with two stools. She gave Gisela a sullen look that seemed to say, "Gisela has always helped me with my work, and must I serve her too now?" She went away, shaking her head and muttering.

Gisela went over and looked into the pitcher. Was her stepmother trying to poison her? She sniffed it. It looked and smelled like water from the well.

She poured a bit of water into a small cup made from a hollow gourd and put it to her lips. She took the tiniest sip. It tasted like water. She waited to see if it would have a bitter aftertaste, or if her throat would suddenly constrict. Nothing happened. But she had better wait to make sure.

She suddenly realized how much she wanted a bath. In the far corner of the room, she poured most of the water in a basin and hurriedly washed herself, keeping an eye on the door.

When she was finished and had put on her best chemise, she sat back down by the window to keep working on her dress. The rip was jagged and frayed. She did her best to conceal her stitches, to prevent the bodice from looking skewed, but even the best she could do still made the dress look quite flawed.

She bit her lip to keep it from trembling. How could Valten be proud to be seen with her if she was wearing this dress? How could she make him see that she was good enough, pretty enough, to be worthy of him?

A tear dripped onto the dark green fabric. Now it would be stained too. She flung the salty drops off her cheeks. Who was she fooling? She was only a servant. When she was seven, her father often told her she was special, that she was beautiful, that she was born to be someone extraordinary. At seven it had seemed possible that she would marry the heir to the duchy of Hagenheim. But her father's words now seemed a foolish jest and not at all the way her life had turned out. At some point she had realized her father, whom she had always adored, had been wrong.

Gisela carefully laid the dress aside and walked to the fireplace. She took out the loose brick and pulled his small portrait out of its hiding place. Somehow his memory had gotten entwined with the memory of Valten as a fourteen-year-old boy, coming to her home to buy a horse. At the time she hadn't seen anything farfetched about her marrying the future duke of Hagenheim. Now . . .

"Father, I didn't want you to die." She touched his portrait face with her fingertip. But he did die, and she must face her problems and take care of them herself.

She sighed and put the picture away, hiding it behind the brick and turning back to the dress. Perhaps she could find something pretty to sew onto the bodice, some kind of border, to disguise the rip. She had to.

Turning back to the trunk, she searched through every inch of it. She decided she could cut up the pink dress and use it to make a border around the hem, the neckline, the waist, and the cuff of the sleeves. She stood staring at the two fabrics. She could work all night, could finish the sewing by morning, but what would it look like when she finished? More like a jester or jongleur's costume than a lady's dress!

Gisela groaned and dropped both dresses back into the trunk. She took a deep breath and let it out slowly. It was already late. She walked to her open doorway and stood still, but she didn't hear a peep. Evfemia must be in bed.

God, what am I to do? She tilted her head back and looked up at the ceiling.

Wear the red dress again. Yes, she could wear the red dress that she'd borrowed from Margaretha. Of course she could. Her shoulders felt lighter, and she sat down on her little straw-filled bed.

She'd wear the red dress. Her stepmother, if she was still pretending to be kind, might even insist she ride in the carriage with them back to the tournament festivities tomorrow. Gisela would see Margaretha again. She might even insist on letting her borrow another dress. But somehow it would all turn out well.

Gisela yawned. Perhaps she should sneak out and ask Ava if she could sleep at her house tonight, but she was so exhausted after the long day. She had sat in full view of practically everyone in the region, been tense and terrified for Valten, and now her bed was the only place she'd like to be.

Her door was still open. *I mustn't sleep too hard or too long.* She had to remain on her guard in case her stepmother tried to keep her from going to the tournament or the ball tomorrow. Truth be told, she didn't care about the tournament. Men would be engaged in competitions of archery and feats of strength, but Gisela had no interest. All she truly cared about was the ball and dancing with Valten, to see him again and talk to him.

She sighed, lying down on her bed in her chemise. She pulled the worn-thin blanket over herself, laid her head on the pillow, and drifted to sleep.

Valten awoke the next morning and immediately felt the pain in his hand. He lifted it and examined the bandage. Frau Lena's wood-and-cloth splint fit snugly to his hand, and was wrapped tightly so that his hand looked like an enormous white stump. The tips of his fingers were barely visible at the end of it, and it came past his wrist, halfway to his elbow.

He growled. Must he put up with such a conspicuous appendage when he was the tournament champion? But he would upset not only Frau Lena but also his mother if he took it off. His mother would cry, and he would put up with almost anything to not make her cry.

He growled again. He'd have to have this thing on his hand when he danced with Gisela at the ball tonight. But he could still dance. He could still hold Gisela with his right hand.

Thinking about Gisela made him restless. He threw the covers off and got up.

"Hugo!"

His young squire came running into Valten's chamber from the small one next to his, blinking and rubbing his face. "Yes, my lord?"

"Find the captain of the guard and tell him I need a report. After you help me get dressed, I won't need you any more today." He winked at the boy. "Go have some fun."

"Yes, my lord." Hugo, with wide eyes, ran back to his little adjoining chamber.

Valten would see Gisela tonight. In spite of the pain in his hand, it was going to be a great day.

Gisela awoke with a start. Her door was closing. She jumped out of bed, but by the time she was halfway across the floor, the door shut and a heavy thud sounded on the other side.

She pushed on the door, but it didn't budge. Despite the fact that Gisela had hidden the crossbar, her stepmother must have found another one to lock her in.

Of course she had.

"Who is there?" Gisela tried to keep her voice calm but forceful. "Who is there? Open this door!"

She listened, but heard nothing. "Who dares to lock me in?" Tears choked her words as despair gripped her.

She pressed her ear against the solid wood door but heard nothing, not even footsteps.

I should have known. What a fool I am. She should have sneaked away to spend the night at Ava's, or even in the stable. Now she was trapped! How would she ever get to the ball now? She would miss her chance to be with Valten. What would he think of her? What would his family think if she didn't show up?

"Let me out!" Gisela pounded on the door. "I'll tell Duke Wilhelm what you did! You'll be thrown into the dungeon."

Evfemia's cackling laugh came from the other side of the door. "You won't be telling anyone. I have sold you to a man who promises to make sure you are never heard from in Hagenheim again."

Gisela's heart pounded harder than her fists. "What man? You're lying!"

"His name is Friedric Ruexner, and he was very interested in getting his hands on you."

Gisela sank to the floor, feeling like she was going to throw up.

"He paid quite handsomely," Evfemia went on, "but don't worry. He's a baron and he promised to marry you. You should be thanking me for arranging this marriage for you. It isn't as if the duke's heir would have married you. Ruexner is the best you could have ever hoped for. And since I can't tell the duke's family the truth, and since we must go to the ball, I shall tell Lord Hamlin you ran away to marry a wealthy merchant."

No. This couldn't happen. She couldn't let this happen! "You will be found out. If you let me out now, I won't tell them what you were planning."

Nothing. Then footsteps, getting farther and farther away as Evfemia descended the stairs.

Gisela stared at the door, too horrified to cry, too numb to think. "God," she whispered. "God, please, please, please ... help me."

Chapter 14

The guard who had been ordered to watch Gisela met him in the corridor as Valten was leaving his chamber.

"My Lord Hamlin." The guard bowed swiftly.

"I wish to know how things stand after our first two days of the tournament. Walk with me." Valten continued down the corridor toward the kitchen. He held his injured hand against his midsection.

"My lord, besides breaking up a few drunken brawls and capturing two pickpockets, we had no problems."

"And what of the two people I asked you to keep a watch over?"

"My lord, our Queen of Beauty and Love remained safe, and no one attempted to bother her all day."

"Where is she now?" A fresh breath seemed to enter his lungs at the thought of seeing her right away. Perhaps even now she was in the kitchen with his sisters, eating breakfast.

"She went home with her family after the tournament yesterday."

Valten stopped in midstride and faced the guard. "What do you mean? I thought she was spending the night with Margaretha."

"No, my lord. I didn't know of any such arrangement. A woman and her two daughters approached her and said she was coming home with them. Lady Margaretha told me they were her family."

"Who was the woman?"

"Lady Margaretha said she was the girl's stepmother, Evfemia Mueller. I was careful to ask the name."

It must have been the woman who treated Gisela so badly in the Marktplatz on the day they'd first met. He supposed she was safe enough with her family, even if they mistreated her, but it annoyed him. He wanted her here, where his guards could watch over her.

"What about Ruexner? Where is he?"

"He left town last night, my lord, immediately after your battle—he and his men."

"Good. But tell the captain of the guard I want you to keep watch for him. He might still be lurking around. If you see him, I want to know immediately."

"Yes, my lord."

An uneasy feeling swept through Valten's gut as the guard strode away. He wanted to send a guard to Gisela's house to check on her, but he didn't know where she lived. He could find out, now that he knew her stepmother's name, but wouldn't he seem … odd and overprotective if he sent guards to her home? After all, they weren't betrothed.

He would wait. She would come back today, and she would be safe in Hagenheim. No one besides Ruexner would dare harm her, and Ruexner was gone.

The sun was just coming up when Gisela stuck her head out her chamber window and shouted for Wido and for Miep. She shouted so much she was becoming hoarse. "Can anyone hear me? Please help me!" Yet no matter how many times she called, no one came.

She waited, watching, staring across the fields. She could just make out the roof of Ava's house past the copse of trees to the north, toward the town of Hagenheim, but it was probably too far away for anyone there to hear her.

The sun was halfway up the sky when Gisela stepped away from the window to get some water.

Now she understood why her stepmother had sent up the pitcher of water. *How kind of her.* She was planning to lock her inside.

The water still might be poisoned, so Gisela took a small sip, then another. It felt good on her raw, burning throat, and since it tasted good, she drank some more.

But no, Evfemia wouldn't poison her now. Ruexner might not pay her if his prey was dead. Terror gripped Gisela, squeezing the air from her chest. "Help me escape, God," she rasped. *I must escape.* To be in Ruexner's clutches would be worse than death.

Her chamber was too high for her to jump out of the window without killing herself, or at least breaking her legs. She studied her door for the hundredth time. The cracks around it were tiny. If she had something small and thin she might be able to stick it through the crack and lift the crossbar. But how would she ever find anything thin enough to fit through the crack that would also be strong enough to lift the bar?

She found a pair of cutting shears and began stabbing it into the door, over and over, but was only able to hack off a few splinters after several minutes.

Why didn't Wido or Miep come to help her? Evfemia must have sent them away, or threatened them, or otherwise made them too afraid to help her.

Gisela alternately prayed, her hands clasped together and her head bowed, her fingers caressing her iron cross, and rushed around the chamber trying to find something she could use to break down her door. She beat at it with a brick from the fireplace.

She hacked yet more with the shears. She sat on the floor and cried. But crying did no good at all.

Footsteps. Someone was coming up the stairs. "Please let me out!" Gisela cried, getting to her knees and leaning against the door.

"Don't worry, my dear," came Evfemia's cheerful voice. "Your new master, Friedric Ruexner, will be here soon—any moment now, in fact—and he will let you out. Irma, Contzel, and I are leaving to go to the tournament and then to the ball. But we will tell your Valten that you won't be there because you have run off with another man. I am sure Rainhilda will help him forget you." She laughed as her footsteps echoed down the stairs.

Gisela's heart froze inside her. No, no, no. *Please, God! Don't let her do it. Don't let her win.*

The window was her only hope. She got up and hurried over to look out, hoping this time someone would be there, on the rutted road that led up to her house, or down below where Wido's flowers grew, the ones he so lovingly cultivated. *Wido.* Why wouldn't he help her? How could he be such a coward?

Of course, he was old, although Miep was not so old, and if they lost their place with Evfemia, they might have a hard time finding another. They could starve if they didn't find work.

Gisela stayed by the window, hearing the crunch of wheels on the road. Soon, Evfemia's carriage came into view around the side of the house.

Gisela stepped back from the window so her stepmother and stepsisters couldn't see and gloat over her. The carriage rolled away, and tears once again fell from her eyes. But she couldn't be crying. She had to do something. But what? She had tried everything she knew, everything she could think of, and she was well and truly trapped.

God had helped her before. Many times in the past, when she prayed for God's intervention, something unexpected would happen. Once when Evfemia was trying to sell Kaeleb, the man who wanted to buy him changed his mind. And when her stepmother tried to marry Gisela off to an odious man from another town, that man couldn't raise the money she was asking for, and he didn't come back.

Not that Gisela would have married him. She had planned to run away to Hagenheim Castle and beg them to give her a job as a servant, a scullery maid, anything. She might have run away anyway, but she couldn't bear to leave her horses, and she still held out hope that somehow, some way, Evfemia would leave, would perhaps remarry and take her ugly daughters with her. Then Gisela would no longer be a nobody, she would be the owner of the Mueller house.

But instead of waiting around for Evfemia to come to some bad end, she should have left. She should have done anything rather than let her trap her like this.

Once when she was a child, she'd imagined her stepmother being killed by a band of knights for her cruelty to Gisela. But she had frightened herself with that dark thought and asked God to forgive her.

Perhaps now she was being punished for having those murderous thoughts.

But no. God was not like that. *Evfemia* was like that. She'd punish a person even after they had repented, but God would not. Besides, God had done good things for her in the past two weeks. Valten had come to her aid when she was accosted by Ruexner in the street. And she had been in the right place at the right time to see Ruexner's squire put deadly water hemlock in Sieger's food, so that she was able to save him.

And best of all, Valten had worn her colors and chosen her as the Queen of Beauty and Love.

But ... it was all for nothing if she couldn't get away. It was more pain than she could bear, to think of Valten waiting for her and not seeing her, of Evfemia lying to him and saying that she had run away with another man. She imagined what he would think of her and she doubled over, pressing her forehead against the floor.

"Oh, God, am I destined for pain?" Her tears fell on her long-sleeved chemise. "God, what will happen to me when Ruexner gets here? I'd rather be nobody than married to him."

Someone was whistling outside her window. She jumped to her feet and stuck her head out.

A boy, one of Ava's servants, whistled as he walked near Wido's flowers.

"Boy! You there!"

The boy looked up, craning his neck back, as he was directly beneath her window.

"Help me, please!"

"You need my help?" The boy's eyes were big and round.

"Yes! Please don't go. I am trapped here in my chamber. I need you to come inside and let me out."

His eyes grew even bigger. "I'm scared of Frau Evfemia. She doesn't like me."

"She isn't here. She's gone and won't be back for a long time. Please. I won't tell anyone you helped me."

"I think I should go tell my mistress, Frau Ava, first." He turned as if to go.

"No, don't go! You must not leave me!" Ruexner could arrive at any moment. Gisela gripped the windowsill so hard a piece of the stone ledge crumbled off into her hand. In desperation, she screamed in her hoarse voice, "I beg you, and I charge you by the Most High God to come and let me out!" She must have heard the words at a miracle play. In her desperation, they must have popped into her mind—and out of her mouth.

The little boy looked hesitant, but finally he nodded. "I am coming." He ran around the side of the house.

Gisela's heart soared. "O God, thank you, thank you!"

Please let the front door be open. She thought she heard it click and creak open. Of course Evfemia would have left it open for Ruexner.

She was only wearing her underdress. She grabbed up the beautiful red gown and pulled it over her head. As she was wriggling into it, she heard the boy's footsteps on the stairs.

"I'm here, I'm here!" she shouted, hoping the sound of her voice would guide him to her room. "Can you hear me?"

"I hear you!" he shouted back. He was now at the door, and she heard him grunting, trying to open the door. *Let the crossbar not be stuck.*

She pulled her dress into place and dug around in the trunk until she found the leather pouch that contained her money, the money her father had made her hide before he died. Then she yanked out the brick in the fireplace, took out her father's picture, and put it in the pouch.

A sound like wood scraping metal came from the other side of the door. The door began to open, creaking slowly, and revealed the boy from Ava's household.

His mouth fell open as he stared at her, looking her up and down.

Gisela squeezed his arm. "Thank you! You saved me." An ecstatic, slightly hysterical laugh escaped her as she looked down at him. "What is your name?"

"Lukas, if you please." He swallowed. "My lady."

"You are a wonderful sight to behold, Lukas, and I shall forever be in your debt. But we must leave here at once, for an evil man is coming—"

She stopped to listen. Horses' hooves thundered toward the house.

Chapter 15

Valten found his sisters, Margaretha and Kirstyn, standing in the courtyard outside the Great Hall. He strode up to Margaretha, but before he could utter a syllable, she cried, "Valten, how is your hand? Are you well enough to dance tonight? I know someone who will be disappointed if you can't dance with—"

"Margaretha, have you seen Gisela?" If he didn't interrupt her, he'd never get a word in. And he wasn't in the mood to listen to her chatter.

"No. I've been wondering where she was. Is she not here?"

"No one has seen her."

Margaretha looked frightened. "I hope nothing bad happened."

Her words made Valten want to shake her. "What do you mean? Why do you say that?"

He didn't realize he was leaning toward her until Margaretha took a step back.

"I'm sure she's fine. But she did have a strange look on her face when she left with her stepmother."

Valten clenched his teeth. Her family had treated her like a servant, with no kindness or respect. What if she was unable to get back to town?

"Don't worry," Margaretha said. "I'm sure she will be here. The ball hasn't started yet. Hardly anyone has arrived."

Valten didn't like his sister telling him not to worry. Only females worried; men took action. He would talk to his father about sending out a couple of soldiers to the Mueller home.

"There is her stepmother now." Margaretha nodded at a woman coming toward them.

"Run."

Gisela took the boy's hand and they ran down the stairs faster than she ever had before. She pulled Lukas along behind her as they headed for the back door. Tugging it open, she darted outside, and she and Lukas hid behind a bush.

Heavy footsteps resounded from inside the house, along with shouts and loud, indistinct talking. Footsteps pounded up the staircase. Instead of waiting to see anything else, she pulled on Lukas's arm and they ran farther into the bushes and trees that separated her home from Ava's.

Not knowing if Ruexner or his men had seen them, she kept running, praying she didn't ruin the beautiful dress. Lukas ran along beside her, and once he even looked up at her and smiled. He was enjoying this little adventure.

If Gisela hadn't been so out of breath, she might have laughed out loud. She *would* go to the ball, she *would* see Valten, and her stepmother would not get away with locking her away and selling her to Ruexner!

If only she could get to the castle before her stepmother told her lies to Valten. Clutching her voluminous skirts in one hand and her money pouch in the other, she and Lukas reached Ava's house and ran through the front door without even knocking.

Ava was just inside, lounging on a bench piled on every side with cushions. She sat up straighter, gaping at Gisela and Lukas. But Gisela was breathing too hard to speak.

"I saved her, Mistress Ava. She said I saved her."

Ava raised herself up. "Gisela, what happened?"

Gisela grew able to talk and told Ava the whole story of being locked in her chamber, and of Evfemia telling her she'd sold her to Friedric Ruexner. "This boy, Lukas, came just before Ruexner arrived."

"I thought I heard someone calling this morning," the boy said, "so when Ernolf offered to finish my chores for me, I went to see who it was."

"Good boy, Lukas." Ava hugged him, then looked at Gisela. "We must get you to that ball." She pursed her lips, her hand on her side, and propped herself up. She looked Gisela up and down and frowned. "That dress is beautiful, but it's soiled and has a rip in it. Come." She turned and started walked toward the back of the house.

Gisela followed her, and Lukas skipped away, no doubt to tell the other servants of his heroics.

Ava opened a large wardrobe and rummaged inside. "Here it is!" She pulled out a beautiful gown of shimmery fabric, a lovely shade of pale blue that was decorated all over with pearls and silver embroidery. It was a dress fit for a duchess, and it took Gisela's breath away.

"Put this on." Ava thrust the dress at her.

"But it's too beautiful. What if I ruin it? Your husband would be upset, and so would you, I imagine."

"Nonsense. He's never seen me in it, it's perfect for you, and I don't think it will ever fit me again. I'm always either pregnant or too fat. And what do I care? He can buy me another. Now put it on. We don't have any time to waste. You must get to Hagenheim Castle before the ball begins."

She would be late. The sun was already sinking, and the ball would begin at twilight.

Ava sent a servant to tell her coachman to get her carriage ready. Then she began helping Gisela off with the red dress.

"Will you hide this for me?" Gisela showed Ava her leather pouch.

Ava took it and stuffed it inside the wardrobe, hiding it behind the clothes inside.

"I can never go home again, and that is the only valuable thing I own. I suppose I'll never see my horses again." Gisela's voice caught and she didn't try to go on. Ava didn't like self-pitying tears.

"You'll see one horse again. Kaeleb has been in my stable since you rode here two days ago."

How could she have forgotten about Kaeleb! "Thank you, Ava! I'm so happy he's safe." God had saved her, and He even saved her favorite horse. When she ran away, she would not only have the money her father left her, she'd have her beloved Kaeleb too.

Ava pulled the dress over Gisela's head, tugging at the bodice until it was straight and fluffing the material down over her hips. "It looks as if it were made for you."

She stepped back and looked at Gisela. "You look absolutely beautiful. The Earl of Hamlin will lose his heart tonight, if he hasn't already."

Gisela felt herself blush.

"Oh, I heard about him choosing you to be the tournament queen." Looking over her shoulder, she yelled, "Bridget! Come now!" Then she grabbed Gisela's hand and led her to a stool and motioned for her to sit. "I know all about him dancing with you at the banquet. And how he couldn't take his eyes off you." She grinned gleefully and patted Gisela's cheek.

Bridget, Ava's maid, came running into the room. "Bridget, we must prepare Gisela's hair for the ball."

They began brushing and styling and discussing Gisela's hair, while Gisela tried not to fidget too much. She was terribly thankful to God for helping her escape her chamber and for saving her from Ruexner, but if Ava didn't stop playing with her hair and let her leave, she would be late.

Valten watched Evfemia Mueller and the two maidens who had called Gisela "Cinders-ela" make their way toward them through the courtyard. When she approached, she bowed low and presented herself and her two daughters to him and his sisters.

Valten was tempted to grab her by the throat and demand she tell him where Gisela was, but Margaretha spoke first.

"Frau Mueller, we were wondering why Gisela isn't with you. Is she well?"

The woman scrunched up her ugly face, looking first at Margaretha and then at him. "I am sorry, more sorry than I can say, but I'm afraid Gisela has … well, I am so ashamed I can hardly speak the words." The woman actually crimped up her face as if she was about to cry.

"What?" Margaretha said, once again helping him to forestall throttling the woman. "What has happened?"

"Gisela met a man, a wealthy merchant from Venice, a few days ago. I'm afraid she has run off with him. He promised to marry her, and she left with him early this morning."

Valten felt the heat welling up inside him. Was she lying? Or had Gisela left with another man? If she hadn't, then where was she?

His betrothed hadn't wanted him either. It was the same thing all over again. She'd chosen another man over him.

Valten turned and stomped back to the Great Hall. He just might put his unbroken hand through someone's face, if given the slightest bit of provocation. Gisela. Could she do this? Would he look like a fool again?

"Ava, I must go!" Gisela's patience was already gone. They had been fussing over her hair for more than an hour. "Please!"

"Very well. You are beautiful. See?" Ava held up the looking glass for Gisela to see for herself.

Gisela only saw an agitated face that desperately wanted to be at the ball with Valten.

"Thank you, Ava. Now I must go!"

"But you have no shoes!"

They all stared down as Gisela pulled the dress up a few inches to show her bare toes peeking out.

"I have the perfect ones." Ava turned and pulled out of the wardrobe a pair of white leather shoes with pointed toes that curled up and over, with a jewel embedded on top.

She had never owned a pair of white shoes before—they were too impractical. These were obviously meant only for leisure parties and feasts ... and for dancing at a ball.

Gisela pulled them on. Amazingly, they fit. Gisela straightened and hugged her friend. "You are an angel from heaven, Ava. Thank you."

"Now go. Valten will be waiting for you." Ava pushed Gisela toward the door, and she was only too willing to leave. She bounded through the doorway, across the marble floor, out the front door, and down the steps to the waiting carriage.

Ava yelled at the coachman, "Don't let any harm come to her."

Otto agreed to keep her safe, and the horses started forward. Gisela was on her way, but the horses seemed to move so slowly, Gisela thought about getting out and running the rest of the way. But she'd certainly destroy her delicate white shoes.

O God, please help me get there, and don't let Ruexner find me. She hadn't even thought about Ruexner for the last hour. If he was riding along this road, he might stop her carriage and look inside. He would surely recognize her, and Ava's coachman, Otto, would be no match for Ruexner and his men.

Chapter 16

Valten stalked through the Great Hall, where the Meistersingers were readying their instruments and getting into place. He kept walking, out into the corridor, not sure where he was going. He came to the library and went inside.

It was dark and quiet, but perhaps not the best choice, as it brought back memories of the day his betrothed, Sophia, and his brother, Gabe, told him in this same room that they had fallen in love with each other. They had asked Valten to relinquish his right to marry her.

Valten ran his hand through his hair, the same anger, the same pain, shooting through his chest. Only this time was much worse. Gisela. He had chosen her. He had thought her the most beautiful, the sweetest, the strongest ... She wasn't afraid to stand up to Ruexner, and she'd saved Sieger from Ruexner's attempt to kill him. She was no ordinary girl. There was no malice, no ugly pride in her eyes when she looked at people. He had even begun to see himself marrying her.

An invisible knife stabbed his heart at the thought of her choosing some other man over him.

Her stepmother had grabbed her in the marketplace. The woman was cruel to her. He'd seen her pinch Gisela's arm. The thought came to him again: What if the stepmother was lying?

Why would the woman be bold enough to try to trick him?

She would pay dearly for lying to the duke's son. Did she hate Gisela so much?

He spun on his heel, ready to look for the captain of the guard, ready to go look for Gisela himself. As he was walking out of the library, Margaretha almost ran into him.

"Valten, that woman, Gisela's stepmother, is lying."

"How do you know this?" Valten sounded like a snarling dog. He blew out a frustrated breath and purposely gentled his voice. "I'm sorry. Why do you think so?"

Margaretha put her hand on her hip and frowned up at him. "I forgive you. I know you're upset, and you have reason to be. Evfemia Mueller is not telling the truth, because Gisela would never run off with another man. You can see it in her face. She would never choose another man over you."

"You only knew her for a few hours, Margaretha. How can you be sure?"

"Trust me, Valten. I know these things. I could see her stepmother was lying by the way she spoke to you. And her two mean girls gave her away, besides. The plump one looked terrified and kept wringing her hands, and the skinny one was smirking and her eyes were twitching back and forth."

"It's not enough proof."

His sister grabbed his arm. "Send someone to her house. I don't believe she ran away with anyone, and she could be in danger."

"That's just what I was about to do."

Valten sent for the captain of the guard, who didn't keep him waiting long. They met in the library. His father, Duke Wilhelm, followed the captain in.

Valten focused on Captain Hartmann. "I want to know where Evfemia Mueller lives. I want to know everything you can learn about her, and I want men sent to her house now to search for Gisela."

"Wait." His father stepped forward. "I can tell you who Evfemia Mueller is. She's the widow of one of my best knights, Christoff Mueller."

Valten waited for his father to go on.

"I had forgotten he had a daughter, but Gisela Mueller is Christoff's only child. And Evfemia took possession of his home and lands and all other property when he died. I had intended to make sure his daughter was taken care of, but I'm ashamed to say I forgot about her. Your little sister, Lindi, died around the same time as Christoff, and I'm afraid your mother and I found it hard to think about anything else for a while. And Evfermia had assured us she would care for Christoff's daughter like she was her own ... The truth is, your mother and I have neglected Gisela, but Lady Rose has spoken to some other ladies today who say Gisela has been treated badly by her stepmother and stepsisters. I think it very likely that Evfemia is lying about Gisela."

"Then where is she? We must find her." Valten spoke between clenched teeth, trying to stay calm. Once again, he was having visions of putting his fist through a wall.

"We'll send guards to her house. We'll find her."

At least Valten knew his father would not rest until he found out what happened to Gisela. But it wasn't enough. "I want to go with them."

"The guards will report back. You should stay at the ball, in case she comes here." Duke Wilhelm lowered his voice. "Besides, Frau Lena says you shouldn't be riding for at least a few weeks."

Valten scowled and turned away from his father.

Duke Wilhelm gave the guard his orders, telling him to head south of the town's western gate to the Mueller house. Valten followed them out, still angry. Angry that his hand was bandaged as fat as a beehive, angry that he didn't know where Gisela was, still angry at the thought she might have run away with another man, even though she had likely done no such thing.

The ball would begin soon. The music would start and the guests would soon be dancing. The night he'd looked forward to was about to commence without Gisela by his side.

Valten joined the festive atmosphere down in the Great Hall, but the song and laughter made his mood even darker. Valten went to find something to drink and then slipped back into the dark quiet of the library. He stayed there, nursing his thoughts, chafing at the time it was taking for the guards to ride to Gisela's house and report back.

It was less than half an hour before a guard, out of breath and being trailed by Duke Wilhelm, burst into the library.

"Your grace, my lord." He addressed each of them and then paused to catch his breath. "We found the house ransacked, and both the front door and the back door were open. We found no trace of Gisela Mueller."

He also said the rest of the men were searching the road and the neighbors' houses. It was the only information the soldier knew, so they dismissed him to stand guard outside the Great Hall.

What could this mean? Valten could hardly stop himself from leaving to go search for her. Why had the house been ransacked? It made no sense.

While they waited to hear the next report, his father talked to him, reassuring him that Gisela would be found, but he hardly heard the words.

Valten paced the floor of the library, imagining the violence he would wreak on the person responsible for hurting Gisela. His father gave up trying to talk to him and waited silently, staring out the small window.

Finally, they heard the heavy footsteps of another guard coming down the corridor and entering the library. "We found her."

After traversing the road toward town and passing through the gate, Gisela's carriage slowly made its way through the crowded streets. The sound of several horses' hooves clacking on the cobblestone streets drew closer until Gisela heard shouts, and the coachman pulled the horses to a stop.

Gisela's heart was in her throat as the door of the carriage was flung open and a strange man stood outside.

"Are you Gisela Mueller?" He was wearing the colors of Duke of Hagenheim's guards.

"I am."

"We shall escort you to the ball."

"I-I thank you." She sank back against the cushioned seat, drawing in a shaky breath.

The man slammed the door shut, there was more shouting, and they started forward again. The carriage began moving faster than before. After several more minutes, it came to a stop outside the castle.

Gisela was helped out by a guard and found herself surrounded by soldiers. Holding her dress's hem out of the dirt, she crossed the empty courtyard toward the Great Hall. Light shone through the windows, and she heard music and singing and lots of voices. She could hardly breathe. Had her stepmother told Valten her lies? Did he believe them? Would he be happy to see her now? Or would he be dancing with some other girl?

Valten's heart leaped at the news.

"What did you find out?" his father asked the guard.

"We went to the closest house and spoke to the owner, Ava von Setenstete, who told us Gisela Mueller was on her way here.

She said Gisela had been locked inside her chamber, and that her stepmother had sold her to Friedric Ruexner."

Valten's hand went for his sword, but it was not there, as he was supposed to be at a ball.

"According to one of the von Setenstete servants, she escaped just ahead of Ruexner. Gisela went to Ava von Setenstete's house, who helped her get ready for the ball, and was on her way here in Frau von Setenstete's carriage. And we found her just as the woman said. She should be here soon."

Valten's father told the guard to apprehend Evfemia Mueller and have her kept in the dungeon. Valten's head was buzzing, but he heard his father also say, "Have every man on high alert, looking for Friedric Ruexner. We must find him and bring him here."

"Yes, your grace."

Gisela was safe. *Thank God.* And she should arrive within moments. Valten headed out of the library and into the Great Hall to wait for her.

Everyone seemed to be having a wonderful time, but Valten could not forget what the guard had said, that Gisela's stepmother had sold her. *Sold* her. To Friedric Ruexner. His blood boiled as he searched the Great Hall and saw Evfemia Mueller standing near the back of the room. He watched as two guards ordered her to go with them. She went pale, as if all the blood had drained from her face. Her two daughters, who were standing nearby, covered their mouths as the guards led their mother away.

"Lord Hamlin!"

Valten turned to see Rainhilda, Sir Edgar's daughter.

"I couldn't wait to tell you." She leaned toward him, as if encouraging him to look down the low bodice of her dress. "You were magnificent in the tournament."

"Thank you." He kept his eyes at the level of hers, refusing to stare at her chest.

She widened her eyes and laid a hand on his arm. "I was so

afraid for you I could hardly breathe." She leaned even closer, and he took a step away from her. "I'm so pleased you were able to defeat them all. You were magnificent."

Not wanting Gisela to see him talking with Rainhilda, he backed away further. "I must go. Excuse me, Rainhilda."

He turned and strode toward the door facing the courtyard, where Gisela would enter. He couldn't stand around waiting for her. He reached the door and opened it, and there was Gisela, walking toward him, her hair in curls piled on top of her head. It was dark, but he could easily see how beautiful she looked.

When he reached her, he put his hand on her shoulder and searched her face in the dim light.

"Valten." She said his name on a happy sigh as she looked into his eyes.

He put his arms around her, pulling her against his chest.

Gisela's heart seemed lodged in her throat as the door opened and Valten came toward her, silhouetted in the light spilling through the doorway. The door closed and the two of them were in the relative darkness of the night, with no one around—except about twenty guards.

She was so happy to see him, to see the concern on his face. When she told him what happened, he wouldn't be angry with her. He touched her shoulder, and joy overwhelmed her.

"Valten." She was just thinking how good his arms would feel around her, when he suddenly pulled her to him.

His chest was warm. She wrapped her arms around him and breathed in the clean smell of his dark blue tunic. The soldiers were backing away, and she'd never felt so safe.

"I thought you would be at the tournament."

"I went home with my stepmother last night, even though I knew it was unwise. I should have known better. The truth is, she locked me in my chamber while I slept." It was embarrassing to admit. What would he think of a girl who could inspire such hatred in her own stepmother? "I-I was afraid you would be angry with me. I couldn't bear for you to think I wasn't coming. I tried everything I could think of to escape, but I was trapped." She held on tight to him, keeping her face pressed again his chest, not wanting to look him in the eye as she told him the shameful truth of her stepmother's treatment. But she seemed compelled to tell him all, wanting him to know that she had not stayed away on purpose,

"Ruexner came just as I escaped with Ava's servant boy. I was terrified I wouldn't get out before he came. We ran as fast as we could, and I'm afraid I tore Margaretha's beautiful dress. Ava gave me this dress and fixed my hair. I'm sorry it took so long. I knew Evfemia would tell you lies, and I desperately wanted to see you and tell you the truth so you would not be angry with me."

He pulled away and held her at arm's length, staring into her face with a strange look in his eyes. "I am not angry with you." She wished he would hold her again, but he seemed to be searching her face, or memorizing it. At least he didn't look angry.

"I wanted to see if you were well." She reached up and lightly brushed her fingertips over the stitches by his eyebrow. Her heart beat fast as his expression changed. "Is your hand well?" Her voice was breathy as the intensity of his gaze made her wonder if she was being too forward.

He slowly bent his head toward her. He was going to kiss her. How she wanted him to kiss her—

"Valten! There you are! I wondered where you went."

Chapter 17

Valten's hand tightened around Gisela arm, and he grunted in frustration. He brushed his finger over her cheek and whispered, "We will continue this conversation later."

"Yes, my lord." The mischievous twinkle in her eye almost made him kiss her anyway, even though Rainhilda was staring at them from the Great Hall door. Half the crowd of guests were craning their necks to see through the door Rainhilda was holding open.

He released Gisela and held out his arm to her.

"Your poor hand," Gisela said softly, for his ears alone, and lightly touched his bandage. "Is it broken?"

"Just one bone."

She looked up at him, her blue eyes wide. "I'm sorry you were hurt by that brute."

"You are the one who was in danger. I thank God for keeping you safe." And he meant it, as gratitude to God welled up inside him. He couldn't bear to think what could have happened to her if Ruexner had gotten there a minute sooner. "I wish I had been there to save you."

But they couldn't speak of that now. The guests were all looking at them, waiting for them to come inside.

Well, he would share her, but only for a little while. When the ball was over, he would make sure she slept inside the castle tonight, with his sister Margaretha. In fact, he might just make sure she never left the castle.

He didn't intend for her to ever be without protection again.

Gisela placed her hand on his arm and they walked together toward the door of the Great Hall.

A pleasant warmth seeped through her, as she could almost feel Valten's arms still around her and his chest against her cheek. She walked by his side through the Great Hall door, and the entire hall erupted in applause. Valten led her to the middle of the floor, then turned and bowed to her. "All hail Queen Gisela."

Gisela felt gratified and embarrassed at the same time. By tomorrow the tournament and its festivities would be over and she wouldn't be anyone's queen, but it was fun to see the smiles on people's faces and their willingness to go along with the charade. They all bowed and seemed in a joyous mood—until her gaze settled on Rainhilda, whose eyes were throwing daggers.

Gisela didn't care. Valten was paying attention to her, was happy to call her his queen, and that was enough to drive out any unhappy thought.

The music began again, and Valten didn't have to say a word. They lined up facing each other. Gisela hoped she would know the steps. Though it was unfamiliar, the dance was slow, and she watched the other dancers and followed their lead. Valten led her carefully, so she made it through without too many missteps.

Valten's eyes never left her. And in her heart, she believed her stepmother had been wrong. From the way he was looking at her now, his marrying her didn't seem so farfetched.

The next dance was a round in which she had to hold Valten's wrist, since his hand was bandaged. His arm brushed hers as the circle became tighter, and he twirled her around with his right hand. Even with a broken hand, he looked more powerful than any other man in the room.

The dance ended, and as everyone else applauded, Valten brushed his shoulder against hers and leaned down to whisper in her ear. "You are beautiful."

She managed to say, "Thank you." He was so close she could see the shadow of facial hair on his jaw, the tiny scars, and the serious glint in his eye that contrasted with the slight upturn of his lips.

Out of the corner of her eye, she couldn't help noticing all the people staring at them.

She smiled playfully at Valten, trying to lighten the mood—for her own sake as well as for all those watching them. "I love dancing with you, but may I get something to drink?"

Valten led her to a table filled with all kinds of food and drink, and she remembered she hadn't eaten all day, except for some cheese and bread Ava gave her while the servants did her hair.

A servant filled a tankard from a pitcher of red liquid and handed it to her. He filled another for Valten.

Valten stood at her elbow, partially blocking her view of the rest of the hall. He leaned his head toward hers. "My father's men are searching for Ruexner, and I want you to spend the night with Margaretha."

Gisela nodded. "Thank you." She was humbled, first by the fact that she now had no home and nowhere to go, and then by the thought that since her stepmother had taken money from Ruexner, some would say she rightfully belonged to him. They would say she must marry him.

He must have seen the troubled look on her face, because he moved closer. "And your stepmother is spending the night in the dungeon."

The thought of her stepmother in a dungeon didn't fill her

with joy, as she might have thought it would. Instead, she felt sadness and relief, mingled with anger.

Trying to banish the picture of her stepmother in a dank, dark dungeon, she sipped her drink, letting the liquid soothe her parched throat. She was still hoarse from the yelling and screaming through her chamber window that morning.

She heard footsteps a moment before Margaretha bounced around Valten's side and threw her arms around Gisela—but carefully, so as not to spill her drink.

"I am so happy you're here! We were afraid something had happened. We waited for you all day. I'm so sorry I didn't tell your stepmother you couldn't go with her, that I needed you to stay with me. You didn't tell me she was cruel to you. Valten was so worried." Margaretha glanced up at her brother. "Valten, why don't you go … walk over there for one minute while I talk to Gisela." She shooed him away with her hand.

Valten stared down at his sister and raised his eyebrows at her. "One minute is all you get. Gisela wants to dance."

"Yes, yes, be assured, she'll dance the very next dance with you. Now go."

Valten's gaze lingered on Gisela before quaffing the rest of his drink and walking away.

"I'm sorry, Gisela, but I wanted to talk with you, and I knew Valten would get irritated with our girl talk. Your dress is divine." She took a step back to get a better look at it. "And that icy-blue color makes your eyes sparkle—oh my! And your hair is so lovely." She gave her another quick hug. "I hope you can stay with me tonight and forever. We could end up as sisters, maybe very soon!"

Did she mean she thought Valten would marry her? No, she probably was only talking about what Valten had said about her staying at the castle. She wanted to ask Margaretha to tell her more about Valten, but their little sister, Adela, came up behind her, crying. The nursemaid shook her head apologetically at Margaretha. "I'm afraid she's overtired and says she won't go to sleep unless you come and sing her a song."

"Oh, of course, my little *liebchen*." Margaretha cupped her little sister's cheek, then turned back to Gisela. "I must go, but it's just as well. Valten isn't known for his patience." Then her expression changed. "Not to say that he can't be patient, but I know he wants to be with you, and if we make him wait too long he won't be happy. I shall return soon!" She waved at Gisela then took her little sister's hand and hurried off with her and the nursemaid.

Gisela looked around and saw Valten talking with a guard—clearly not one of the guests, as he had on partial armor and a sword at his hip. Not wishing to interrupt him, Gisela drank some more of her spiced wine and water, then put the tankard down on the table. She started to walk over to look at the fresco painted on the wall, but before she could note much more than a couple of knights on horseback and ladies in pink and blue and green gowns, someone tapped her on the shoulder.

Rainhilda stood just behind her, her eyes wide and solemn. "Pardon me, Gisela? Is that your name?" She scrunched her face as if it pained her to utter it. "Your sister Irma is upset and crying. Won't you please talk to her? She's over there." She gestured to the doorway to her left.

Gisela turned her head toward the darkened corridor where Rainhilda pointed. A girl was crying into her hands. She looked up and locked eyes with Gisela.

Irma. Gisela's stomach twisted. The last thing she wanted to feel was pity for her stepsister.

"Gisela, please come and help Contzel." Irma sniffed, wiping her face with a handkerchief. "She's thinking of doing harm to herself."

"What can I do?" Gisela felt a stab of pity in spite of herself.

Contzel had never been as cruel to her as Irma and Evfemia. She had gone along with her mother and stepsister, but Gisela had sometimes wondered if she would have been a kind person if it had not been for them.

"She's wracked with guilt and wishes she had talked mother out of selling you to Ruexner. She thinks you could never forgive us for what we did."

"I don't hold any grudge against Contzel."

"Please, won't you tell her that yourself? Perhaps she won't do herself harm if you will only tell her you forgive her."

Gisela glanced over her shoulder. Rainhilda had disappeared and Valten was still talking with the guard and wasn't looking her way. She probably should have someone come with her. However, she didn't want anyone being privy to the conversation she was about to have with Contzel, where she forgave her for any involvement in selling her to Ruexner, trapping her in her chamber, and all the myriad of things they had done to her over the years, not least of which was forcing her to work as their servant.

Gisela looked from Irma to Valten and back again. "Where is she? I shouldn't leave the Great Hall."

"She's just inside the corridor." Irma started crying again. "She's all I have left, now that Mother is . . ." She sobbed rather loudly before blubbering, "In the dungeon."

Her tears seemed more real than any she'd seen her cry before. "All right. But I can't be gone long."

Gisela stepped through the doorway into the darkened corridor. Why was it so dark? Someone should light the torch in the wall sconce. "Where did you say Contzel was?"

Irma let the door close behind them. The back of Gisela's neck prickled. Her heart began to pound. Something was amiss. Irma was trying to trick her, she was sure, but before she could voice her alarm, someone threw something over Gisela's face.

A hand clamped over her mouth as she tried to scream. Biting fingers dug into her arms. She kicked but lost her footing and felt herself being dragged down the corridor, away from the ball and away from Valten.

"We are still searching for Ruexner, but there's no sign of him," the soldier told Valten. "We're questioning people as well. So far no one has seen him."

"Keep all guards on the search, except for the ones guarding the castle."

"Yes, my lord."

As the guard walked away, Valten turned to find Gisela. She was not where he had left her. He looked around but she didn't appear to be anywhere in the room. Perhaps she had left with Margaretha.

He growled under his breath. Would she leave without telling him? During the ball?

He didn't want to act like a worried nursemaid. She was probably with his sister and they had gone to the garderobe.

"Dance with me." Rainhilda was at his elbow, smiling up at him. "It is a ball, after all. Aren't we supposed to dance?"

He was supposed to be dancing with Gisela. He wanted to be dancing with her. But where was she?

He shook his head at Rainhilda. Just then he noticed another guard striding in and walking quickly toward his father, who was at the other end of the room. "You will excuse me." Valten started toward his father and the guard. "What?" He got their attention as he approached.

Father's look was grim as the guard said, "The soldier guarding the castle gate was found knocked senseless from a blow to the head. We are rallying our men to surround the castle and look for intruders."

Gisela. Was it a coincidence he suddenly couldn't find her?

Just then, a few more guards entered the Great Hall. They stationed themselves at the doors, making the ladies gasp and a frightened murmur break out among the guests.

"Gisela is missing." His hand went to his hip again out of habit, looking for his sword.

"Missing?" His father looked quite dangerous, as dangerous as Valten felt. He needed his sword. Just then a servant boy walked past with an empty platter. "You. Fetch my squire and tell him to bring me my sword. Then go to the stable and have my horse saddled and ready."

"Yes, my lord!" The boy ran off.

"She was standing over there"—he nodded at the other side of the room—"talking to Margaretha a few minutes ago. Now they're both gone."

Father pointed at the guard. "Get three trusted men and have them scour the castle for Margaretha and Gisela."

"Yes, your grace." The guard barely took time to nod before hurrying off.

"Let's check the west door." Father headed toward the door Gisela had been standing near the last time Valten had seen her. Valten walked briskly by his father's side, then broke into a run. The guard moved aside to let him pass.

Holding the door open, he looked around. His father came up beside him.

"These torches on the wall should be lighted."

"There's something on the floor over there." His father pointed several feet down the corridor.

Valten walked over and picked it up. The guard came back with a lighted torch. "It's a shoe." A woman's shoe of white leather. A surge of energy went through Valten. "I think it's Gisela's."

"My lord, I have your sword." His squire's voice broke through the haze of rage that had settled in his head. He brushed past his father, took the sword and scabbard, and fastened them around his waist as he walked.

"Ruexner will pay dearly for this," Valten promised, speaking to no one in particular, but imagining he had the fiend's neck between his hands. If he dared hurt Gisela . . .

He started running down the corridor that led outside.

Chapter 18

Gisela struggled to stay conscious, but the cloth bag was clinging to her nose. She managed to get a hand free and pulled the cloth away from her nose so she could breathe.

The man dragged her feet along the ground. She'd lost both her shoes by now — Ava's beautiful shoes — and the man was holding her around her shoulders, his hand tight over her mouthlips, his other hand gripping her arm.

She struggled but he only gripped her tighter. She tried to drive her elbow into his side, but the way he was holding her, her elbow couldn't reach.

It was useless. He was much stronger than she was. Her only chance would be to get turned around so she could knee him where it would really hurt, or punch him in the throat.

Behind them she heard men's voices. She tried to make as much noise as she could, but with being hoarse, and the cloth bag and the man's hand firmly clamped over her mouth, the sound was so muffled she doubted they heard her.

Her captor dragged her over rocks. She lifted her feet completely off the ground, hoping to slow him down by forcing him to carry all her weight. But he seemed to move faster, not slower.

She pulled at the man's hand, trying to dislodge it so she could scream, but in response he dug his fingers harder into her cheeks, until the pain was almost unbearable and she was afraid he would break her jawbone.

She stopped clawing at his hand and settled for holding the bag away from her nose so she could breathe.

If only she could get away. If only God would send Valten. If only he would come in time!

They seemed to be moving from dirt to cobblestones, and then she was being lifted. A second set of hands grabbed her. She was transferred from one man to another, and for one brief moment, the hand let go of her mouth. She tried to scream, but her scream was muffled and hoarse. The second man's hand clamped over her mouth, and she was lifted up onto what felt like a horse's back. Someone was holding on to her, and the horse started forward, throwing her back against the rider. Other horses started moving at the same time and the same speed, their hooves clopping loudly on the cobblestone street.

Gisela clung to the pommel of the saddle, finding it hard to balance herself when she couldn't see anything. They must be riding through Hagenheim. She tried to think of something she could do to stop the horse, to get away. She struggled and twisted but the man only held her tighter. Finally, she could think of nothing else to try.

Valten and his men, including some of his father's best knights and trackers, rode through Hagenheim like the devil was at their heels, speeding through the dark, deserted streets. They headed for the east gate, which led outside the city by the southeast road. When they talked to the guard, Valten found he had guessed correctly; three horses carrying three men and a woman, who was sitting in front of one of the men, had ridden out just a few minutes before.

"What did the woman look like?" Valten yelled the words louder than necessary.

"I couldn't see her face. There was something covering her head, I don't know what. It was dark. But her dress was pale blue and glowed in the moonlight."

Valten and his men urged their horses forward, through the gate and past the city wall. Ruexner was likely taking Gisela to his castle several days' ride to the south. The men spread out to try to track which direction they went, while Valten and three of his best knights headed south.

They rode hard and fast for an hour, and then Valten caught a glimpse of them ahead. Ruexner was riding double, which meant his horse couldn't go quite as fast. Valten would soon be upon him, and when more of Valten's guards caught up to them, Ruexner would be outnumbered.

But could he afford to engage Ruexner and his men in a fight? Gisela might get hurt. And Ruexner wasn't above threatening to kill her to keep Valten away.

Valten slowed his horse and motioned for his men to gather around. In a low voice, he said, "We will stay just behind Ruexner and his men, and when they stop to make camp, we will sneak in and attack, snatching Gisela away to safety. But for this to work, we can't let Ruexner know we are so close behind him."

But it was possible Ruexner had already spotted them. So, thinking ahead, Valten said, "If I am captured trying to save Gisela, you must not follow us or try to rescue me, but ride on ahead of him to his castle. Hartmann here knows where it is. If Ruexner does capture me, he will take us to his castle"—*if he doesn't kill me first*—"and you can join with the rest of Father's men and storm the castle."

The men nodded their agreement, even though a few of them grumbled at not being allowed to rescue him if he were caught. They quickly spurred their mounts forward and resumed the chase.

Valten's blood boiled at the thought of Ruexner holding Gisela, of him taking her by force, dragging her away from underneath Valten's nose, from his own home. Ruexner had violated every code of chivalry in existence. He'd behaved without honor and didn't deserve to be called a knight of the Holy Roman Empire. Valten would make sure the king heard of Ruexner's dastardly conduct. And if he hurt Gisela in any way ... Valten clenched his fists. As many times as he'd fought and jousted and crossed swords with opponents, he'd never felt such a killing rage before, so strong it was a fire that pounded in his ears and filled his mind with vengeful images. At the same time, the thought of Gisela suffering at Ruexner's hands sent ice water through his veins, along with a stab of guilt. If Gisela should suffer pain and distress at Ruexner's hands, it would be his fault. Ruexner had only taken her because of his hatred for Valten.

God, I must save her. I must not fail.

Gisela sensed the horse beneath her getting tired. The poor, poor horses. They'd been riding for a while, and Ruexner had not let up or slowed from their gallop. At least, she assumed it was Ruexner holding her. He had only spoken once, when he removed his hand from her mouth and growled in her ear, "If you scream, I'll put a gag in your mouth."

A few minutes later, Gisela tore the hood off her face and threw it down. She expected him to punish her, but he didn't do anything.

They were following a narrow road, and on either side of them was a dense forest. It was the middle of the night and there were no houses, no one around that she could call to for help.

Did Valten know Ruexner had taken her? Was it reasonable to hope he would come? But she couldn't imagine he wouldn't try to save her, if he knew she was in danger.

He was a knight. Even if he didn't care as much for her as she did for him, she was sure he would still come. Valten was too honorable to let a young maiden be taken from his own castle and not go to rescue her. And he was sure to notice she was missing. She only hoped he didn't think she had left of her own accord. But he had told his sister, Margaretha, "Gisela wants to dance," so he knew she wanted to be with him. Surely it was obvious. *He will come for me.* But his hand was broken. He wasn't supposed to be riding. Perhaps he would send his men after her, but her heart sank at the thought. Even a dozen soldiers couldn't make her feel as safe as Valten could.

Since there was no escaping Ruexner's iron grip around her stomach and his uncomfortably hard chest behind her, and since she'd probably be killed if she flung herself to the ground, she tried to relax and rest without falling asleep. She wanted to be ready if some opportunity to escape presented itself.

More time passed. The men around her kept looking to Ruexner, but he didn't say anything. The horses slowed but still kept up a fairly brisk pace. Gisela couldn't help worrying that the poor animals would collapse in exhaustion.

Eventually, Gisela closed her eyes, lulled by the rhythm of the horse's pounding legs, and the night became an even more torturous experience. She was exhausted, but afraid to fall asleep. And when her head began to drift to one side or the other, or to tilt forward, she would jerk herself awake. Still, they rode on, the horse's hooves pounding into the ground. *Poor horse.* He must rest soon or he would die.

The sky began to lighten and turn gray. Dawn was breaking, although it was still quite dark. When the sun started sending pink tendrils over the sky, her captor motioned with his hand and they turned their horses off the road, descending through a shallow ditch into a dense, wooded area. The horses were made to trot through the underbrush and trees. They moved rather noisily as the tree branches swept over them, and as they passed through the undergrowth, twigs, and leaves.

"Are we going to make camp?" one of the men asked.

Ruexner motioned for him to stay quiet as the sound of horses' hooves came from behind them, from the road they had just left.

Valten! He, or his guards, were following them, she was sure of it. Would they pass by without noticing that Ruexner had left the road?

The horses on the road stopped. Then came the muted sound of their hooves on the thick ground covering of leaves, and the slap of the branches from behind them. She could barely keep from crying out in joy and relief.

Ruexner kicked his horse into a run, dodging tree limbs and forcing the horse to jump over bushes. Gisela ducked her head as a branch slapped her. She wanted to scream out to Valten's men, but that would probably only enrage Ruexner. They knew she was there and screaming would serve no purpose, at least for now.

Valten spied Ruexner and his men a hundred feet ahead. He pushed Sieger to go as fast as he dared. He ignored the sting of the tree limbs slapping his face and tearing at his arms, and Sieger nimbly jumped the larger bushes as they got closer and closer to Ruexner.

He had not been able to sneak up on Ruexner, but Ruexner had not stopped to make camp, riding all night instead, as if he already knew Valten was following him. They would have to run Ruexner down and hope he surrendered, although he knew that was unlikely.

The dense foliage continued to punish them. Valten lost them from sight, but then they came back into view. The trees seemed to be getting thinner. The gray light of dawn showed through the leaves ahead, and then Ruexner and his men broke out of the trees and into a clearing.

When Valten and his men emerged from the woods, Ruexner and his men were dashing across a great meadow, scattering a flock of sheep. Valten raced after them. Ruexner topped a small hill, and a bit of silvery-blue fabric could be seen on either side of his body. Then he and Gisela vanished over the crest of the hill.

Ruexner had seen them, which ruined Valten's plans. Since Ruexner had Gisela, all he had to do was threaten to kill her and he would have Valten completely in his power. Still, Valten couldn't just let him get away. His instincts screamed at him to follow.

Valten pushed Sieger to go faster. The destrier's hooves pounded the ground until he topped the knoll. Ruexner stood facing Valten from another hill just opposite them, with a little valley in between. Ruexner's arm was around Gisela's neck, and he was holding her head against his shoulder, a dagger to her chin.

"Halt!" Ruexner called. "Or I'll kill her!"

Valten and his men stopped their advance.

"Give her to me, Ruexner." Valten's heart was in his throat. He knew he couldn't get to Gisela in time if he truly wanted to kill her. "Don't hurt her and I'll give you gold, jewels, anything you want."

Ruexner laughed. "Why would I turn over my prize to you? You don't have the gold with you, do you?"

"No, but I can get it."

"You would take her and go, then have your men kill me! At least, that's what I would do." Ruexner laughed again.

Gisela looked pale, but also brave. Ruexner could kill her in the blink of an eye, and still she had a look of courageous defiance in her eyes. The point of the knife had pricked her chin and a dribble of blood dripped off his blade. *O God.*

Valten forced himself to focus. "What do you want, Ruexner?"

"I want what I've always wanted—your defeat and humiliation. I want you to grovel before me. I want you to lose something you care about." He yanked Gisela's hair, pulling her head back, but she didn't scream. "I want you to surrender to me now and send your men back home. You must come with me, and your men must swear they will not follow."

Valten couldn't let Ruexner hurt Gisela. Just seeing her in anguish was like a sword piercing his heart. There was a chance that Ruexner wouldn't kill her, that he wasn't evil enough to slay an innocent maiden, but Valten wasn't about to take that risk.

"I will surrender, but let the girl go home with my men. You only took her to get to me. Take me and let her go."

"No!" Gisela's eyes were wild and she seemed about to throw herself off the saddle, but Ruexner held fast, his arm her around her waist.

"Why would I let her go when I can use her to make you do whatever I want?" He laughed his wicked laugh again. "Now come, or she dies." He pressed the knife blade flat against her throat and ran his grimy finger down her cheek.

Gisela's face was stoic.

"I am coming. My men will go home." Valten started walking his horse toward Ruexner. Valten's guards mumbled behind him, sounding angry, unsure.

"If your men follow us, I will kill their lord. Do you hear?"

"We hear," Valten's men shouted sullenly behind him.

"Throw down your sword, Valten."

He took off his scabbard and threw it to the ground. Somehow he would find a way to free Gisela and escape with her. Ruexner would make a mistake and Valten would take advantage of it. He simply had to keep his head and not fly into a killing rage until the timing was right.

Valten walked his horse slowly toward Ruexner and his

men. Gisela looked more frightened now than she had before—frightened for him rather than for herself, if he read her expression correctly. He looked her in the eye. *I won't let you down. I will save you.*

When Valten reached them, Ruexner barked, "Tie his hands." A man dismounted and approached Valten with a piece of rough hemp rope. He could kick the man away, could probably take out his other man with the dagger concealed in his boot, but by the time he did, Ruexner could have slit Gisela's throat. So he held out his hands and let Ruexner's henchman jerk them downward, crushing Valten's broken hand in a viselike grip that sent a searing pain up his arm.

"Don't hurt him!" Gisela cried out. "Stop it!"

The henchman laughed and began wrapping the rope around his wrists, then tied it, cinching it so tight it cut into his skin.

Ruexner chuckled and put away his knife. Gisela kept her eyes on Valten. Even though her bottom lip trembled, she still looked like the bravest woman he had ever seen. *Hold on*, he wanted to tell her. *I* will *save you.* But then he thought he'd better pray, because, if he was honest with himself, he knew Ruexner could easily kill him before he had a chance to do anything. He was completely at Ruexner's mercy.

Chapter 19

Ruexner's man put a lead rope on Valten's horse, helped Valten back into the saddle, and took away the reins.

"Let's ride." Ruexner turned his horse around and headed down the other side of the small hill.

He was thankful for Sieger's sake that the pace was slower now. Valten's hand throbbed; the man had moved the broken bone out of place. Frau Lena would not be happy with having to set it again. If he ever made it back to Hagenheim and Frau Lena. But he wouldn't think like that. He would escape from Ruexner and his men and return with Gisela too.

What was it he'd once said to his brother Gabe? *I'll just have to rescue my own damsel in distress.* His words seemed prophetic now. At least, if he didn't get killed. He'd spent the last two years dwelling on the fact that his betrothed had chosen his little brother over him. He'd always thought that, because he was the oldest, he had to be stronger, more responsible, win tournaments, and be the best at everything. He had to do more. How would it look if he failed now?

But even worse than his petty fear of humiliation, if he couldn't save her, Gisela would be at Ruexner's mercy. She'd have to marry the man. After all she'd suffered at the hands of her cruel stepmother . . .

Something from the Bible popped into his mind. "In this world you will have trouble." Jesus had said that. "But take heart. I have overcome the world." He certainly needed Jesus now, to overcome this trouble.

They had been riding all night, and weariness was evident in the men's postures, as their shoulders rounded forward and their eyelids hung heavy. They hadn't eaten either. Gisela must be the most weary and hungry of all, after being trapped in her chamber all the day before. When was the last time she had food? The thought of her discomfort made him all the angrier and more determined to make Ruexner sorry he had been born.

Another verse came to mind. "'It is mine to avenge; I will repay,' says the Lord."

His parents would be surprised he'd learned so much from them.

The thought almost made him smile.

Ruexner had dropped back and was looking at Valten. "What makes you so happy? I shall kill you, and then I shall marry this fair young maiden, the one you named the Queen of Beauty and Love. What do you think of that?"

Valten tried to look nonchalant. "You can do nothing unless God allows it. And God will not allow it."

Rage descended over Ruexner's face. "You think God will stop me? I paid for her. Her stepmother has agreed that we should marry. I will have our marriage blessed in a church, and neither you nor God will stop me. Even in God's eyes she will belong to me, and there will be naught you can do about it."

Gisela's eyes were the only thing that betrayed her fear as she leaned forward, her hands on the pommel of the saddle in an attempt to get as far away from Ruexner as she could. But Ruexner tightened his hold around her and jerked her back.

"With your words," Valten said slowly, "you tempt God, Ruexner. A dangerous thing to do."

Ruexner's face turned redder. "I do not fear God, and I do not fear you." Ruexner's features twisted into a sneer as he glared at Valten with bloodshot eyes. The man needed sleep. They all did.

Valten let the silence lengthen before saying, "That is not wise."

Ruexner snorted, then forced his horse to bolt forward, causing his men to spur their horses forward too and pull Sieger along.

As they neared the end of the meadow, a well-worn path led through the forest on one side, probably leading to the house whose owner tended the sheep they had passed. Ruexner steered his horse to the other side and entered the stand of trees. Valten and the rest of the men followed. Ruexner had dismounted and was helping Gisela off the horse. Valten grit his teeth at the way Ruexner was holding her around the waist. He hated this feeling, of his hands tied, literally and every other way.

Ruexner instructed his men to bring Valten to the small, empty space in the center of the trees where there was enough room for all of them to stand in a circle. Ruexner stepped up to Valten, while Valten pretended complacency. His hands were tied in front of him, so he possibly could defeat one of them. But even if his hands were free, he realized he could not defeat all three of the heavily armed men.

Gisela stood to the side where Ruexner had placed her, looking on with anxious eyes.

Ruexner stood so close they were nose to nose — except that Ruexner was two or three inches shorter.

"Don't hurt him." Gisela stood with her shoulders squared, her head tilted defiantly, but her voice quivered.

Ruexner glanced back at Gisela, then met Valten's eye. "Your presence here is upsetting my betrothed. We'll take a walk."

Now Valten would find out if he was to be killed, or only beaten and tortured.

Ruexner motioned at the larger man, the one with a long scar across his chin. "Malbert, you come with me and our illustrious guest, Lord Hamlin." He turned to the smaller of his men. "Lew, you stay here with her."

He poked Valten in the back with something sharp. "Move." They started walking deeper into the woods.

The trees were relatively thin here, so even though they walked thirty feet or more, he could still see Gisela and the other man. Ruexner stopped him and came around to stand in front. Malbert came to stand just to the side, looking on, his hand on his sword hilt.

"What do you want with me, Ruexner?"

His smile was sinister. "Do you remember the tournament in Saillenay, how you made me look foolish? You knew I wanted to marry Count d'Arcy's daughter, Carmelita, and yet you humiliated me in front of her."

Valten searched his memory for the incident he was talking about.

"You and her brother made a bet that you could defeat me in a sword fight. I had been drinking, or I would have trounced you. You chose to fight me in her father's courtyard, in front of her. You made me look a fool, and now I will take my revenge."

Valten had a vague memory of defeating Ruexner in a nobleman's courtyard, but he remembered it another way. "I did not challenge you to that duel. You challenged me. And as for betting on the outcome … the young man insisted. What can I say? I did not know you were in love with his sister." Ruexner was drunk and entirely to blame. But he would not listen to reason, not now. Probably not ever.

"Now I have stolen your 'queen' to make you pay for all the times you defeated me, for humiliating me in front of Carmelita, and for giving me this scar." He pointed to the one on his cheek, from when Valten had unhelmed him in a tournament in

Burgundy. It had been a fair fight. Scars were part of tournaments and battles—Valten's own face was proof.

"Can I help it if I am better at fighting than you?"

Ruexner drew back his fist and aimed for Valten's nose. Instinctively, Valten raised his hands and blocked the blow with his arm. Then he brought his elbow around and struck Ruexner's jaw with a satisfying crunch.

Malbert struck Valten in the side of the head with the hilt of his sword, knocking Valten to his knees. He blinked at the stars exploding in front of his eyes.

Gisela screamed.

"You are upsetting my betrothed again." Ruexner put his boot on Valten's shoulder and shoved, but Valten caught him around the ankle using his bound hands and jerked his foot out from under him. He landed on his back beside Valten.

Malbert promptly kicked Valten in the stomach. He fell to his side, unable to bite back a grunt of pain.

Ruexner got up, breathing hard, and kicked Valten again. He tightened his stomach muscles, making the blow less effective. But he'd still be black and blue and very sore. He prepared himself for the next blow, which came swiftly.

From the small clearing, Gisela screamed, "Stop!"

But Ruexner did not stop. He kicked Valten again and again in the side and the stomach. Valten felt one of his ribs crack. *God, this can't be how I die, leaving Gisela at the mercy of this fiend.* He was beyond being able to fight back as darkness encroached on his vision and the roaring in his ears increased.

It seemed as if Gisela's screams were growing closer. The brutal kicking stopped. He heard a loud thud and several startled yells.

He forced his eyes open. Gisela was on top of Ruexner on the ground, pummeling his head with her fists, while Ruexner held his arms up to protect his face.

Valten struggled to get up, desperate to protect her. But the pain in his head and stomach almost caused him to black out. He fell onto his side.

Ruexner would kill her. *God, no.*

His two men pulled her off him, with Gisela kicking and fighting like a lioness. "Leave her alone," Valten growled through clenched teeth.

"Take that she-devil back to the clearing!"

Lew began trying to pull Gisela away, holding on to both her wrists.

Ruexner stood and brushed himself off. Then he knelt beside Valten and leaned close to his ear. "I am not finished with you. Next time I plan to give you a scar for a scar. 'An eye for an eye and a tooth for a tooth,' eh? And even your little she-devil spitfire will not stop me."

Ruexner stood and Malbert pulled on Valten's shoulder.

"Get up," Ruexner ordered.

Valten swayed as he slowly got to his feet, keeping his eyes on Gisela, who looked to be holding her own. The blow to his head had made him dizzy. Blood ran down his brow, tickling him. But his stomach and ribs hurt worse. Breathing almost wasn't worth the pain. He groaned before he could stop himself.

Gisela struggled against Lew, who was holding her by her arms but didn't appear to be hurting her. She lunged toward Valten, but Lew's grip held.

Ruexner pushed him forward, making him stumble. He caught himself, but stayed bent over. When they entered the tiny clearing among the trees, Gisela turned and kneed her captor in the groin. The man went down, falling on his knees on the ground. Gisela ran to Valten.

She grabbed his arm. "Are you badly hurt?"

He tried to smile at her, to lessen her anxiety. "No."

Her hand trembled as she reached toward his temple, where

he felt the trickle of blood. But then she placed her soft little hand against his cheek.

"I am well. Don't worry." He longed to wipe away the tear from her face with his fingertip, but he was afraid he'd become too unbalanced and fall.

"I'm so sorry," she whispered. "I'm so sorry I caused all this."

"You didn't cause it." How could she think that?

Ruexner snorted derisively, looking at Gisela. "He doesn't look so strong and fierce now, does he?"

She turned on Ruexner. "You're a fiend. He never did anything to you. Why do you hate him so much?"

"Because, my dear. He had what I wanted. It's a harsh world. A man must take what he wants or he's a weakling and a fool." He stepped closer to her and lowered his voice. "My father taught me that."

"How does it feel"—he turned now to Valten—"to look like a weakling in front of this fair maiden? You're no longer the proud, arrogant future Duke of Hagenheim. You're just a broken man, at my mercy. And I have no mercy." He drew his fist back. Valten wasn't quick enough to block it this time. The fist slammed into cheekbone. The pain in his head thundered like a rainstorm, making him see stars again.

Something soft and warm pressed against his midsection. He blinked. Gisela wrapped her arms around him, getting between him and Ruexner.

"No! I won't let you hurt him!" She held on until Ruexner grabbed her arm and pulled her away.

Ruexner stared at her. "Why should I stop? I intend to kill him ... eventually."

"No." She shook her head. "Let him go, please."

"Why should I?" Ruexner's cold black eyes glinted.

"If you will let him go, I-I will marry you."

Ruexner rubbed his bearded chin. "You'll marry me anyway."

"No, I won't. Not if you keep hurting this man."

"You'll have no choice. I'll find a priest who will marry us against your will."

She faced him defiantly, but there was fear in her eyes.

"But I will take your offer into consideration." He rubbed his chin again.

"So you agree not to hurt him anymore?"

"Perhaps ... for now."

Chapter 20

The men's eyelids drooped. Gisela was ex-hausted but too tense to sleep, and was still trembling after watching Ruexner and his men beat and kick Valten mercilessly. Her whole body ached and sand seemed to have lodged inside her lids, scraping her eyes every time she blinked. When Ruexner announced they would make camp, she nearly fainted with relief.

They ordered Valten to sit in the center of the open space, then they tied his ankles together. Gisela sat down beside him, although not too close, hoping they wouldn't order her to move.

Ruexner started walking toward her, and she noticed bloodstains on his shirt, under his armpits, and down his sides, obviously from the wounds he'd received from the sword fight with Valten in the tournament. The blood was dry, so someone must have bandaged the wounds, or they had stopped bleeding. It was a shame the injuries didn't seem to be slowing him down.

Ruexner handed her a flask. Then he muttered something to the other two men and stalked into the woods, probably to relieve himself.

Gisela uncorked the flask and sniffed; it was water. She moved to Valten and held it up. He placed his bound hands over hers and drank. When he finished, she put the flask to her own lips and swallowed the water, with Ruexner's two men watching her. She hadn't drunk much in the last two days, and the water felt good going down her parched throat.

Ruexner came back and let one of the other men head into the woods. Ruexner glared at Gisela, then went to rummage through his saddlebag. He came and handed her some dried meat and an apple. He looked at Valten for a moment and then turned and walked to where Valten's horse was tied. He rummaged through Valten's saddlebag and found some dried fruit and nuts and gave some to his men.

When Ruexner's head was turned, Gisela shared the food with Valten.

No one spoke as they ate and then stretched out on the ground. Ruexner threw a blanket in Gisela's direction, and she got up to retrieve it. Gisela folded the blanket, and she and Valten used it as a pillow as they lay facing each other.

Would Ruexner and his men keep watch? Or would they all fall asleep? If they did, she was sure she and Valten could escape. But Ruexner didn't lie down. He only propped his back against a tree and watched them while whittling a piece of wood with a knife. Almost immediately, his two men started snoring, but Ruexner looked wide awake.

The next thing Gisela knew, she was blinking her eyes open and the sun was high overhead. Had she actually been asleep?

Valten's eyes were also open. She turned her head to follow his gaze. Ruexner's head was lolled onto his shoulder and his eyes were closed. The other two men were still snoring.

Valten whispered, "In my left boot is a dagger."

Gisela sat up, looking over her shoulder at Ruexner. He still looked asleep. She crawled as quietly as she could to Valten's feet and slipped her hand inside his shoe, felt the hard handle of the dagger, and drew it out. She immediately went to work sawing through the rope around his ankles. It took longer than she thought. Valten kept his eyes on Ruexner while she worked.

Suddenly, she broke through the rope and his feet were freed. She crawled back toward Valten's head, holding the knife, and started trying to cut the rope around his hands. The hemp made a soft squeaking sound as she sawed through the tough fibers.

"Wait." Valten's hoarse warning made her cease and look at Ruexner. He was moving. Any moment he might open his eyes and see her kneeling in front of Valten's hands. She dropped the knife on the ground and held her hand over it to hide it. Ruexner mumbled a bit and rubbed his face. Gisela quickly lay down, only now she was close to Valten, and they were lying face to face. She turned her head so she could better see Ruexner, who was still rubbing his cheek.

Suddenly, Ruexner jerked himself upright, his eyes popping open.

Gisela closed her eyes, feigning sleep. Her heart was pounding, making it hard to keep her breathing under control. As much as she wanted to know what Ruexner was doing, she kept her eyes closed.

She heard faint rustling sounds coming from his direction. Then the crunching of leaves, then more rustling. Someone mumbled something that sounded like, "Your turn."

Gisela dared open her eyes just a bit. One of Ruexner's men was walking over to where Ruexner had been sitting and Ruexner was now lying down. Gisela waited, trying not to move. Soon, their guard's head drifted to the side, and he started snoring again.

Gisela waited. She wanted to make sure Ruexner was asleep. When she couldn't wait any longer, she turned to face Valten. His gray-green eyes were staring right at her. How could he look so handsome with a bruised eye and dried blood at his temple? She sat up on her knees and he held his hands out to her as she took up the dagger again and started sawing the thick rope. How tight it was on his wrists! His fingers were purple. She was desperate to get the cruel twine off him, but she didn't seem to be making much progress.

"You are very brave," Valten whispered.

She stopped, only for a moment, to look into his eyes. The admiration in them made her heart grow and press against her chest. She kept sawing even harder, but trying not to cut his arm or fingers in the process.

"But don't tell Ruexner you will marry him. Because you won't." His jaw seemed to have turned to stone and the soft expression disappeared.

His words made a warmth come over her neck and travel up to her head that had more to do with anger than his handsome face.

"I said that so he would stop beating you," she huffed. "Would you rather I let him pound you to death?"

She kept working on cutting through the rope instead of looking him in the eye.

"You won't have to marry him," he continued, as if she hadn't said anything, "because I *will* rescue you."

The determination in his voice sent more warmth through her. "I couldn't bear to see him hit you again. But I would never marry him. I would get away from him somehow." She couldn't help adding mischievously, "Maybe *I* will rescue *you*."

He made a growling noise in his throat, and she was hard-pressed to keep from laughing. Her amusement at least took her mind off how horrible she felt seeing him get beaten. After all, it was only happening because she had been foolish enough to get herself captured by that despicable Ruexner. Earlier, when they'd stopped to face their pursuers, how elated she had been to find that Valten had actually come himself to rescue her! Immediately afterward, she'd felt horribly guilty, since he was certain to get hurt, or killed. She should have prayed for him to stay away, to let his men rescue her.

The rope was so tight that her sawing at it was causing it to chafe his skin. She became afraid his wrists would bleed. "I'm so sorry I'm hurting you."

"It doesn't matter. Keep cutting."

He shifted his weight a bit, and Gisela paused to get a better grip on the knife.

"My men have orders from me not to follow us. They will gather the rest of our men and come to Ruexner's castle in Bruchen, which is where Ruexner is taking us. But we can avoid any of them getting killed if we can escape."

"I am afraid Ruexner will kill you before we ever reach his castle."

"No. He's jealous and cruel and wants to humiliate me. But he has some kind of plan for when we reach his castle. He'll keep me alive until then."

She could feel the intensity of his gaze on her. She stopped and looked up at him.

"He's already hurt you." She had a sudden thought and grabbed his arm, squeezing to ensure that he was listening. "Promise me that if you get a chance to escape without me, you will do it. He won't kill me. Go find your men and come back for me."

His eyelids and brows lowered. "You don't know me very well or you wouldn't say such a thing. I *won't* leave you."

He was angry. How could he be angry with her for wanting him to be safe?

Frustrating man. At the same time, hadn't he performed enough feats of skill and strength and bravery in the tournament to inspire her belief that he could save her? If anybody could, it was Valten.

She whispered, "Even with a broken hand, you are the knight I'd most want and trust to rescue me—and I know you can do it. You are the boldest, bravest, most noble knight in the Holy Roman Empire."

That seemed to soothe him. His brow lifted and he gave her a good long gaze that made her wonder if he would like to kiss her as much as she would like to kiss him. But no … they didn't have time for such thoughts. He would surely scold her for them.

Abruptly, the knife sliced through the last fiber of the rope. His hands were free.

Her heart beat faster. What would Ruexner do if he caught them trying to escape? Would he kill them? He would at least beat Valten again.

"What are you doing?"

Gisela's heart leaped painfully inside her.

She turned with a jerk while hiding the knife in the leaves. Ruexner came toward them with his sword drawn.

His two men roused themselves and were soon on their feet, arming themselves with swords.

Gisela froze. Valten's right hand, positioned beside her, was as tense and hard as steel. What could they do, armed only with a knife, against three men armed with swords? Best to pretend that Valten was still bound.

"You have a knife. I saw it. Throw it down to me," Ruexner ordered, slowly advancing toward her.

Gisela glanced at Valten. He gave a barely perceptible nod.

She threw the knife on the ground. "His hands were bound too tightly." She wasn't about to apologize to him. "You beast. I insist you loosen his bonds."

"I believe you already loosened them for him." Ruexner sneered, showing the chipped tooth on top and a missing tooth on the bottom. "How kind of you. Now stand up, both of you. Lew." He turned to his henchman. "Pick up that knife and tie his hands again."

Lew looked at him strangely, but after a slight hesitation he picked up the knife and moved toward them. Gisela helped Valten to his feet.

Ruexner threw Lew another rope.

"Not so tight this time," Gisela ordered.

Lew moved toward him with the rope. Valten lifted his hands toward the guard. When he did, Lew jumped back, as though expecting Valten to attack him. But Valten just stared.

Gisela moved back in front of Valten to look at his hands. The left wrist was protected by the splint on his broken hand, which reached past his wrist. But his right wrist was bloody and raw from the rough rope. She sucked in an anguished breath at the sight of it.

"Tie him up again, now." Ruexner sounded like he was running out of patience.

"No!" Gisela glared at Ruexner and pulled Valten's arms around in front of her as she pressed her back against his chest. "You are purposely hurting him in any way you can."

"I suppose you would like to tie it yourself?" Ruexner's smile suddenly vanished. "Do you think me a fool?"

"No, but there's no reason to tie the rope so tight. He'll lose his hand."

Valten cleared his throat just above her head. It occurred to her that he might be embarrassed at the way she was defending him. But she was only trying to save him from pain and permanent injuries.

But he would appreciate her interference if Ruexner actually listened to her. She hoped.

Ruexner snatched the rope out of Lew's hands. He waited for Gisela to step aside, but she refused.

"I won't let you hurt him." She tugged Valten's arms tighter around her, careful not to touch his broken hand or his bloody wrist.

She felt Valten shrug. "What can I say? Women are softhearted creatures."

He was pretending to be amused.

Ruexner's face twisted when he looked at Valten over her head, then he stared down at her a long time before saying, "I will allow you to first wrap a cloth around his wrist."

Gisela watched as the villain cut a piece off the end of Valten's bandage and handed it to her. She took it from him and wrapped it gently around Valten's raw wrist.

"Now step aside, and I will not tie the rope so tight." He smiled through clenched teeth.

She wasn't sure she should believe him, but she hardly had a choice. She moved as Ruexner asked but watched closely as he tied the rope. The man did indeed seem to be making it looser this time. *Thank you, God.*

Ruexner finished tying the rope and stepped away from Valten.

"You see? I am not a beast."

He took a step toward Gisela, and she took a step back.

"I don't wish to hurt you. But I also can't have you trying to escape. You must tell me where you got the knife."

Gisela involuntarily glanced at Valten, then back to Ruexner. She said nothing.

"Where did you get it? Do you have any other weapons hidden on your person? Must I search you?"

"No!" Gisela took another step back, then perceived his two henchmen hovering just behind her. "I don't have any weapons. I was at a ball." She had the urge to call the man a number of unflattering names, including *lack-wit* and *jackal-pate*. "What would I be doing with a weapon at a ball, where I'd planned to dance all night?"

"She got the dagger from me." Valten looked almost bored, as if the answer should be obvious. "But that was the only weapon I had."

"Search him," Ruexner ordered.

The other two men cautiously approached Valten. Even

with his hands tied, he looked dangerous. But Valten stood still while the two men searched him for weapons. They made him sit down, and they took off his boots and looked inside them, but found no more weapons. After all, he'd been at a ball too.

They allowed Gisela to help Valten put his boots back on.

"Since you have both obviously had enough rest," Ruexner said with false cheer, "we shall get back on our horses and continue on our journey."

Gisela felt as if she'd hardly taken more than a two-minute nap, but she clamped her lips together and walked to the horses. Ruexner's men held Valten's reins and the lead rope while he mounted his horse. Then Ruexner mounted and pulled Gisela up in front of him while one of his men lifted her by her waist.

God, let this nightmare come to an end soon.

Chapter 21

They rode the rest of the day, but stopped at Gisela's request to rest the horses. Valten knew better than anyone else that Gisela truly was concerned about the horses. He was only surprised that Ruexner would listen to her.

Valten kept his eye on Ruexner and Gisela. Ruexner's allowing Gisela to talk him into sparing the horses was a sign that he might have a soft spot in his black heart for her — a soft spot Valten could well understand. She was beautiful, strong, capable, and brave, sweet and compassionate; how could any man not fall in love with her?

It was unfortunate their earlier escape attempt had failed. Not only were Ruexner and his men more watchful, Valten had lost his only weapon when Ruexner took his dagger. But Gisela had done her best. It chafed to have her see him at Ruexner's mercy, tied up and vulnerable. But that didn't matter so much. Her safety was what mattered.

God, let me not show weakness in front of her. But more importantly, keep her safe.

And even though he knew she had only been trying to save him from a beating that morning, it galled him to hear her offer to marry Ruexner. Didn't she understand how her saying such a thing would eat at him?

Women were strange creatures. But he already knew this,

having so many sisters. His father had admitted as much to him one day, but had added that when he found the right woman, she would be worth any confusion she would cause him.

He was right. Gisela was worth it. Even her strangeness somehow endeared her to him. The way she looked at him sometimes, especially when they had danced together, made him feel like a king. And the way she'd put her arms around him to keep Ruexner from hitting him was imprinted on his memory.

But if Ruexner had wanted to cause him to suffer, he'd found the perfect tactic. Thinking of Gisela being forced to marry Ruexner made Valten physically ill and filled him with thoughts of the justice he'd like to bring down on Ruexner's head.

As twilight descended, Ruexner stopped to make camp again. One of Ruexner's men had stolen a mince pie and bread rolls stuffed with cabbage from a house at the edge of a village they had passed. They ate the fresh food along with their dried fruit, jerky, and nuts. As before, Gisela made sure to give food and drink to Valten, since their captors would not.

Just as Valten had hoped, Ruexner forced Gisela and Valten to once again lie down in the middle with the three men surrounding them. Ruexner made Malbert stand guard, since he'd had the most sleep that morning. He kept his hand on his sword hilt and his eyes on Valten and Gisela.

"Are you well?" Gisela whispered as soon as Ruexner began to snore.

"Yes."

"Your eye is swollen."

"I am well. Are you?" He could see her face but faintly in the moonlight filtering through the trees. She looked tired.

"I am."

"Get some sleep."

"Do you have a plan to escape?"

Her question took him aback. "I have no weapon, you have

no horse, and my hands are tied. I'm not familiar with this place, and we have only seen one village. No, I have no plan." It hurt his pride to admit that.

"If the men all fall asleep, perhaps we could sneak away on foot. Or we could take Sieger and another horse and get away."

The guard was eyeing them suspiciously, probably trying to hear what they were saying.

"I don't want to endanger you. For the moment, I think it's better to be patient." If only they'd been able to get away earlier. But with no weapon or way to cut themselves free now, it seemed impossible.

"But if the guard falls asleep, perhaps I could steal his sword." Gisela's soft voice vibrated with excitement.

"No. If he falls asleep, tell me, and I'll steal the sword."

"It's best to let me do it. They won't harm me, but if he wakes up and sees you coming toward him, he will kill you."

"You don't know that they won't harm you, and he won't know who is coming at him in the dark and might kill you by mistake. No, I won't have you putting yourself in danger."

"Silence!" The guard spoke in a harsh whisper, stepping toward them and holding up his sword menacingly. "Go to sleep, both of you."

Gisela had an obstinate look on her face, reminding Valten of his sister Margaretha when she was angry or determined to get her way. But she was looking at Valten, not at the guard.

Ach, but she was stubborn. He was only trying to protect her. But once again, in spite of his frustration, he admired her bravery and determination. And he surprised himself by realizing ... he even liked arguing with her.

They both lay still, and he couldn't quite tell if her eyes were open or closed. His own eyelids were beginning to feel so heavy he could barely keep them open. He wouldn't have to worry about her. She was probably already asleep and would sleep all night.

"Good night, Valten," she whispered.

His eyes popped open as irritation warred with admiration again. "Good night, Gisela."

Gisela found herself waking up to Ruexner relieving Malbert of guard duty.

Valten's eyes were open. He'd probably been awakened by Ruexner too. But as she watched, he closed his eyes. He must be exhausted. How she wished they had been able to escape yesterday. Perhaps now they would be safe in the keeping of his men, and Valten could get the sleep he needed. But it was comforting, too, that he was a light sleeper and had awakened when the guard changed. He wanted to keep her safe; such a sweet sentiment, but likely to get him killed. He believed his men would rescue them after Ruexner brought them to his castle, but how could he be sure? Ruexner would kill Valten rather than let his men take him.

And since she couldn't bear to see Ruexner hurt Valten anymore, she would do whatever she could to escape.

Surely God would not allow Irma and Evfemia—and Rainhilda too—to get away with their cruel trick. By selling her to Ruexner, then helping him kidnap her, they had certainly satisfied their desire to hurt her.

Gisela awoke again when the sun was already above the horizon and Ruexner's men were milling about the camp, packing up to leave. Valten was nowhere to be seen.

She sat up quickly and looked around. Had he escaped? Had he left her there? She should be glad he had gotten away. Hadn't she told Valten to find his men, to leave her if needed? After all, there was no need in him getting himself killed if he could help it. But still, the thought of him leaving her behind felt like a sack of flour on her chest.

Then she saw Ruexner walking with Valten. "Your turn, Lew."

They were taking turns going into the woods to relieve themselves, and Ruexner had gone with Valten.

Her heart leaped, then sank. How could she be happy about Valten still being a prisoner?

Valten came and held out his hands to her. She reached up and let him help her to her feet.

Realizing how awful she must look, she tried to smooth her hair. "I'm a mess." Her dress was torn and dirty, and it broke her heart to see the once-beautiful gown getting ruined.

"You look pretty, as always."

She wanted to believe him. She didn't.

While their captors were busy, Gisela looked up at Valten, wincing at the swollen, bruised state of his eye, and whispered, "If you get a chance to escape without me, you should take it."

He lowered his brows at her in his dangerous way.

She quickly went on. "I couldn't bear it if Ruexner hurt you again." She reached up and touched his swollen cheekbone, but lightly.

Valten half frowned. He lifted his hands and ran his knuckles over her jawline. "You shouldn't worry about me."

"Hey!" Ruexner shouted. "No talking amongst the captives." He motioned to Gisela. "Go relieve yourself and get back here."

Gisela turned reluctantly from Valten and obeyed. At least she could be thankful Ruexner didn't follow her into the woods when she had to go.

Soon, they were back on the horses and starting on their way again.

The day slowly crept by. As she traveled with Ruexner on his horse, a few hours after noon, he spoke into her ear, "You look like someone I once knew. Who were your parents?"

It seemed an odd thing for him to say, and Gisela refused to reply.

After a few moments, he asked, "You are from Hagenheim? And your parents are from Hagenheim?"

Gisela could have told him she wasn't sure where her parents were from and didn't even know her grandparents' names, but she didn't want to encourage his friendliness, so she simply said, "Yes."

"And your surname is Mueller?"

"Yes."

He said no more as they entered rougher terrain now, and often their trail led them around small mountains, or down steep hillsides and back up again. They seemed to be following any path that kept them away from the roads. Ruexner must have been afraid of Valten's men following them.

When they stopped to make camp, Gisela watched for an opportunity to talk to Valten. She found it when Ruexner and his men decided to build a fire against the chill of the evening air and cook the deer Malbert had killed with his crossbow.

"Do you think we're close to Ruexner's castle?"

"Two more days, maybe three," he whispered back. His gaze lingered on her face.

"Listen." He spoke quickly. "Tonight I want you to try to untie the rope around my wrists, and then I will watch for a chance to escape."

Gisela nodded, her heart rising into her throat.

Ruexner yelled at them to stop talking, so she stepped away from him, trying not to look as excited as she felt.

As they all sat down to eat, they heard someone whistling on the trail nearby. Ruexner glanced at their fire, then at one of his men. "Go see who that is."

The men put their hands to their swords, as if to make sure they were there, and Lew cautiously stalked toward the sound of whistling, then faint singing. It seemed to be coming toward them, coming quite close.

"A good evening to you!" a voice sang out.

"Don't come any closer," Lew warned.

Gisela couldn't see the person through the dense trees but sensed that he was very close.

"My good man, I mean you no harm," the cheerful, rather meek voice went on. "I am but a poor friar on a mission to encourage all men everywhere to repent and believe in the goodness of God. I smelled the smoke from your fire—"

"You're not welcome here. Be gone."

"Perhaps your companions would be interested in the saving message—"

"Be gone, I say!"

"As you wish, as you wish." Through a small break in the leaves, a man in a friar's robe and with a tonsured head passed by on a donkey. His eye darted her way, and she was sure he saw her. She opened her mouth to call out to the man. But what could a friar, undoubtedly unarmed, do to help them? She might get the poor man killed if she alerted him to their plight. So she closed her mouth and stayed quiet as he and his donkey continued out of sight.

As night fell, Gisela lay close to Valten again, and Lew was left to guard them. Valten faced away from the guard, and Gisela plucked at the knot that secured the rope around Valten's wrists, working to loosen it while keeping her shoulders still. When Gisela didn't seem to be making any progress, Valten began wriggling his hands, using his thumbs to push the ropes, trying to ease them off. Gisela tried to help him, but eventually went back to trying to loosen the knot.

Gisela kept glancing at Lew. He was whittling something, probably the same thing she'd seen him working on the first time he'd watched them. He didn't seem to be paying them any attention. Gisela hoped she looked like she was asleep. Fortunately, she could see both Valten and the guard without opening her eyes too wide.

She forced her eyes open and realized she had dozed off. Lew was still whittling and Valten was still working quietly and with little movement, pulling at the ropes around his wrists. He had let her fall asleep.

She pinched her arm, hard, to force herself fully awake, then started trying to loosen the knot again.

"I can do it," Valten whispered, so low she could barely hear him, even though she was only a few inches away. "Go back to sleep."

"No, I can help." She also wanted to stay awake so she could tell Valten when Lew fell asleep. In spite of the way he had reacted to her recent suggestions, she thought he would appreciate her help now.

Valten had made some progress, but the ropes now seemed to be stuck at the joint of his thumb due to the splint around his left hand. He shifted his focus toward trying to work the coils over his right hand. It was slow going, and she wasn't sure he would be able to do it. If Ruexner caught him, he would no doubt go back to tying it so tight it turned his fingers purple and rubbed the skin off his wrist.

God, please don't let him get caught. She was almost afraid to hope. God had saved her when she was locked in her room the day of the ball. She had begged for God's help and he'd sent Ava's servant boy, Lukas. Perhaps she only had to believe that he would help her again. She needed to have faith.

She had once seen a miracle play about Shadrach, Meshach, and Abednego, who got thrown into the king of Babylon's fiery furnace. They told the evil king that they believed God would save them from the fire. But even if he did not, they still would not worship the king's false god.

Perhaps that was the kind of faith God required of her now.

I believe you will rescue me, God. But even if I don't escape, please let Valten escape. He has a family who loves him.

Valten suddenly seemed close to getting his hand free. He kept pulling. She glanced at the guard, whose attention was still focused on his carving.

Valten slipped the rope off his right wrist.

Gisela gasped. Valten pressed a finger to his lips. While working to keep her breathing steady, she glanced at Lew; he was still placidly whittling his piece of wood.

Valten held her gaze. Now what? She assumed they would have to wait until Lew fell asleep. Valten pointed to her and mouthed the words, "You sleep. I will watch the guard." Then he closed his eyes, put his hands back together, and turned over, as if turning in his sleep. The guard noticed, stared, but then went back to whittling his piece of wood.

Gisela didn't want to lie there while Valten plotted their escape. She wanted to watch with Valten, to be ready as soon as the guard fell asleep. But this guard didn't seem tired at all, so she started praying again. *God, please let this guard fall asleep. Or let the next one come soon to take his place, one who cannot keep his eyes open.*

Gisela had so often eased her pain by telling herself she didn't care what happened. But she couldn't tell herself she didn't care if Ruexner forced her to marry him. To be his wife was a detestable prospect. So she kept praying to God to help Valten and her escape, and to keep them safe. It was comforting to ask for God's help, to believe that he was listening and that he cared. She felt herself relaxing and letting go of her fear …

"You there. Pssst."

Gisela's eyes popped open, and she realized she'd fallen asleep again. The guard had changed, and the new guard, Malbert, was lying against a tree trunk, snoring.

Slowly, Valten rolled over, making no noise. But he was not looking at Gisela, but at someone behind her.

Her heart in her throat, Gisela rolled over as well, to find herself face to face with a stranger. It was the friar she'd glimpsed as he passed by their camp on his donkey.

The man was bending over so that his face was almost level with Gisela's. His smile seemed so out of place that Gisela could only stare.

"Do you need help?" the man whispered.

Gisela nodded while Valten quietly jumped to his feet. Then he and the friar each took one of Gisela's hands and helped her up.

Looking over his shoulder, Valten put his hand under her elbow, and all three of them carefully picked their way away from the three men. When they were fifty feet away, they began walking a bit faster. About a hundred feet away, they came upon the friar's donkey.

"Wait here," Valten said. "I'm going back to get my horse. If I don't return soon, go on without me."

Before she could think of anything to say, he was walking back toward Ruexner's camp. She stared after him until he disappeared in the dark woods.

What had she been thinking? They had escaped! She should never have let him go back for Sieger. Because if Ruexner were to catch him and find Gisela gone, Valten was a dead man.

Chapter 22

Valten walked more carefully the closer he got to Ruexner's camp. He avoided stepping on sticks, and he dodged tree limbs that might brush against his shoulders and make a noise. He was only a few feet from the sleeping guard when he had to step over an enormous rotting tree. A loud snap made him freeze—his foot had landed on a large twig. He watched the nearby guard, as well as Ruexner and his other man a few feet farther on. No one moved, and he could still hear the sounds of soft snoring.

Valten stepped his other foot over the log and pressed forward.

Sieger stood silently next to the other three horses. But before he made off with Sieger, he wanted to steal a sword, preferably his own, which he had forfeited to Ruexner when he'd turned himself over to him to save Gisela. Unfortunately, he didn't know where Ruexner was keeping it, and he had to hurry before the next guard came to take his turn watching them and discovered them missing.

Valten crept closer to the sleeping guard, Malbert, until he could see that his sword lay across his lap with one hand laying limply over it. He couldn't possibly take it without waking the man. So he crept backward and made a wide arc through the trees to get closer to Ruexner and Lew.

They lay on blankets in the leaves. Ruexner's sword was by his side, and he too had his hand resting on its handle. Valten moved on to check on Lew, but he couldn't see Lew's weapon at first. Then Valten spied it on his blanket, half of the blade under his thigh.

Valten gritted his teeth. He didn't dare try to steal either sword, for he would be too likely to wake the men. He turned back toward the horses. Just as he turned, something near the ground, propped against a tree trunk, caught his eye: Malbert's crossbow.

Valten almost groaned out loud. He'd never been very good with a crossbow, but if he couldn't have a sword, the bow was better than no weapon at all. He picked it up, then gently lifted the quiver of arrows lying on the ground beside it. Holding them carefully against his chest, he moved quietly away from the sleeping men.

The horses were sleeping as well. He'd like to steal one of their horses so Gisela would have her own to ride, as well as to put Ruexner and his men at a disadvantage, but as he drew near, the horses began to snuffle warily, obviously awake and not liking his presence. Valten moved extra carefully around the suspicious animals and made his way to Sieger. He untied his horse, who thankfully stayed quiet, and led him away from Ruexner's camp.

"Were those men holding you against your will?"

Gisela liked the friar's kindly, clean-shaven face. He looked to be about twice her age, maybe thirty-eight or forty, and he wore a rough brown mantle.

She nodded.

He shook his head, compassion in his eyes. "That is very wicked of them. And the man with you?"

"He is a knight from Hagenheim and Duke Gerstenberg's son—Valten, the Earl of Hamlin. He was trying to rescue me and was captured."

He shook his head again, making a clicking sound with his tongue.

"I am very grateful to you for coming back for us. We were planning to try to escape tonight, and Valten—Lord Hamlin, I should say—had freed himself from the rope tied around his wrists. While we were waiting for our guard to fall asleep, I'm afraid Lord Hamlin and I fell asleep."

"It is indeed a good thing I came along," the friar said. "For another reason as well. If I had not come, and if you had both escaped, your virtue would have been compromised. You and the knight would have been alone together. You would need to marry, or your reputation would be ruined."

"Oh." She'd started to hope that Valten might marry her because he wanted to, because she was the tournament queen. She knew it wasn't customary for a future duke to marry a woman simply because he liked being with her, or because he cared about her. Unfortunately, Gisela had begun to hope that very thing. Future dukes married women from wealthy noble families. But if Valten felt forced to marry her, he would come to resent it, especially when he discovered she was only a peasant girl, no more than a servant.

It was indeed good that the friar came when he did. She didn't want Valten to feel forced to marry her.

"To whom do I owe my gratitude, sir?"

"You may call me Friar Daniel, my dear maiden."

"And I am Gisela Mueller, from Hagenheim."

He bowed to her. "God's flower," he murmured.

"Thank you again, Friar Daniel, for so kindly coming back for us. How did you know we needed help?"

"I saw a glimpse of your face through the trees. From the

man's brusque manner, he didn't want me to see you, and from your expression ... well, you didn't look like you belonged with that bunch of rough, bearded men. I came back around through the woods and observed your camp, saw that you and this noble knight were captives, and I decided to wait until an opportune moment to help."

"You are very brave, Friar Daniel. I shall never forget your kindness, and I'm sure Val—Lord Hamlin—is very grateful as well." Valten. Where was he now? He could so easily get caught. He could step on a twig and wake up the guard. Perhaps Malbert, or Ruexner or Lew, had already awakened and seen that she and Valten had escaped. Perhaps they were watching the horses, waiting for Valten to come for Sieger. If they caught him ... Gisela couldn't bear to think what they might do to him without her there to defend him. She should go back and help him. He would never leave her, and she wouldn't leave him either. She would give herself up to Ruexner if it would save Valten.

"You are worried about him, aren't you?"

Tears pricked Gisela's eyes. She nodded.

"Shall we pray for him?"

New gratitude welled inside her. "Yes, please."

He lifted the crucifix around his neck and clasped it between his hands and bowed his head. Gisela clasped her hands and bowed her head as well, and she concentrated on the friar's quiet words.

"O God our Father, we extol you. Your name alone is holy, and all your ways are holy and just. I thank you that you sent me to aid this woman and this man, and I ask that you look down in your infinite mercy and save the young man, the Earl of Hamlin, who is a noble knight, no doubt in your service and with a heart to save young damsels in distress. Give him the furtiveness to accomplish his goal and come back to us. Keep him safe, O God.

We put our lives in your hands. No one can take us out of your hand, Almighty God. Strike your enemies with blindness so that they cannot see, and give us your servants supernatural speed and stamina to—"

"Amen."

Gisela turned to see Valten just behind her with Sieger beside him. Gisela threw her arms around him. "Thank you, God."

Valten squeezed her shoulder, then pulled away. "We must go." He turned to Friar Daniel. "My good friar, do you know of a place to hide, a place big enough for my horse?"

"I do indeed," Friar Daniel responded. "I grew up nearby, and a cave I used to play in as a boy is but two miles away. I only hope we can find it in the dark."

"Lead on, Friar."

They had not walked far when Valten stopped Gisela with a hand on her arm. "Come. You ride." Without waiting for an answer, he placed his hands on her waist and lifted her onto Sieger's back, letting her sit sidesaddle. He took up Sieger's reins and followed Friar Daniel and his donkey.

Gisela shivered, probably from a combination of the excitement of escaping from Ruexner and his men and the cold night air, which was unusually cold for this time of year. There was nothing for her to do but try to keep her seat on Sieger's back and feel comforted by how strong Valten looked, with his broad, muscular shoulders and his large, capable hands. Then she noticed the crossbow hanging from his shoulder by a leather strap. He must have taken it from Ruexner's henchman. The sight made her feel even more comforted.

Just then, Gisela heard wolves howling in the distance. She shivered again. *Thank you, God, for Valten's safety, and for how you will save us from all danger.*

Valten was glad he'd been able to steal a weapon, even if it was a crossbow, which was definitely not his preferred weapon. If they could only avoid getting caught by Ruexner, he could make it back to Hagenheim with Gisela where she would be safe. Then he could gather his father's knights and soldiers and go teach Ruexner a lesson he'd never forget.

But for now, Valten had never felt so ill equipped. Without a sword, he felt exposed and vulnerable. If a wolf attacked, he would have one shot, and one shot only. If he missed, or if there were more than one, he wouldn't have time to reload. But he would do whatever it took to protect Gisela, even if he had to take that wolf apart with his bare hands.

Another problem he would never admit was that he was in a lot of pain, and still dizzy, from the beating he'd taken from Ruexner and his men.

God, are you trying to humble me? Because it's working. If you're trying to show me that I need your help, I'm seeing it. I want to rescue Gisela in my own strength, but right now I'll just be thankful to get her to safety any way that comes about. Even if it came in the form of a round-faced friar.

He'd actually fallen asleep waiting and watching for the guard to fall asleep. The friar had not only saved him and Gisela, but now he was leading them to a cave, a hiding place Valten could neither have known about nor found. Though his initial reaction had been frustration that a friar could do something for Gisela that he couldn't do, he'd better humble himself and thank God for sending him. He should not and would not argue with God about his mode of provision.

Valten and the friar continued walking for about half an hour before Valten began to wonder if they were lost. The forest seemed to go on forever, and all the trees looked alike. It was so dark that it was hard to distinguish anything out of the ordinary, and the moon was sometimes blocked out altogether by the dense foliage. He glanced back at Gisela every now and then. Her shoulders drooped, but whenever he looked at her she gave him a brave smile. Even with her blonde hair falling around her face and shoulders in a tangled mass, she was just as beautiful to him now as she had been at the ball.

The friar turned and said, "We're not far now." As he rounded a slight hill, overgrown with small trees and bushes, they faced a gaping hole in the side of the hill. "Be careful. It slopes downward sharply, and the floor is wet and slippery."

Valten turned and grasped Gisela around the waist to help her down. She placed her hands on his shoulders and he set her on her feet, but slowly. After all, when one has a pleasant task to do, there's no reason to rush it.

He wrapped his fingers around Gisela's small hand and entered the dark cave, unable to see more than three feet in front of them. He had been inside the secret tunnel that ran under the town wall around Hagenheim Castle many times, but he liked the idea of being inside a cave created by nature—God's own hiding place.

The rocky floor was indeed wet, and he could hear water dripping somewhere ahead. The open mouth of the cave was like a giant swallowing them up as they were plunged into complete darkness. The floor of the cave was uneven, and became quite steep as they continued farther into the darkness. It was a strange feeling not to be able to see where he was going. Gisela held on to his arm in the blackness of the cavern.

"We'd better stop here," the friar said. "There are probably bats farther in, and we don't want to fall into a hole."

That sounded like sage advice. Valten patted Sieger, then opened his saddlebag. Ruexner and his men had plundered it, but there was still one blanket attached to the back of his saddle.

"We shall try to sleep now." Valten's voice sounded hollow as it bounced off the walls and sank into the dark hole at the back of the cave, from which it never returned. He directed his voice toward where he thought the friar was standing. "We are greatly indebted to you, Friar, for helping us escape from Ruexner and his men, and for leading us to this cave. I am sorry I do not have the means to reward you for your act of bravery. You will always have a bed and a place at our table at Hagenheim Castle."

"That is very kind of you, noble knight."

"And tomorrow you may go on your way and never mention that you met us."

"Oh, but perhaps I can be of further assistance to you. I have nowhere particular that I need to go."

He wasn't sure what further assistance the friar might be offering, but he said to Gisela, "We may as well stay in this cave for a day or two and hope Ruexner and his men search for us elsewhere. My hope is that they will think we've taken the road back to Hagenheim."

"You will need someone to stay with you," the friar said. "I could not leave an unmarried lord and lady alone together."

So that was the *further assistance* he had been talking about. "That is unnecessary. I shall marry the lady as soon as we get back to Hagenheim."

He expected Gisela to have something to say about his statement, but she was silent. She did let go of his arm.

"That is well and good, my lord, but I believe I shall stay all the same."

"As you wish, brother friar."

"I have an extra blanket. Please take it."

Valten took the friar's offered blanket and handed Gisela his blanket.

He and Gisela bumped into each other several times as they laid their blankets near each other on the hard floor of the cave.

When they lay down, the silence was broken only by the dripping of water in the distance, which echoed as if it was falling down a great hole. He only hoped some light would come in through the entrance in the morning. Otherwise, he wasn't even sure he knew in which direction was the entrance.

He closed his eyes and tried to sleep.

She couldn't understand why Valten's words, *I shall marry the lady as soon as we get back to Hagenheim*, should make her cry, but she found herself remembering them when she lay down, and the tears flowed into her hairline, chilling her in the dark cave, as she positioned herself facing Valten. At least, she thought she was facing Valten. It was impossible to tell. She wanted to reach out and touch him and make sure he was there, but she also didn't want him to think she wanted him to take advantage of the darkness and her nearness.

She rarely ever cried anymore, probably because she always told herself she didn't care, and that stopped them. But she couldn't say now that she didn't care.

Was Valten only willing to marry her to save her reputation? The thought of marrying him was wonderful, but it filled her soul with pain to think of him marrying her only out of a sense of duty. She had hoped that he had begun to care for her. But the way he had said the words, so coldly, instead of tenderly, or expressing love for her, stating his intent to Friar Daniel as if she wasn't even there ... It was like a dagger in her heart.

Was she being foolish? Perhaps. She only knew she wanted his undivided love, and she couldn't bear him marrying her out of pity.

Ava had once told her, "Never let yourself fall in love with someone who doesn't love you. Or at least don't tell them you love them, whatever you do." It had seemed like wise counsel.

A person who didn't love you could use the knowledge of your love against you.

With Friar Daniel here, Valten would have no reason to marry her. She would tell him as soon as possible that she would not hold him to his statement if he was only being chivalrous.

She tried hard not to sniff and wiped her nose with her hand, hoping no one heard her crying, and closed her eyes to sleep.

Chapter 23

Gisela awoke to someone moving beside her. She sucked in a quick breath and backed away. "Ow!" Her head hit something solid behind her.

"Are you all right?" Valten's voice came from very close by, but now her head was throbbing.

Gisela stifled a moan; she'd apparently hit her head on the wall of the cave.

"Give me your hand."

Gisela reached out and Valten helped her up. It was disorienting to be in the pitch-black cave. She lost her footing and stumbled face-first against his chest.

He put his arms around her and held her so tight she couldn't have broken away from him if she'd wanted to. And resting her cheek against his warm chest, she most definitely did not want to.

She sensed and heard, rather than saw, Friar Daniel loading his things on his donkey's back a few feet away from them.

Valten's arms were gentle and warm around her shoulders. His breath fanned her hair as he whispered, "Why were you crying last night?"

"Oh. I wasn't . . ." She wanted to say she wasn't crying, but that would be a lie.

"Are you afraid?"

"A little." Let him think she was simply afraid. She tightened her arms around him, allowing herself to imprint this moment of warmth and tenderness in her memory forever. He was so solid, so safe. And so far above her as the heir of Hagenheim.

She took a deep breath and plunged in. "I know you said you would marry me when we go back to Hagenheim, but I don't want you to think you have to marry me."

"What do you mean?" Valten's hands went stiff. He pulled away slightly. "I didn't say I *had* to marry you."

Was he angry? She whispered, "I just don't want you to feel *forced* to marry me."

He pulled away even more. "I don't feel forced. I want to marry you." But the tone of his voice had an edge to it that didn't sound like a person in love. She couldn't see his expression, as it was too dark, but she was fairly sure he was wearing his rock-hard, square-jawed, lowered-brow look.

She let her arms drop and felt the tears well up again behind her eyes. Trying to keep them from flowing, she bent to pick up her blanket. She rolled it up then handed it to Valten, but he grabbed her arm. His voice came from mere inches away. "Are you sad because you don't want to marry me?"

"Of course not. No, no." She didn't want him to feel hurt. Still, this was not the way she wanted him to ask her to marry him. But it was all so foolish of her! He shouldn't be marrying her at all. He should marry the king's daughter, or a duke's daughter, not her.

"We shall speak of this again." He took her hand and led her and Sieger toward the entrance.

When they were close enough to the entrance that she could see Valten's face, she noted that he looked grave. "I think we need to stay close to the cave, as we are still near Ruexner's camp. They may find us here, but if we leave, I think it's even more likely they will find us. If we stay a day and a night here, we might have a better chance of evading them."

"Then I shall stay with you also." Friar Daniel lifted his chin, as if he had just volunteered for a dangerous mission. Which he very well might have if Ruexner caught them.

Gisela didn't think Valten looked happy, whether about the friar staying with them or about something else, she didn't know.

Valten took several minutes to make sure no one was around before coming back inside. Gisela and Friar Daniel each went out, in opposite directions, to tend to their personal needs, but he instructed them not to go far. Then Valten took Sieger out for a drink and to fetch water from a small stream they'd passed last night on their way to the cave.

Back inside, Friar Daniel and Gisela were chatting away.

"Do you think God has a different purpose for every person," Gisela asked, "or is his purpose the same for everyone?"

Friar Daniel wrinkled his forehead, not noticing that Valten was holding out his flask of water until Valten nudged his shoulder.

"Oh, thank you, brother knight." Friar Daniel smiled up at him from his seat on the cave floor. The man was always smiling.

Friar Daniel went on. "Some things are the same for everyone. God wants us all to strive to grow more like Jesus, to become holy as he is holy, but God also has a specific purpose for each person. How could it not be so? Everyone in a village cannot be a baker, because who would then make the candles or shoe the horses or grow the food? God says we are like a body. 'The eye cannot say to the hand, "I don't need you." And the head cannot say to the feet, "I don't need you."'"

"Does the Bible say that?"

"Oh, yes, and it says, 'Now you are the body of Christ, and

each one of you is a part of it.' Just as the villagers are part of a village and have different tasks, we all have tasks to do for the Lord God." He smiled, looking rather foolish, with his round, cheeky face and the bald circle on his head.

Valten felt a twinge of envy that the friar seemed so sure of his purpose. To envy the man was absurd. But when had Valten ever felt as if he was doing what he was supposed to be doing, that he was fulfilling a purpose? He had once thought his purpose was to train to be the best at jousting and sword fighting and all kinds of combat. But it had been a long time since he'd thought about what God might want him to do. He'd been so focused on being the best, on winning recognition for himself.

He rubbed his face, feeling the itch of three days' growth of beard. He didn't want to dwell on such things, to realize he'd lost his usual confidence. With no weapon except a crossbow and no real plan, nothing to do but wait, his mood grew darker, especially with Gisela telling him he didn't have to marry her. What did she mean by that?

"My dear," the friar was saying to Gisela, "I'm sure God has a purpose for you. You must realize that God loves you and that He places great worth on you. Do not doubt it. If you ask for it in prayer, I am sure God will give you direction and a purpose."

A purpose for Gisela? Valten wasn't sure when it had started, but he had begun to imagine her married to him, having his children, and living at Hagenheim Castle with him. But what if God had another purpose for Gisela, one that didn't include him?

Why did the friar have to stir up these disturbing thoughts?

Friar Daniel stood and drew something out of his saddlebag. "I wish to share with you. 'Such as I have, I give you.'" He handed Gisela and Valten a small roll of bread. "I must say my prayers, for I never eat until I've prayed at least half an hour." Still smiling, the friar made his way farther into the cave and disappeared in the darkness.

Gisela looked up at him, her eyebrows raised. She looked sweet enough to . . . kiss, but he probably shouldn't, not with the way she kept telling him he didn't have to marry her. Did she not want to be his wife?

He sat down in front of her and let her smile lift his spirits a little.

"Thank you for the water."

He nodded. "I think we should rest as much as we can today and then start toward home when it gets dark. If we travel at night, we have a better chance of getting away."

Gisela nodded, taking a bite of her roll. "That makes sense."

Moments later Valten was taking the last bite of his bread, thinking about going hunting for some game, when Gisela suddenly gasped. She was staring down at something, then she grabbed his right hand.

Gisela couldn't believe she'd forgotten to look at Valten's right wrist. She had noticed several times the somewhat untidy state of the splint on his left hand, but hadn't paid attention to his right. Of course it would be bloody after he'd struggled so long to get the rope off. Dried blood plastered the piece of cloth to his skin, and there were rope burns on the back of his hand.

She sucked in a breath as she examined his strong, broad hand and the damage to it. "You must let me take care of this. We should go to the stream and wash it."

"You can't go to the stream. It's too dangerous. Ruexner may follow the stream looking for us."

"At least hold still and let me wash it." She held his hand over the grass. She poured water from the flask over his bloody wrist and the abrasions on his hand. When the bandage was soaked through, she carefully worked it loose. As she stared at his poor hand, she had a sudden urge to kiss it, so strong it made her heart slam against her chest.

"It's nothing," he said. "It will heal."

She poured some more water on it, trying to clean enough blood off so that she could see how bad it looked. She swallowed. "Perhaps Friar Daniel will have some clean bandages I could use." Her voice wavered.

She turned his hand palm up and admired the structure of his fingers. Her face heated and she wished she had something to dry his hand off with, just so she'd have an excuse to keep holding it. She let go and raised her head. He was looking at her so tenderly. Was he feeling the same way?

"Your cheek isn't swollen as much anymore. That's good." But his left eye was still bruised purple and blue below and above his eye. The stitches over his eye seemed to be holding well, and that cut looked like it was healing. Her gaze wandered from his eye to the growth of hair on his face. She'd always thought he looked dangerous, but he looked even more so with the short stubble on his face.

His eyes met hers, and it seemed as if she could see a longing in the intensity of their gray-green depths. She felt as if she could never stop caring about him, as if he had captured her and she would never escape … would never want to. A terrifying thought. Her heart pounded even harder, especially when his gaze moved from her eyes to her lips. He moved closer as his head bent toward her.

"There is nothing like communing with God first thing in the morning."

Gisela sat back on her heels as Friar Daniel emerged from the dark cave.

Trying to recover her composure, Gisela jumped to her feet and asked, "Friar Daniel, do you have any clean bandages?

Valten—I mean, Lord Hamlin, has some wounds on his wrist and hand—"

"Of course, my dear." Friar Daniel turned to look through the supplies on his donkey's back. He brought forth a roll of clean cloth.

"Thank you so much." She turned back to Valten, who was also standing. Feeling a bit awkward now that Friar Daniel was watching them, she took Valten's hand and carefully wrapped it with the bandage, tying it securely.

Friar Daniel sat eating some bread and no doubt watching them. Not trusting herself to look up at Valten, she turned away.

Valten went and picked up his crossbow from where it was leaning against the wall. "I'm going to find fresh meat. Stay close to the cave."

Gisela and Friar Daniel both agreed to do so, and Valten was soon gone, walking quietly into the woods.

Valten came back with two large pheasants. He said he would wait until it was dark to build a fire and cook it. Meanwhile, Gisela slept most of the rest of the day. She hadn't realized how tired she was.

As night fell, hoping Ruexner and his men were far away, Valten built a small fire at the entrance to the cave.

Valten took the first pheasant and put it on the ground, spreading out the wings. Then he took the legs and pulled until the skin slipped off the breast, and the wings came loose from the legs and entrails.

Gisela watched in fascination as he had the bird dressed and ready to be cooked in less time than it would take Ava's nursemaid to change a diaper. He made a spit out of sticks and placed both the birds over the fire.

As Valten got more wood and Gisela turned the pheasants on

the spit, Friar Daniel was in the dark part of the cave, praying—or sleeping, Gisela wasn't sure which.

Valten sat down beside Gisela on the fallen tree. "I've been wanting to ask you ... How did Ruexner abduct you from the ball? You were standing in the Great Hall one minute, and the next minute, you were gone."

Gisela shook her head. It had been her fault. She hated to admit to him how gullible she had been, but he deserved to hear the story. "Rainhilda came and told me my stepsister Irma wanted to speak with me. Irma was standing in the doorway to the corridor, crying. She said she was afraid Contzel, my other stepsister, was about to do harm to herself, and she needed me to come and talk to her." Gisela shook her head. "I should have known better, but I stepped into the corridor and someone—Ruexner or one of his men—threw something over my head and dragged me away."

For a long moment, Valten didn't say anything. Was he angry with her? She could understand it if he was. He could accuse her of being foolish and she would agree with him.

"I'm so sorry you had such a terrible stepmother and stepsisters." His voice was low and kind.

The compassion in his eyes made her sigh. "I should have known not to trust her, that she would trick me. I was foolish."

"No." He picked up her hand and held it, caressing her knuckles with his thumb. "You couldn't have known. I can't imagine a sister of mine doing anything so evil and heartless."

"I'm sure your sisters wouldn't. They all seem so sweet. And your mother too." A pleasant warmth went all through her at the way he was touching her hand.

"They like you very much."

The way Valten was looking at her made her glad Friar Daniel was not around. But his mentioning his family only reminded her how she had fallen in love with them too, as surely as she had fallen in love with Valten. Could he feel the same about her? She thought back to what Friar Daniel had said about God loving her and placing great worth on her. Might the reason she struggled to believe that also be why she also struggled to believe that Valten might be falling in love with her?

"My father told me your father was one of his most trusted knights, Sir Christoff Mueller."

"I didn't know. I didn't even know he was a knight." The information settled over her like a blanket. It would explain how her father and Duke Wilhelm had seemed to know each other so well.

"How old were you when your father died?"

"I was seven, almost eight." It had been so long since she'd talked about him. In fact, she never talked about her father.

"He was a kind man," Gisela went on, staring down at the small crackling flames of the fire. "He never would have allowed my stepmother to treat me the way she did. Evfemia wouldn't even allow me to have a fire in my chamber. When I was very young, sometimes I would build a fire in my fireplace anyway. And then when she made me put it out, I would sleep inside near the coals for warmth." Now he would know just how different their childhoods had been.

She focused on the fire, on its friendly color, and listened to its cheerful crackling sounds. Valten didn't say anything for so long that she looked up at him. He was staring intently at her face. He reached out and stroked her cheek with his thumb and cupped her chin with his palm.

"You deserved better."

His warm fingers on her skin, together with the gruff compassion in his voice, seemed to melt something inside her that had long been hard and cold. She looked down, unable to bear the kindness in his. He was rubbing her cheek with his thumb and sending a tingling warmth all through her, a warmth that seemed to be melting away all her anger and pain. If Valten loved her, truly loved her, and wanted to marry her, she could do anything, even stop hating her stepmother and stepsisters and forgive them.

He leaned toward her. Her eyes wavered closed just as his lips touched her forehead. His lips were warm on her skin. His hand slipped behind her neck, and he turned slightly and kissed her temple. She was afraid to move, afraid to breathe, for fear she would ruin the moment and he would stop.

Someone cleared his throat behind them.

Gisela froze. A low growling sound came from Valten's throat as he pulled away, but he kept his hand behind her neck. Her face burned as she realized Friar Daniel had seen Valten kissing her.

Valten frowned and removed his hand from her neck. She ducked her head.

"I see there's more cooking out here than the pheasant."

Valten leaned over to turn the roasting birds on the spit and mumbled, "Not anymore."

"That sure smells good." Friar Daniel cheerfully rubbed his hands together. "Tonight we feast, then we travel, eh, brother knight?"

Gisela could still feel Valten's lips on her brow and temple. She sat quietly, imagining what might have happened if Friar Daniel had not come out of the cave when he did. Did Valten love her? Would he have kissed her if he didn't? She was afraid to believe it, afraid to hope.

Valten didn't attempt to hold her hand anymore, but he stayed near her while Friar Daniel sat on the ground and told them about some of the people he had encountered in all his wandering. "My message is so simple," he said. "Repent and believe in God's goodness. Can you believe some people don't know that God is good? That he will forgive their sins? No one had ever told them. They think God wants to punish them, not that he wants to forgive them. Imagine my joy at being the one to tell them the good news!"

Gisela couldn't help smiling back at the friar's beaming face.

The three of them ate both of the pheasants and the last of Friar Daniel's bread. She hadn't realized how hungry she was, either.

When they finished their meal, they dumped the bones and scraps into a hole Valten had dug, then filled the hole with dirt and heaped dirt onto what remained of their fire. Once all traces of the fire and meal were gone, they prepared to leave.

It was already dark, with clouds rolling in and threatening to blot out the moon's meager light. Valten seemed anxious to be off. He lifted Gisela into Sieger's saddle, then hoisted himself up behind her. Friar Daniel mounted his donkey and followed.

Chapter 24

Riding with Ruexner, Gisela had taken pains to try to avoid touching him as much as possible. The heat of his chest had made her feel clammy and disgusted. Even though he had behaved well and had not taken any liberties, she'd hated the feel of his arms around her as he held the reins, or put his arm around her waist to make sure she didn't fall or try to get away.

But riding with Valten was a completely different experience. His warmth was reassuring. The feel of his muscular arms around her as he held the reins and guided the horse made her feel safe. He had said he wanted to marry her, and he had seemed about to kiss her more than once, so he must at least have some feelings for her. She wanted his love so desperately it was terrifying, but she was afraid to hope. After all, even her own stepmother and stepsisters didn't love her. It would be safer, and less painful, if she could stop herself from caring whether or not Valten loved her.

They stayed off the main road, traveling under cover of the trees whenever possible. Gisela prayed they wouldn't encounter Ruexner. She chose to believe Ruexner had missed their trail, that he had gone the wrong direction and was wandering around and would soon give up and go home.

After an hour or two of traveling, she allowed herself to rest her cheek against Valten's chest and close her eyes.

Gisela couldn't be thinking as much about kissing him as he thought about kissing her or she wouldn't be able to fall asleep. With her in his arms, he was too restless to think about anything but her.

He had never felt this way before. He always assumed if he fell in love with a girl, she would naturally love him too. What made a girl fall in love? What could he do to make Gisela love him? He had no idea, and that complete lack of knowledge about women made him feel like he'd been punched in the stomach.

He was used to feeling powerful, to having the upper hand. But with Gisela, he often felt vulnerable. He knew he wasn't particularly handsome, with his short hair and scars. Some children at one of his tournaments in Burgundy had taken to calling him "Goliath." Not the most endearing biblical character. And though he'd had many women openly offer themselves to him, he'd never been interested in their brazen advances.

The truth was, he had no experience with women. He had no idea what they wanted. All his expertise was in fighting. He knew how to command men of every age and status, he knew how to relate to horses and men, but women? He knew nothing.

He tried to think about his sisters, the kinds of things they responded to. Certainly they were gentler than his brothers, and they became angry when someone treated them roughly or disrespectfully.

How had he treated Gisela the last few days? Had he been gentle and respectful? She had seemed to like it when he caressed her hand and kissed her forehead. At least she hadn't pushed him away, and he had been gathering his courage to *truly* kiss her when Friar Daniel had appeared and spoiled it.

His sisters also seemed to expect compliments. They often called the rest of the family's attention to a new dress or a new way of doing their hair, hoping for flattering remarks. When they received them, they were happy. When their brothers teased them, they grew angry.

Since Valten would much prefer Gisela smiling at him than scowling, he tried to think of ways he could compliment her. He had told her once that she was beautiful; he distinctly remembered that. So she already knew he thought she was beautiful. He didn't need to tell her that again, did he? What other compliments were there? She was beautiful. What else could he say?

She was fierce. He had admired her tremendously when she'd jumped on Ruexner and started beating him with her fists. But he had already told her he thought she was brave.

He thought of his father and mother, who had a happy relationship. What had his father done to make his mother happy, to win her over and make her love him? His father had told a story of how he and his men had rescued his mother from an evil conjurer. He had also seen his father kiss his mother whenever he returned after being away, even if he had only been gone a few hours. Valten had tried to kiss Gisela, but so far they'd always been interrupted. But she had understood his intention to kiss her, hadn't she?

But perhaps kissing was more of a married thing. He was sure Friar Daniel thought so.

And then there was his younger brother, Gabe. Every maiden in the region seemed to love him. Even though he was married now and had no interest in their flirtations, in the past they had all smiled at him whenever they saw him, batted their eyelashes at him, and tried to talk to him. Gisela had never done that around Valten. Did that mean she didn't like him?

What was it about Gabe that drew pretty girls like moths to a flame? Valten had always thought it was his good looks and his glib way of talking. When Gabe was still unmarried, maidens seemed to love the way he could always think of something to say, something clever and charming. It had annoyed Valten. True chivalry was being able to fight for your woman, to protect her. But Gabe seemed to inherit all the talk, and Valten seemed to get all the fight. Girls liked talk more, apparently, because the only ones who seemed interested in Valten were the ones who wanted the status of being the future duchess of Hagenheim.

These thoughts were not improving his mood. Although it was pleasant to have Gisela fall asleep on his chest, he was even less confident now that he could make Gisela fall in love with him. He wasn't handsome or a smooth talker like Gabe. Friar Daniel wouldn't let him kiss her. He was doing his best to rescue her but had yet to accomplish it. And he'd already told Gisela she was beautiful. What else could he do?

Valten groaned inwardly when the friar came sidling up to him. A sliver of light snaked through the trees and shone on his face, lighting up that perpetual smile on his face.

Valten scowled at him, hoping he would not wake up Gisela.

"Good knight," Friar Daniel began, and Valten cringed at his loud voice. "I can't help noticing that you scowl a lot. Do you have peace in your life? Because God offers us all peace, in addition to eternal salvation."

Aggravated at his question, Valten thought about just letting the silence stretch and not answering the friar, but Friar Daniel would probably just ask again. "No, at this moment I don't have peace." How could he have peace when a madman was chasing them and Gisela was not safe?

Gisela lay relaxed and still against his chest as Sieger and Friar Daniel's mule picked their way over rocks and around trees, not making very good time as they rode a safe distance from, but parallel to, the road.

"That is a common problem I have found among noblemen." Friar Daniel nodded soberly. "The solution is to cast your burdens on Jesus and let him give you his peace."

The friar's words did not apply to Valten's situation at all. "I will have peace when I can get Gisela safely back to Hagenheim."

"But that is exactly the reason you don't have peace. You are trusting your own strength to get the lady to safety. You must entrust her to God, who is the One who will ultimately make us safe, if we are to be safe."

What kind of reasoning was that? But in his heart, Valten knew the friar was right. He had felt, almost since he met Gisela, that God was trying to humble him, to make him realize he should be asking for God's help and trusting in His strength instead of his own. Perhaps that was what the Bible meant when it said, "When I am weak, then I am strong." His tutor had made him memorize that passage of Scripture when he was younger, about delighting in weaknesses and difficulties. It had never made sense to him before.

Friar Daniel was quiet.

If God wanted him to humble himself, he supposed he must start with admitting to the friar that he was right. "I have been trusting too much in my own strength. But if I live to see Gisela safe and justice done to Ruexner, it will be because of you, friar."

"Not because of me. It is because of God." He smiled his nonjudgmental, cheerful smile.

"You are right. The Bible says it is God who rescues us from the hand of wicked."

"This is true. And where did you hear this Scripture?"

"I've read the Bible for myself."

"Ah! You are indeed knowledgeable, then! God says, 'My people perish for lack of knowledge,' but you, brother knight, shall not perish, but have eternal life."

After a short pause, the friar went on. "I have been roaming the Holy Roman Empire telling as many people as I can that God is good and faithful and will forgive us if we repent. You are one of the few people I don't have to convince."

"Our priests in Hagenheim teach this."

The friar grinned. "Glory to God!"

Valten couldn't deny that the man seemed truly joyful and at peace with the life he had chosen, wandering about, telling strangers to repent and believe in God's goodness. When was the last time Valten felt joyful, at peace, and as if his life had purpose? Two tournaments ago? Five? Ten? He couldn't remember.

I will discover a new purpose for my life. Valten spoke the words in his spirit, determined to start anew. As soon as he made it back to Hagenheim, he would start learning more about governing and leading and negotiating. He'd fight a new battle, but a more peaceful one. Perhaps he would build a new castle, atop a hill, where he and Gisela would live and raise their children. Perhaps then he would feel at peace, would find new purpose and joy.

Only ... Gisela hadn't agreed to marry him yet.

Gisela heard voices as she drifted in and out of sleep. Friar Daniel was talking. Every time Valten answered him, his chest rumbled beneath her ear, quite pleasantly. She felt him sigh. Did he not like what Friar Daniel was saying? She tried to pay closer attention, pretending to still be asleep so she could continue relaxing against Valten's heavenly warm chest.

"You, brother knight, shall not perish, but have eternal life."

Valten must have said something that pleased Friar Daniel. Gisela was glad. She enjoyed talking with the friar, but she sensed Valten didn't like his questions.

Valten was a man of action, but few words.

Not so Friar Daniel. He began regaling Valten again with stories of people he had given his message to, of people who rejected him, some who mistreated him, and some who gratefully accepted his words, invited him to stay and teach them more, and eventually sent him on his way with extra food and supplies.

Gisela felt bad for eavesdropping and pretending to be asleep, but she was enjoying the softness of Valten's tunic against her face and his familiar scent — she breathed in deeply — filling her senses.

She sat forward and rubbed her eyes. A sound in the distance, like thunder, grew louder. No, not thunder. Horses' hooves.

The noise was in front of them, behind them, everywhere. They were soon surrounded by men on horseback. Valten's arms went taut as he gripped the reins.

Ruexner rode right up in front of them, grinning his gap-toothed sneer.

"Thought you could escape from me, did you?" Ruexner laughed.

Gisela's heart sank. *Not again.*

Chapter 25

At least twenty men surrounded them.

Valten couldn't fight them all, especially when Gisela was in front of him and any aggressive action on his part could get her killed.

He braced himself. Ruexner could beat him senseless if he wanted to, or simply kill him.

Even though Valten couldn't see Ruexner's face, as it was completely shaded from the first gray light of dawn, he could tell Ruexner was looking straight at him. "Help the girl down from the horse. I'm taking her with me."

Valten tightened his arms around Gisela. She buried her face against his chest, holding on to him as if her life depended on her grip.

"That's my crossbow!" Malbert shouted, urging his horse toward Valten.

Valten took off the weapon, which was slung over his back. It was fairly useless anyway while he was on horseback, surrounded by so many of Ruexner's men. He handed it to Malbert as if he had intended to give it back to him all along.

"Where did all these men come from?" Valten glanced around, hoping he might recognize some of them, that he might sway their loyalty and convince them to come over to his side.

"These are my men." Ruexner sounded as if he was enjoying every moment of this. "I sent for them before the tournament was over. They are completely loyal to me and are all from Bruchen. My enemy is their enemy."

Valten suspected they were little more than nominally trained peasants, forced to take up arms whenever Ruexner demanded it. No doubt they and their families had been living on Ruexner's family's lands for generations and were, in truth, loyal to him. Valten would get no help from them. Had they been knights of the Holy Roman Empire, sworn to uphold the code of chivalry, then maybe.

"What do you intend to do?" Valten said, trying to buy some time.

Ruexner chuckled. "I don't have to tell you anything. Put her down and I will let you go. You're only a few days' ride from Hagenheim. But if you want the girl, you'll have to come to my castle and fight for her." A long pause, then Ruexner said, "I intend for us to settle our score forever, in front of witnesses at my castle in three days. If you win, you may take the lovely maiden and go home. If I win, she shall be my bride and you shall swear never to challenge me."

"You cannot mean to do this evil thing," Friar Daniel said.

"Shut up."

"It is not lawful for you to force this maiden—"

"This does not concern you, friar," Ruexner growled.

Valten could feel Gisela breathing hard, her hands still gripping his clothing. He buried his lips in her hair next to her ear. "I will come for you," he whispered. "Trust me."

Friar Daniel spoke up again. "You are a noble knight, sworn to protect innocent maidens. You must not take this maiden—"

"Quiet, you pathetic lump," Ruexner ground out. "Or I'll force you to marry us this moment, on pain of death."

Friar Daniel fell silent.

"Now, Valten." Ruexner dismounted and started walking toward them.

For a moment Valten calculated how easy it would be to kick Ruexner in the face and send him sprawling. But it would do no good; he and Gisela couldn't escape with twenty men surrounding him. Ruexner or one of his men would kill him if he resisted. He must bide his time and defeat Ruexner when the odds were more in his favor. He had to stay alive for Gisela's sake.

"Trust me." He whispered this last instruction, then pulled on her arms to loosen her grip. His heart was ripping in two at having to force her away from him and hand her to Ruexner.

He gently removed her arms from around his back and slid her from the saddle. The stricken, horrified look on her face felt like a knife through his gut. *Please trust me.*

"Very well. Take her," Valten said loudly, his voice sounding gruff. "But I shall accept your challenge and see you in Bruchen in three days."

Ruexner grabbed her around the waist and hauled her to his side. Enough light shone on his face to highlight his ugly grin.

Valten hardened his features to show no emotion or concern as he watched Ruexner drag her to his horse. The vile man mounted his horse and then dragged her up in front of him by her arms.

"No!" Gisela screamed, sending another jolt of pain through Valten. Never had he felt so helpless or so enraged. He could kill Ruexner with his bare hands, but Ruexner's men would immediately kill him, and that wouldn't help Gisela.

Ruexner pulled on his horse's reins and turned him around, one arm around Gisela's torso.

Valten and Friar Daniel were left to stare after them.

He fought back the curses that rose up and threatened to explode from his lips. But he had to stay calm and think.

He had two choices: He could either send Friar Daniel to

follow Gisela while he went to Hagenheim to round up a small army, or he could follow Gisela himself and send the friar to Hagenheim and hope his father was there to rally enough soldiers to come rescue Gisela—and Valten too, as he was likely to get captured again.

Since he couldn't bear the thought of leaving Gisela, he decided to go after her and send Friar Daniel to Hagenheim. The friar was so persistent, Father would have to listen.

But this time, Valten would pray his heart out to God to save them—in God's mighty strength, not his. Another verse jumped into his thoughts. *I lift up my eyes to the mountains—where does my help come from? My help comes from the Lord, the Maker of heaven and earth.*

Valten turned to Friar Daniel. "Do you know the way to Hagenheim?"

The friar looked perturbed, his brows drawn together and his eyes misty. "Hagenheim?... I think so."

"Go there and tell them I sent you—Valten Gerstenberg, Earl of Hamlin. Ask to speak to Duke Wilhelm. Tell him to send an army, as many soldiers as he can muster, and come after Ruexner, who is on his way to his castle in Bruchen. I will follow that fiend and do my best to make sure he doesn't harm Gisela."

The friar started wiping his face with his sleeve. "I must say, I am glad. I was wondrous sorry for the girl."

"Go. Ride as fast as you can."

Valten urged Sieger after Ruexner and his men—and Gisela. He turned back to Friar Daniel, who was nudging his donkey into a trot. *Thank you.*

Someday Valten would thank the friar properly. Now he had to do what he could to get to Gisela. He'd do anything to get her back safely, but the most important thing he could do was pray and believe that, even though he was wounded, broken, exhausted, and desperate, God was strong. *God, help me. Help Gisela.*

The way Valten had pulled her away from him and handed her over to Ruexner haunted Gisela. Of course, he didn't have a choice. He couldn't defeat twenty men. But no matter how often she repeated Valten's whispered words—"I will come for you. Trust me. Trust me"—being torn away from him had felt horrible. She feared being at Ruexner's mercy again, after escaping from him. Besides, Valten would risk his life again, would suffer pain, danger, and exhaustion to save her. Her greatest fear was that he wouldn't survive this time—or that he wouldn't think she was worth what he would have to go through to save her.

Always before, if something brought a pain to her heart, she could say, *I don't care.* Even if she did care, saying she didn't lessened the pain. But it was too blatant a lie where Valten was concerned. She did care, very much, and if she ever got another chance to tell him, she would. She would tell him she loved him. If he was still willing to marry her, she would marry him. And if what he wanted was love and complete devotion, he wouldn't be sorry for marrying her.

But would she ever get a chance?

Valten stayed far enough back that he never saw Ruexner or his men, only followed their easy-to-read trail. After riding for several hours, staying alert for any sign of either Ruexner's men or his own, Valten's shoulders ached, the pain encompassing the base of his skull. His eyes burned and he found himself losing his balance, but the memory of Gisela on Ruexner's horse and the terror on her face kept him going, kept him pushing himself, punishing himself for failing to evade Ruexner. How had the man found him? He must have met up with an expert tracker.

No doubt the devil was on his side. *But God, aren't you supposed to be on my side?*

Until now, he had depended more on himself than God.

Valten took a deep breath, tamping down the frustration that threatened to take over his thoughts. He rubbed the back of his neck, then ran his hand over his eyes. After riding all night, and now all morning, he had to stay awake. He couldn't fail Gisela. He had to get her back. It was all his fault Ruexner had kidnapped her, and was using her to exact his revenge. He'd never be able to live with himself if he failed her.

The memory came rushing back, of lying in bed with a broken leg while his little brother, Gabe, rescued Valten's betrothed. It was as if his careless little brother, who never had a serious, responsible thought in his life until he ran off to rescue Sophie, had bested him again.

But his desire to not let his little brother make him look bad didn't matter now. Nothing mattered except saving Gisela. This was not about Valten looking like a hero. It was about relying on God to save the woman he loved.

Gisela, with her soft voice, perfect lips, and her beautiful blue eyes ... "God, please. You can't let her suffer at Ruexner's hands. Please help me save her."

What had his life meant? All his success, all the tournaments he'd won ... they were like dust and ashes. Meaningless. Without Gisela, his life was meaningless.

By the time the sun sank behind the trees, Gisela was so weary she could barely keep her eyes open. There were moments she even forgot where she was, as the horse's constant, jostling gait lulled her into something akin to sleep.

When they finally stopped to make camp for the night, Gisela let Ruexner lift her off the saddle. But when her feet touched the ground, her legs wouldn't hold her up, and she crumpled to the ground, too exhausted to stand. What did it matter anyway? Maybe Ruexner would leave her where she lay.

Hands grabbed her under her arms and lifted her up, then slid under her knees. She found herself being picked up and carried.

She decided not to bother even opening her eyes, as long as he didn't try to molest her. Soon, she felt herself being lowered to the ground. Moments later, a warm blanket was spread over her. She never opened her eyes, but let herself drift away.

Gisela gradually awakened, wondering why her bed had grown so hard. She had replaced the straw in the mattress not long ago; it should be softer than this. One particularly prickly piece of straw was jabbing her hip. She rolled over on her side, but something felt different. She opened her eyes and realized she was sleeping on the ground outside, surrounded by sleeping men.

Then it all came back to her.

Was Valten following them? Or would he go to Ruexner's castle to fight Ruexner in two more days? *God, please help him get his men first, then come and defeat Ruexner and rescue me.* She wouldn't even pray that she would not have to marry Ruexner. She would just believe she would get away.

She trusted that Valten was coming for her. He might even come alone, and she couldn't let him be killed. She had to find a way to escape her captors herself, to keep Valten from getting recaptured or hurt.

An owl hooted in the darkness, somewhere hidden in the dark forest. It was still night, and the sound of snores and heavy breathing was all around her. As she looked around, her watchman stared back at her, wide awake. No chance that he would fall asleep any time soon. So she let herself drift back to sleep.

The next morning, with the sun spreading the first vestiges of light over the dark forest, Gisela sat up. Ruexner and his men were milling about. A man with a deep scar on his upper lip, which cut a line all the way to the outer corner of his eye, stood propped against a tree, watching her with narrowed eyes.

She'd have to stay alert and wait for a better chance to escape. This oaf wouldn't let her get away. Perhaps if she pretended to be docile and scared, some guard would get careless and give her an opportunity. But with this many men around, she needed to think of a clever plan.

Ruexner walked over, approaching cautiously.

Gisela purposely held back the defiance she was feeling and stared at him blank-faced. He might not be such an ugly man if he was not always sneering and behaving like a brute. He was not at all handsome compared to Valten, but she was sure the man didn't have to kidnap a woman to get a bride. He was a baron, with a castle and most likely a great number of vassals and servants in his ancestral town of Bruchen. Perhaps Gisela could reason with him.

While he was eyeing her, she decided to give it a try. "I am sure there are many maidens — very pretty and sweet ones — in Bruchen who would be happy to marry you. Why would you want to force me to marry you? I have no fortune, lands, or title."

"Don't you know, my dear? I want to marry you for one simple reason — for revenge." His smile was cold. "Besides, you remind me of my mother. She had the same shade of hair and eyes as you."

"So I am only a pawn in your game."

He did not deny it, and she felt heat creep up the back of her neck as anger rose up within her. "I won't marry you."

"I'm afraid you'll have no choice."

"You cannot marry me without my consent."

"Do you think I can't find a priest who will marry us against your will if I tell him to? It will not be so hard."

Gisela forced herself to push away her anger and think rationally. "What will your people and your family say when you bring an unwilling bride to your castle? I will not go with you calmly. I will scream and tell everyone that you have taken me against my will."

"And I will say that you are a peasant, and that I paid for you fairly, which is the truth. No one will question my right to marry you." He stepped even closer and ran a finger down her cheek. "Besides, my father took my mother against her will and married her. Over time she came to accept her place as his wife. She bore two sons and one daughter before she died. In time you will come to accept your role as the Baroness of Bruchen."

"I shall never accept you." Gisela actually felt sorry for this man. Pity and outrage warred inside her as she stared at his weatherworn, battle-scarred face. "I'm sorry your father gave you such a bad example, but I assure you ... I love Valten and I cannot love anyone else. I will never accept a life with you."

"Perhaps, perhaps not." The sneer came back, curling his lip, but he made no threatening moves.

"Don't you wish your father had cared about your mother's happiness?"

"If he'd cared about her happiness, she wouldn't have been my mother."

In spite of her efforts to stay calm, Gisela huffed. "Don't you have any fear of God?"

"Why should I fear someone I've never seen?"

"Just because your father didn't respect God doesn't mean you shouldn't. If you want to escape damnation and unhappiness in this life, you'd better start to care."

Was she talking to Ruexner? Or to herself? If she wanted to escape unhappiness, she'd better start to care. That seemed to be the lesson God wanted to teach *her*.

Ruexner was staring hard at her as he seemed to be trying to decide what to say. "Your features are so much like my mother's." He shook his head. "She didn't have your spirit, but she had the same look about her. It is too bad you are in love with Valten, because my greatest desire is to make him suffer. My father used to say, 'In this life, a man must take what he wants. He's a fool if he doesn't.' "

"You don't have to live your father's life. You can be your own person. Did your mother ever pray for you?" She asked that last question on a whim. Perhaps if she could remind him of his mother praying for him, he might feel some remorse for trying to force her to become his wife.

He spat on the ground near her foot. "You waste your time." Turning away from her, he told his men, "Get ready. We're leaving."

Chapter 26

As Gisela was hauled into the saddle in front of Ruexner, she told herself she shouldn't wonder if Valten was following them. She should assume he was not, that she wouldn't see him until he showed up at Ruexner's castle in two more days.

Her mind was constantly working to think of a way to escape from Ruexner. After an hour of riding, they drew near a town. Surrounded by his men, Ruexner boldly rode right through the middle of it.

There must be something she could do to escape. But if she jumped down off the horse, Ruexner would only drag her back. If she screamed and begged the townspeople, who were milling about, to save her from this man who had taken her against her will, would they help her? After all, what could they do against Ruexner and his armed men?

She looked around at the faces of the people. None of them made eye contact with her. A few looked curiously at them, but then looked away, and she guessed that Ruexner had glared at them and intimidated them into losing their curiosity. They soon reached a gray stone church on the edge of town, and at the front stood a large, square tower watching over the church and the town like a sentinel. Ruexner rode straight up to the high, circular steps that led up to massive wooden doors, and he dismounted.

"Why are we stopping here?" Gisela demanded.

Without even looking at her, he reached up and grabbed her around the waist and pulled her off the horse. He practically dragged her up the steps of the stone cathedral.

"What are you doing?" Her voice sounded a bit hysterical. "Where are you taking me?" She purposely made her voice loud so anyone nearby could hear her. "I won't marry you!"

"Quiet," Ruexner growled, as he opened the door with one hand and dragged her inside.

Valten followed Ruexner and his men as they entered a town. Why would Ruexner be so bold? He was up to something, so Valten closed in, not worrying about being seen, as he could get lost in the milling townspeople on the street.

Valten got closer until he was only a hundred feet behind Ruexner and his men. Gisela looked pale and frightened as Ruexner rode straight up to the town's cathedral. Valten's heart contracted in his chest.

Ruexner pulled Gisela off the horse, and by the time he was pulling her up the steps and inside the church, Valten had closed half the distance between them.

If Friar Daniel had to go all the way to Hagenheim to get help, then the soonest he could expect his father's knights was tomorrow or the next day. But he couldn't wait for them. He had to do something now.

Gisela blinked, trying to focus her eyes in the dim light. Torches flickered along the two walls that led back to an altar and baptismal font. Candles lit up the altar, but she didn't see anyone.

"Where is the priest?" Ruexner shouted, sending an echo through the high-ceilinged nave. "Anyone here?"

They listened, but heard nothing.

"No one is here," Gisela said, hoping he would leave, afraid she knew too well why he was looking for a priest.

"We shall wait."

Gisela racked her brain for a way of escape. But Ruexner's fingers were like iron bands around her arm, and she had no weapon, nothing within reach.

Finally, a dark figure appeared, emerging from the confessional along one wall.

"You there," Ruexner called. "I require to speak with Bishop Fulco."

The figure moved slowly, as if unmoved by Ruexner's urgent shout. He wore a long dark robe with a hood covering his head and shading his entire face. When he reached them, he quietly asked, "May I help you?"

"Where is Bishop Fulco?" Ruexner demanded gruffly. He held Gisela so tight to his side that she could feel his hip bone painfully kneading her side.

"Bishop Fulco is not here," the unperturbed voice answered. "May I assist you in some way?"

"Where is Bishop Fulco?" Ruexner held tight to her arm while he drew his sword. He held the sword's point a mere inch from the priest's face, who kept his head bowed and obscured. "I won't ask you again, and I am not squeamish of killing priests."

The priest did not in any way indicate fear. He didn't move. "As I said before, Bishop Fulco is not here."

As soon as he spoke the last word, the priest jumped behind Ruexner and threw a rope over his head and jerked it tight around his neck, choking him.

Ruexner let go of Gisela's arm, but was still holding his sword in his other hand. Ruexner clawed at the rope around his neck, his eyes bulging and desperate. Gisela clasped her hands together and brought them down as hard as she could on Ruexner's wrist, causing him to drop the sword. She picked it up and held it pointed at Ruexner's chest.

The priest's hooded cowl had slipped back, revealing Valten's face.

Gisela's heart jumped for a moment at seeing him, but then pounded in fear for Valten, her mind on Ruexner's men just outside the church door.

Valten started dragging Ruexner backward, no doubt to find a place to hide him. Suddenly, the front door of the church burst open and Ruexner's men began yelling and running toward them.

"Stop, or we'll kill him!" Gisela screamed, holding the point of Ruexner's sword against his chest.

Ruexner's men stopped. Then their expressions changed as they stared at Valten, Ruexner, and Gisela — no, they were staring at someone, or something, behind them.

"Drop that sword, or I will kill the Earl of Hamlin."

Gisela turned to see one of Ruexner's men holding a knife to Valten's throat.

She threw down the sword.

"Now stop choking him," Ruexner's man ordered. He stuck the point of the dagger under Valten's chin.

Valten loosened the rope around Ruexner's neck, and Ruexner immediately broke free, lifting the rope off his head. He spun around to face Valten, gasping and coughing, as the rest of his men closed in on them, surrounding them.

"Pardon me, but may I be of service?"

A young man dressed in a priestly robe stood near the altar behind them.

Ruexner picked up his sword and grabbed Gisela's arm, squeezing it painfully. But Gisela's eyes were trained on Valten and the dagger that was so close to slitting his throat.

No one paid the priest any attention as Ruexner shoved

Gisela into one of his men. "Hold on to her." He took the rope from Valten and started tying his hands behind his back.

"I do not know what you men are doing," the priest said, walking slowly toward them, "but I will remind you that this is a house of God and sanctuary for the oppressed. You may not do harm or violence here."

"Where is Bishop Fulco?" Ruexner's animallike voice reverberated against the ceiling.

"Bishop Fulco will be back tomorrow. He went to visit his mother in Bolbentberg."

Ruexner let out a strange growl. "Then you will perform the rites and speak the vows for our marriage, while Valten watches." He jerked the rope taut on Valten's hands.

"No," Gisela said stoutly. "I will not marry this man. I am not willing and I refuse to accept his troth."

Ruexner left Valten and grabbed Gisela's arm again.

Quietly, the priest asked, "You are Baron Ruexner, are you not?"

"I am."

"My lord baron," the priest said, "have you had the banns cried or posted?"

"No, nor will they be." Ruexner spoke through clenched teeth.

"Will you force this lady to wed you?"

"I will, and you will perform the rites. Otherwise I shall strike you dead where you stand." Ruexner shoved the sword point at the priest's chest.

"Very well. If you will follow me." The priest turned just as calmly and walked toward the front doors of the church.

"No!" Gisela struggled against Ruexner's hold, but it was no use. He only held her tighter. She let him pull her along, but stayed on her feet to prevent being dragged across the floor. "You cannot force me to speak the vows!"

Ruexner wore his usual sneer. "And why wouldn't a girl like you want to be a baroness? You are being foolish."

Ruexner's men pulled Valten along behind.

The young priest opened the heavy wooden door, letting in the light from outside, bright in spite of the cloudy sky.

"Where are you going?" Ruexner barked.

The priest said patiently, "If you wish to have the blessing of the church on your marriage, you must say your vows in front of the church doors."

Ruexner grunted, then pulled on Gisela's arm. "Come." Gisela stumbled after him until they stood on the top step, which was quite expansive enough to accommodate the priest, with his back to the door, and Ruexner and Gisela facing him.

Would the priest help them escape from Ruexner? He didn't seem inclined to. Besides, Ruexner would kill him if he tried.

Chapter 27

Gisela caught a glimpse of a small crowd of people gathering around the bottom of the steps, watching her and Ruexner and the priest. The townspeople wore various styles and kinds of clothing, from peasant to middle-class burghers, and they stared at the strangers standing at the top of the massive cathedral steps.

Gisela couldn't let Ruexner force her into marriage. She could not let anyone bully her again. Her stepmother and stepsisters had required her to do things she didn't want to do, when Gisela could have run away or even refused. She had not stood up for herself. Now she would do whatever she had to do. If she had to fight to the point of losing her life, she would not let Ruexner force her to marry him.

"Someone, help me!" Gisela cried out, trying to stare down individual townspeople as they glanced up at her. "I am being forced to marry this man! Help me!" She yanked her arm, trying to break free from Ruexner, but he jerked her closer and clamped his hand over her mouth.

"Get on with it," Ruexner growled at the priest.

"What are your names?" the priest asked, as though nothing seemed amiss.

"Friedric Ruexner and Gisela Mueller." Ruexner removed

his hand from Gisela's mouth and whispered harshly in her ear, "Stop it now, or I'll break your neck."

"And what are your parents' names?"

Ruexner growled like an angry bear, then answered, "Baron Arnold Tockler Ruexner and Gisela Russdorffer Ruexner."

Ruexner's mother's name was Gisela? How odd. Especially since her own mother's maiden name was Russdorffer.

"And the lady? What are your parents' names?"

"Christoff Theodemar Mueller and Fordola Russdorffer Mueller. My father was a knight— "

"Shut up." Ruexner clamped his hand over her mouth again. He looked at the priest. "Go on."

Gisela bit his hand and screamed. Ruexner clamped his hand over her mouth again and squeezed her face.

"Get on with it," Ruexner said through clenched teeth. "Speak the marriage vows. Now."

Where was Valten? She thought she saw him standing in the doorway, with three men holding him, a cloth gag tied around his mouth. She couldn't let him see her married to Ruexner. But how could she stop him? She couldn't get away from Ruexner. He was holding her so tightly she couldn't even wriggle.

The priest said in a loud voice, speaking slowly and pausing every few words, "Does anyone here ... know of any reason ... why this man, Friedric Ruexner ... and this woman, Gisela Mueller ... should not be married? If so, speak now."

Gisela could now only see a few people out of the corner of her eye, but she sensed there were many more behind her.

Someone cleared his throat. Then a woman shouted, "Their mothers were sisters!"

"They can't marry then," a man drawled somewhere behind her.

The townspeople were trying to help her!

"Who said that?" Ruexner roared, turning around and facing down the crowd. "It's a lie!"

Of course it was a lie. None of these people knew her, but if she and Ruexner were cousins, the marriage could not take place. The church would forbid it.

In his rush to see who had spoken, Ruexner had removed his hand from her mouth again. Gisela yelled, "I won't marry this man! I do not give my consent!"

Ruexner glared at Gisela, then at the priest. "On with it."

"I'm afraid I cannot." The priest gave him stare for stare. "Someone has declared the impediment of consanguinity, and this young maiden does not give her consent." The people must have emboldened him.

Ruexner turned around to face the crowd, pulling Gisela around with him as if she were a rag doll. "If anyone says another word, my men will cut out their hearts and feed them to the vultures! I, Friedric Ruexner, take this woman, Gisela Mueller, to be my wife. And no one, not even the church, can stop me."

Ruexner pushed the priest aside and pulled Gisela through the door of the church, his hand like a vise on her arm. Gisela caught a glimpse of Valten, being held by three men, as Ruexner shut the door behind him and started up the steps to one of the towers.

"Where are you taking me?"

"If we can't be married, then you will be my prisoner."

"You don't have to do this," Gisela said, trying to reason with him. "You can let me go. You and your men can—"

"You lied about your mother's name being Fordola Russdorffer, didn't you?"

"No. That was her name. She died when I was very young." Perhaps their mothers really were sisters.

"I don't want to hear anything else from you." Ruexner

halted on the steps, blocking her escape, and pulled a piece of cloth from his pocket.

Gisela tried to run back down the steps, but he grabbed her arm. She fought him, tearing at his fingers and their grip on her arm until he wrapped his big arms around hers and pinned them to her sides. He pulled her hands around her back and tied her wrists together.

"You will be sorry for this." Gisela was so angry she felt tears of pure fury in her eyes. "Duke Wilhelm will bring justice on you. You will not get away with it if you hurt me or Valten."

Ruexner continued pulling her up the stairs of the tower by her arms.

"You're hurting me."

She heard a door open, and Ruexner dragged her inside. He sat her down on a wooden bench. Something went around her ankles. Ruexner was tying them together, just as he'd tied her hands together behind her back. Then he tied a cloth over her eyes, knotting it behind her head.

"Why are you doing this?"

He didn't say anything for a moment. "This is about Valten and me. He has to pay for what he did to me."

"What do you plan to do to him? Haven't you hurt him enough? Just please let us go," she whispered out of desperation. Perhaps the man possessed a shred of goodness.

"Almost." Ruexner's voice was low and gentle. "Almost you persuade me. But Valten and I must end our fight now, once and for all. I will take him to my castle in Bruchen, and there we shall have our final duel."

She heard him turn and start to walk away. "Please, don't hurt him. You don't have to do this. You don't have to fight Valten. You can let us go and never have to see us again."

"I don't expect you to understand." He seemed to hesitate

at the door. For long moments she didn't hear anything. Had he left?

The door squeaked open, then closed with a bang.

"O God, please help Valten. Please protect him. Please."

Ruexner's grimy henchmen held on to Valten and surrounded him, his hands tied behind his back, when Ruexner came back down the stairs without Gisela.

"Where is she?" Valten demanded, looking straight at Ruexner.

"She is safe," Ruexner said, his eyes flashing with malice.

"Will you kill an unarmed man, inside a church?"

"I'm trying to decide if I want to take her with us when I bring you to Bruchen."

"I'm ready to fight you. Give me a sword now and let's fight. Even with a broken hand and broken ribs, I can still defeat you."

Ruexner seemed to be savoring the moment, based on his evil grin. "No, I don't think so."

Ruexner went to speak to his men, leaving two in charge of Valten. When he came back, he told the priest, "We're taking over this place tonight. My men are tired and need sleep. Now get out."

"You can't do that. This is a church." The priest seemed genuinely upset, unlike how he had reacted when Ruexner had almost forced Gisela to marry him against her will. Although he had delayed the marriage, speaking slowly, as if hoping someone would come to their aid. He'd also refused to go on once someone had declared an impediment.

"Get out, or my men will throw you out," Ruexner growled in the priest's face.

"Bishop Fulco will hear about this."

Ruexner ignored the priest as one of his men escorted him out the back door.

Ruexner wrapped a piece of cloth around Valten's eyes, blindfolding him. "I shall keep you upstairs. Perhaps we will bring you some supper in a few hours, if you are quiet." Ruexner then pulled him forward.

"Why blindfold me?"

"Oh, I don't know. I suppose I want you to feel helpless. If you can't see where you are, you might not be able to escape."

"You're a sick and deviant brute." Valten's rage was beginning to get the better of him. Lack of sleep was making it difficult to think. He needed to try to reason with him and project confidence. "You know the king will not approve of what you are doing. He will strip you of your knighthood, and possibly worse."

Rough hands forced him to climb some stairs. Undoubtedly they were the stairs leading up inside the church tower. Gisela had been taken up the same stairs.

"I don't worry about the king. He will reprimand me, but if I give him a few valuable trinkets for his coffers, I suspect he will forgive me. And instead of killing you, perhaps I will demand a ransom from Duke Wilhelm when I defeat you in a few days." Still guiding him up the stairs, Ruexner added nonchalantly, "As it turns out, Gisela is the daughter of my mother's sister. Strange, but it is apparently true. Therefore I shall marry her off to one of my knights. Who do you think she would better suit—Malbert or Lew?"

A door creaked opened, then Valten was pushed into a room of some sort. Hands on his shoulders forced him to sit, then they tied his ankles together.

The men shuffled away, Ruexner laughed, and the door shut.

He was already working his feet, trying to take off his boots. If he could get one of his boots off, the rope might slip off with it.

All was quiet, then he heard a sniff, and a woman's voice from several feet away said, "Who is there?"

"Gisela? Is that you?" His heart tripped at her being in the same room.

"Valten!" She sounded like she was crying.

"Are you hurt?"

"No." Her voice cracked and she sniffed again. "Are you?"

"No." He managed to hold one boot down with the other and pull his foot out. Then he was able to shake off the rope binding his ankles. Then, after fumbling for several moments with his boot, he gradually worked it back onto his foot.

Now he could walk. He stood up and took a step forward, his hands still tied behind his back. But with his vision completely obscured by the blindfold, he wasn't sure where to go, and he could easily lose his balance if he ran into something.

"Valten," Gisela was saying, "I'm so sorry for all the trouble I've caused you."

"You didn't cause this trouble, Gisela. Ruexner did. And it's more my fault than yours."

"But you risked your life to save me."

"Of course. You were in danger." He moved slowly toward her voice.

She sniffed again. "There's something I have to tell you."

His shin bumped into something, another bench or stool, maybe, and something slid to the floor with a thump. He hoped Ruexner didn't hear it below them and come to check on them.

"Keep talking." He needed to hear her voice to find her.

"I pretended I didn't know you because I knew you didn't remember me."

Remember her? What was she talking about?

"I was there when you bought Sieger. You bought him from my father."

"I did?"

"You were fourteen years old, and I was seven."

She must have been the little blonde girl who'd looked so

upset that he was taking her horse. "So Sieger did know you." No wonder his horse had acted so happy to see her that day at the stables. He had thought she had placed a magic spell on his horse, but instead, they had known each other from when Sieger had been only a foal.

"The truth is—" Her words were interrupted by a sob.

It tore at his heart to hear her crying, she who had been so brave and fierce in the face of so much danger. If only he could get to her. If only he could comfort her, but he couldn't see her, couldn't even put his arms around her, since his hands were tied behind his back. But at least he had thought of a way to get their blindfolds off. If he could just get to her.

"The truth is," she went on, "I pretended I didn't care about anything. I tried to tell myself I didn't care about you. But I do care. The truth is, I love you."

She loved him. The words made him stumble and pause to restore his balance.

"You are brave and strong and good, noble and kind. I love you and I think you're ..."

His knee bumped into the bench she was sitting on, and he sat down beside her, so close their shoulders and knees were touching.

He leaned down until his cheek touched her soft hair. She caught her breath but didn't pull away. He lowered his face until he felt her breath on his chin.

"You think I'm ... what?"

Chapter 28

Gisela's heart faltered, then started pounding against her chest at Valten's warm breath against her cheek.

"You think I'm ... what?"

His nose touched hers. He was pressed against her shoulder. He radiated heat, as he'd no doubt been fighting and struggling against his attackers earlier. She leaned forward until she felt his stubbly beard prickling her face.

He seemed to be waiting.

"I think you're wonderful," she whispered.

His warm lips brushed her cheek and his voice was gruff. "Will you marry me, Gisela?"

Her heart seemed to leap into her throat. She had to swallow it down so she could say, "Yes."

More deliberately this time, he rubbed his cheek against hers, melting her insides at the strangely wonderful prickling sensation. Slowly, he moved his lips over her face, kissing her cheek, closer and closer to her lips. Gisela moved her head slightly. Valten's breath caressed her lips, then he covered the corner of her mouth, gradually slanting his lips over hers until he was kissing her, and she was kissing him back.

She couldn't see him and couldn't touch him with her hands, but she was keenly aware of his lips touching hers in her first true kiss, her senses filled with Valten's own smell of leather and the outdoors.

He'd come back for her, risked his life yet again for her, and from the way he was kissing her, she didn't think he asked her to marry him out of obligation. Maybe he even loved her.

After several moments, his lips moved across her cheek, stopping at her blindfold, which slipped up and off her head.

She could see him. Oh! He was so beautiful! She leaned forward and kissed him again.

Valten pulled her blindfold off with his teeth. He had to stop kissing her so he could figure out a way to escape, and he needed to be able to see to—

Her lips were suddenly on his again, and he lost his balance and almost fell backward off the bench. Now that he'd *finally* been able to kiss her, she apparently liked it. He had thought she would take off his blindfold first, but he wasn't about to complain.

When she pulled away, he couldn't think about anything but her and her kiss. Then he felt his blindfold slip off his face.

She was so beautiful, with her lips all red from his kisses, her hair tumbling around her shoulders and forehead, and her cheeks blushing pink. She made him restless to kiss her again.

But he had to get them out of there before Ruexner came back.

"Turn around," Valten said, slipping off the bench to kneel beside her.

"What?"

"Turn around so I can try to free your hands."

Gisela turned so that her back was facing him. This was going to be awkward, given his broken hand, but he couldn't think of any other way to get them free. The cloth that Ruexner had tied around her wrists was knotted tightly. He set about pulling at the knot with his teeth, trying to loosen it.

Gisela was silent as he chewed on the knotted cloth, pulling and yanking at one side of the knot, then the other.

"I'm sorry you had to come after me again."

Valten stopped long enough to say, "Stop saying that." He tugged on the cloth some more, not seeing any progress yet. "I told you, it's more my fault than yours. Ruexner is my enemy. I should be begging forgiveness from you for allowing him to get within a foot of you."

She was quiet as he worked on the knot some more. He began to think the knot was loosening ever so slightly, so he got up and, with his back to her on the bench, he began using his fingers to try to pull the knot loose. His hand throbbed so painfully he caught his breath, but he kept working.

"But you were the one who was hurt. You were beaten and pummeled—" Her breath hitched, as if she was starting to cry again.

"Please, don't cry. It's nothing that won't heal. Besides, you're worth it."

A sniffle. "That's the sweetest thing anyone has ever said to me."

"I'm sure I can do better than that, if you won't cry anymore."

She laughed, sniffed, then drew in a long, deep breath. "All right. I promise not to cry ... if you want to say more pleasant things."

He liked the smile in her voice. He pulled at the knot while he thought. "You have the most beautiful hair, eyes, nose, and especially lips, that I've ever seen."

She sighed. "That's very pleasant."

"I like the way you don't become hysterical in dangerous situations."

"Thank you."

"And you are very good with horses."

"Yes?"

"And you kiss exceptionally."

"Compared to whom?"

He continued to work hard on the knot, deciding how to phrase this. "Truthfully, you are the first girl I've ever kissed."

"Oh." She sounded pleased. "And you are the first boy — or man — I've ever kissed."

If he'd been feeling warm and happy before, now he felt downright sunny, like the rays were filling his insides and radiating from every finger and toe.

What foolish things went through a man's mind when he was contemplating marriage to the most beautiful girl in the world.

He worked harder at the knot, plucking at one side, then the other until, he felt it slipping free. *Yes!* The cloth fell from her wrists.

She turned and threw her arms around him, and he found himself kissing her lips again. She was so wonderfully eager, it made him groan.

"Sorry," she said, pulling away, but keeping her soft little hands around his neck, apologizing as if she were to blame for the kiss. "I should untie you first." She started to get up, then seemed to notice that her ankles were still tied together. She bent and pulled at the knot.

Valten got to his feet and watched her make quick work of her ankle bonds.

"There." The cloth around her ankles came loose and she tossed it onto the floor.

She stood up and moved behind him. "Oh. Your poor hand." The splint that Frau Lena had made for him had fallen off in the struggle with Ruexner earlier. Her fingers lightly caressed his throbbing left hand. "You need a healer. Your hand is so swollen and bruised." She started working at the bonds around his wrists, but her touch was too gentle.

"Don't worry about my hand. Just get me loose any way you can. Yank on it if you need to."

"Very well, but I will try not to hurt you."

"Ruexner will cause much more pain if we don't escape."

She pulled harder at the rope around his wrist, her fingers slipping and bumping against his broken bone. The pain was intense, but he'd been living with it for days now. He could endure it better if he was free and Gisela was safe.

Finally, he felt the rope loosen, then Gisela pulled it free. "Got it!"

Valten turned to face her and she threw her arms around him again. *We have to get out of here*, his mind told him, but he decided he had enough time for another kiss. And Gisela obviously agreed.

Gisela could hardly believe she was kissing Valten. If it didn't feel so much more exciting than she'd ever imagined, she might think she was dreaming. But this was too real to be a dream—his warm arms around her, the tenderness in his kiss, the eager way he pulled her in . . .

Valten pulled away, stared hard at her for a moment, then quickly strode to the only window in the entire room, which seemed to be some kind of storage space.

Could it be true that she was going to marry this man? "Heaven."

"What?" Valten looked over his shoulder.

"Nothing."

He opened the shutters and pulled the glass casement open. Gisela hurried to his side and looked out too. It was a long way down. That side of the church faced the woods on the edge of town. No one was within sight.

There was no sign of the tenderness that came into his eyes when he had kissed her. Instead, his face was a picture of cold determination as he turned away from the window.

"Help me collect all the cloths and ropes they used to tie us."

She and Valten picked up their discarded blindfolds and bonds, and Valten began tying them together. First he tied the two blindfolds together. Then he added the two cloths that had been around Gisela's wrists and ankles, then the ropes from Valten's ankles and wrists. He tied them carefully, testing each knot by having her hold one end while he yanked the other end.

Valten searched the room for any other bit of cloth or rope but found only one short piece of rope. After tying it on, he said, "Take this end." They stretched it out between them.

"This will only reach halfway to the ground, if that." Gisela frowned.

"It will be enough." He went to the window and started tying it to the window casement.

"Do you really think so?"

"I'll climb to the end of it and jump the rest of the way."

"But what about your hand?"

"I'll manage."

Was he always so tough, so unflinching? How much abuse could his poor broken hand take? The bone would end up growing back wrong, or worse. Might his hand become septic? If so, he could die. Her stomach lurched.

He tightened the knot, then threw the other end of the makeshift rope out the window, watching it dangle high above the ground. He started to climb out the window.

"Wait." Gisela held on to his arm, which felt as hard and solid as a tree trunk. But he wasn't a tree. He was a man. And even trees could be cut down.

"Don't worry," he said, caressing her cheek with the back of his fingers. "Just climb to the end and I'll catch you."

"I want you to promise me something first."

"What is it, *liebchen*?"

The term of endearment, and the tenderness that had returned to his eyes, made her knees weak. She wanted to throw her arms around him and kiss him once more, but she resisted. Just barely. "I want you to promise me we will seek out an experienced healer for your hand as soon as we escape, and promise you will follow all their instructions."

"I promise." He cupped her chin with his palm and kissed her so sweetly it stole her breath.

He pulled away, took a deep breath, then went out the window, holding on to the rope.

Gisela watched him go, flinching at how painful it must be for him to grip the rope with his broken hand. He looked powerful, in any case, as he maneuvered down. The sight of his massive shoulders made her sigh.

She didn't know she could be so . . . shallow? Enamored? Just plain silly? But she didn't care. She also didn't know she could be so happy.

Valten made it to the end of the rope, then dropped the rest of the way to the ground. He looked up at her. "Just put one leg out the window and grab the rope."

Gisela took the hem of her skirt and tucked it between her legs and into the belt around her waist, to preserve her modesty. She stuck one leg out the window, sitting on the edge, grabbed the makeshift rope with both hands, and pulled her other leg out.

She swayed a bit as she clutched the rope as tightly as possible. Her stomach flipped as she hung high above the ground.

"That's good," Valten said in a soothing voice. "You're doing well. Now move one hand at a time down the rope."

Carefully she shifted one hand down, then the other. Her

hands slipped a bit and she clung tighter, terrified of falling the entire way and landing on top of Valten. Slowly, she moved one hand, then the other, and inched her way down. Would Ruexner or his men see them and recapture them? She forced herself to concentrate on her task.

"You're doing well," Valten assured her. "Keep coming."

He was probably clenching his teeth at how slowly she was moving, but to his credit, he kept his voice calm and encouraging. *He wants to marry me! Thank you, God!*

Gisela's hand slipped. She clung tighter, letting the rough cloth burn the skin on her palm as she clutched it as tightly as possible. *Concentrate. He can't marry me if I fall on his head and break his neck.*

"You can do it," Valten's deep voice crooned below her. "Careful."

Gisela inched down. All at once the rope ran out. She was at the end of it before she knew it. Her hands slipped off the end and she was falling.

She forced herself not to make any noise. Squeezing her eyes shut, she braced herself to hit something solid.

She landed in Valten's strong arms. They held her like iron bands, one under her knees, the other under her back.

"You are so strong."

"I have to find Sieger now."

"Of course."

Still, they stared at each other. Still, he held her in his arms.

Shouts split the air, coming from the front of the church.

Valten set her on her feet, grabbed her hand, and started running toward the trees.

Chapter 29

Gisela ran as fast as she could, tree limbs slapping her in the face and snatching at her clothes. Suddenly, her foot sank into a hole, her ankle twisting painfully, and she went down.

Valten knelt at her side.

"I'm sorry. I stepped in a hole."

"Can you walk?"

"I don't know."

Valten helped her up, holding her under her arms. She put weight on her left foot and gasped. "I think I can— " She took a step and bit her lip at the pain.

Valten swept her up in his arms and started walking.

"You can't carry me."

"I don't mind."

"Where are we going?"

"I want to get you far enough away from the church so that Ruexner won't see you. Then I'm going back for my horse."

"Do you think they know we escaped?"

He didn't say anything for a moment, as if he was listening. Then he turned around and started walking back toward the church.

"What?"

"I thought I heard the captain of the guard."

Whose guard? Gisela wanted to ask, but kept quiet so he could hear.

As he continued to walk toward the church, Gisela watched his face for signs of what he was thinking.

Valten gazed through the trees. Men rushed around, and Gisela thought she recognized the Gerstenberg colors.

Valten set her on her feet beside a tree.

"Where are you going?"

"My men and Ruexner's are fighting. They must have found us somehow."

"But you don't have a sword!"

"I'll find one."

Gisela held on to his arm. "Don't! Please don't leave me!" If she had to pretend to be fearful to keep him safe, she would do it.

Valten looked out at the fighting men while Gisela kept hold of him with both hands. He turned to her. "I must go help my men." He pried her fingers off his arm in a moment, as if her strength was nothing.

"No!"

Her voice had no effect as he ran away from her and into the melee.

Gisela left her place at the tree and hobbled closer, until she was standing at the edge of the woods and could see the men battling in the grassy courtyard of the church. Friar Daniel stood on the outskirts, at odds with the swarm of fighting men in his brown robe, his eyes and hands lifted in prayer.

She quickly spotted Valten. He had apparently found a sword and was taking on two men at once. And then one of his men came to his aid and started fighting the extra opponent. Valten quickly divested his adversary of his sword and sent him to stand with several of Ruexner's men who had lost their weapons and were being guarded by two of the Hagenheim knights.

Duke Wilhelm was also among the men from Hagenheim. He defeated his challengers almost as efficiently as did Valten. Most of Ruexner's men went down easily to Duke Wilhelm's well-trained knights and soldiers. It was clear Ruexner was outmatched, with less than half of Ruexner's men still fighting. Soon, the few that had not been captured surrendered—everyone except Ruexner.

Ruexner battled his way to Valten and raised his sword in a massive arc, aiming for Valten's head. Valten blocked the blow, and Ruexner retreated.

"Surrender, Ruexner!" Duke Wilhelm shouted.

But Ruexner continued fighting, roaring with each blow he inflicted.

Valten was obviously tired. He was fighting with a broken hand, a broken rib, and little sleep. But Ruexner was also injured, since Valten had stabbed both his sides with his sword in the tournament, and Ruexner had gone without sleep just as Valten had. But Ruexner seemed to fight with an unearthly strength, as though his rage was driving him.

Valten's sword suddenly seemed to take on new life. He took the offensive and struck with new speed and force. He came at Ruexner with blow after blow at a rapid pace, forcing Ruexner to retreat, until he was bent backward over the front steps of the church.

"Surrender to me!" Valten yelled.

Ruexner said nothing, only growled and tried to kick Valten's feet out from under him. Valten sidestepped and slammed his sword into Ruexner's so hard that the weapon went flying, landing harmlessly on the stone steps several feet away.

Valten pressed the point against Ruexner's chest, over his heart. "Tie him up!" Valten yelled. "He has harassed my betrothed and showed himself unworthy to be called a knight of the Holy Roman Empire."

Several men moved forward and took charge of Ruexner, whose expression was stoic now that he was surrounded. After wrongfully capturing her and Valten more than once, tying them up and lording over them, now he was the captive.

Valten and his father, Duke Wilhelm, stood talking as the men led Ruexner away. They would have to decide what to do with Ruexner and all his men. One knight shouted for someone to go fetch the town barber, or healer, if there was one. A couple of men ran off down the street. Meanwhile, the townspeople milled about, talking and trying to stand on their toes to see what was happening, while the Hagenheim men seemed busy, checking on the injured and watching the prisoners.

A woman walked toward Gisela. She was well dressed, with plump, pink cheeks and a ready smile. "Gisela Mueller?"

"Yes?"

"I am Hette Schwarcz, and I knew the Baroness, Ruexner's mother. I was telling the truth when I said you were her sister's daughter."

Gisela shook her head. "So it was you who said our mothers were sisters. How do you know this?"

She squeezed Gisela's arm. "Because you look so much like her, and her name was Gisela Russdorffer. Baron Ruexner's mother and her sister promised to name their first daughters after each other. I knew who you were as soon as you said your name was Gisela. But you are tired now, I can see, and no doubt famished. Come with me to the baker's shop. The baker's wife is my friend and she will give you whatever you want to eat. Come."

Feeling curious, but also thirsty and hungry, Gisela started to go with Frau Schwarcz. The woman looked down at her foot, as Gisela was limping.

"Oh, you are hurt!" The woman moaned. "You poor thing."

"I injured my ankle, but it is nothing."

Out of the corner of her eye, she saw Valten coming toward her. "Where are you going?"

"I—"

The woman interrupted. "I am taking her to get some food, just here," and she pointed to a shop barely thirty feet down the dirt street. "I promise I shall take good care of her."

Valten looked at the woman, then at Gisela. He moved closer. "Can you walk?"

"Of course. It is only a little sprain. But you come with us. You need to eat too."

"I will. You go with this woman, but only there. I shall come soon."

Gisela followed the woman, who took her arm and insisted she lean on her. Once inside the little bakery, which was warm and smelled of bread and roast pig, the woman sat her at a small wooden table and brought out a bowl of pork stew and hot buttered bread, with wine and water to drink. Gisela hadn't realized how tired and hungry she was, and as she ate, Hette Schwarcz told her about becoming friends with Friedric Ruexner's mother when Hette was married to her first husband, a merchant who lived in Bruchen.

"Gisela Ruexner, your aunt, was taken by Baron Ruexner when she was but sixteen. He forced her to marry him, since her father was dead and she had no one to object for her. By the time she had her first child, she became resigned to her fate and stayed on with the baron."

"That is terrible. Did my mother know what had happened to her?"

"Not at first. Baron Ruexner wouldn't let her write to anyone. By the time she got word to your mother, Gisela had two babes and felt she must stay for her children's sake. But it wasn't a happy marriage."

Hette Schwarcz sighed wistfully. "She loved her children,

and then she died in childbirth, bringing forth her third baby. I believe your mother died about the same time. You must have been still a child when your mother died."

"Yes. I was only two."

"You are as beautiful as your namesake." Frau Schwarcz patted Gisela's cheek. "I couldn't bear for you to marry that Friedric, and against your will."

"Thank you for that. I was very grateful." Gisela felt much better after eating.

"And now everything is well. Ruexner is captured and you will be with your love." Frau Schwarcz shook her finger at Gisela. "Don't think I couldn't see the love in his eyes when he looked at you. He would have fought to the death for you, that handsome Valten Gerstenberg." She patted her cheek again. "You shall have a happy marriage."

Valten came into the little bakery with his father and several other men, and Frau Schwarcz served them herself. Gisela didn't get a chance to talk to Valten, as he and the men discussed what had happened to them the last few days. She didn't mind, as she happily watched Valten eat, thankful their long ordeal was over.

Gisela learned, as she listened to their conversation, that on his way back to Hagenheim, Friar Daniel had encountered Duke Wilhelm and his men, and he had led them to where they had been when Ruexner had taken Gisela. From there they had tracked them to this town and to the cathedral.

Duke Wilhelm spoke of what would happen with Ruexner and his men now. It seemed Valten's father would be taking Ruexner and his two knights, Malbert and Lew, to face King Sigismund and to answer for their crimes against Gisela and Valten. His other men, little more than farmers who had been pressed into service, would be allowed to go home to their families.

Gisela was glad when the men got up to leave, but Valten stayed behind, all his attention on her as the others left.

He moved his chair close to her. "I need to get you to a healer," he said.

"You need a healer worse than I do. Your hand is badly swollen. How far are we from Hagenheim?"

"Almost three days. But we are only a half day's ride from the Cottage of the Seven, where we can rest. There is also a healer there who will look at your ankle."

"Cottage of the Seven?"

"There isn't a good healer in town, from what I hear, and the town barber has more than he can do to take care of the men who were injured in the fight. My brother, Gabe, is well acquainted with the men at the Cottage of the Seven and their healer, Bartel. He helped Gabe when he was shot with an arrow two years ago."

Valten held her hand. "We can be there in a few hours if we leave now."

It was a great relief to think that someone knowledgeable in the healing arts would tend Valten's hand. And perhaps she could even take a bath.

She could hardly wait.

Once outside, Gisela saw Friar Daniel coming toward them. He immediately told her the story of how he had come upon Duke Wilhelm and a contingent of his knights and soldiers on their way to Ruexner's castle in Bruchen. They had easily been able to find Ruexner and his men's careless trail.

As they walked, they passed Ruexner and his men, who were tied up and sitting on the ground. "Brother Daniel," Valten said, his arm around Gisela's waist, "I do believe there are some men here who are in great need of your good message."

"Indeed." Friar Daniel smiled as though the prospect was a happy one. "I have already arranged it with Duke Wilhelm. He is taking me with him when he travels to King Sigismund's court with these nefarious men. I have been given his full blessing to speak to them on the trip and to tell them of God's goodness and how they might repent."

"I am happy to hear it." Though Gisela still was reeling over the fact that Ruexner was her cousin, her own mother's nephew, she knew she would have to forgive him. She might never want to see him again, but she could pray for Friar Daniel's success in turning him from his evil ways. "I hope you don't mind the difficult task before you, of attempting to reform such depraved men."

"My dear, I could not have asked for anything better. I am pleased to tell the good news to men such as these. After all, who needs the gospel message more?"

"Amen to that." Valten looked rather grim as they walked slowly back to the church, but when Gisela caught his eye, he winked. "Brother Daniel, if anyone can reach these men with truth and goodness, it would be you. I have a great respect for your sincerity."

Gisela's heart filled with gratitude at how Valten's attitude toward Friar Daniel seemed to have changed. Could it be that she and Valten had learned some important lessons since beginning this ordeal?

Valten clasped hands with Friar Daniel.

"It is the Lord's truth that shall win their hearts and minds." Friar Daniel looked adamant. "And while I am fulfilling my mission, I will pray blessings on your marriage, and that you will be a joy to each other and to your people in Hagenheim."

Someone brought Sieger to Valten, and a mount was quickly rounded up for Gisela. The captain of the guard supplied two men to escort Valten and Gisela, and half of the rest were to travel with Duke Wilhelm to escort Ruexner to the king, and the other half would return to Hagenheim. They set out.

As their horses settled into a comfortable trot, Gisela asked, "Why do they call it the Cottage of the Seven?"

Valten raised his eyebrows, remembering. "It is a cottage where live seven ... rather unusual men."

"Unusual?"

"They are good men, but society's misfits, living away from people and their superstitions and fears. The important thing for us is that there is a healer who lives there who will take care of your foot."

"And your hand?"

"And my hand."

"Good, because I think my ankle will be well in a few days, but looking at your hand makes me want to cry."

He hoped she wouldn't cry. He didn't like seeing her cry.

As they rode in silence, his mind went back to the image of Friar Daniel getting on his donkey, preparing to go with Ruexner and his men. Friar Daniel might not carry a sword, but the man was brave nevertheless. And though he didn't own a sword of steel, the sword he did carry was more powerful in the spirit realm.

It was time. Valten knew it. Time to exchange his sword for a new life. He no longer had a taste for his old one. And just as Friar Daniel lived his life for more than tangible, earthly rewards, Valten wanted his life to be about more than winning tournaments and gaining prizes. He had fed his pride long enough, and now it was time to feed his spirit and live life at a deeper level.

Chapter 30

Gisela sighed at the luxury of sitting in an actual tub full of warm water. She had to draw her knees up almost to her chin to fit in it, but it was wonderful. The tub was metal with leather strips to reinforce the seams and make it more leakproof. And the soap smelled even more wonderful than the foreign soaps her stepmother and stepsisters used—like roses and lilacs. Roslind, the kind and generous maiden who had helped her fill the tub, told her the soap was made by Bartel, the former monk who was also a healer and one of the seven men who lived at the cottage.

Valten and his guards had gone to the creek to wash up, so Gisela took her time. Roslind had offered to help her wash her hair, but Gisela was accustomed to doing such things for herself.

Gisela dried herself, then she put on the dress that Roslind had brought for her to borrow while her other one—the beautiful, blue silk gown she had worn ever since the ball at Hagenheim—was being washed. The gown's sleeves were torn and the skirt had a few rips in it, but it still looked better than any of the dresses her stepmother had allowed her to wear.

Roslind had lent her a simple brown work dress, but it was clean and fit Gisela well. Her ankle still hurt when she put her weight on it, but it was already feeling better than it had a few hours ago when she first injured it. She picked up a bucket and filled it with her bathwater and limped as she carried it outside. As she dumped it on the ground, Gisela met the pretty brunette, who seemed to be the only female living at the house of seven men.

"Lord Valten tells us you are his fiancée."

Gisela was smiling even more on the inside at the thought of Valten telling people they were to be married. He wasn't the most talkative man, after all.

"I am married." Roslind wore a pleased look in her pale blue eyes as she helped Gisela empty the bathtub. "His name is Siegfried, but everyone calls him Siggy. I fell in love with him as soon as I saw him." The girl sighed dreamily.

"How long have you been married?"

"Two years."

Two years and she was still sighing. Gisela hoped for the same. Truly, she could hardly think beyond the moment, and certainly not beyond the next four weeks, for Valten had declared they would be married then. He'd already sent a messenger back to Hagenheim to tell his parents.

She was afraid to believe it, afraid it was too good to be true. After all, only a few days ago Valten knew her only as the girl who had a way with horses, with whom he had spent a couple of hours walking around Hagenheim. But after what they had been through together the last few days, she felt they knew each other well.

After they finished dumping out the bathwater, she and Roslind worked together to make dinner. As they prepared the meat pies, she wondered if Valten had finished his cold bath in the creek and was finally letting Bartel tend to his hand.

They set the food and drink on the table, and Roslind told her the names of each of the men as they all trouped in. The men looked like a band of traveling miracle players, or jongleurs and circus performers, instead of the woodsmen that they were.

Dominyk, their leader, who barely stood as tall as the other men's waists, sported a thick black moustache and black hair. He was as dignified as any duke as he seated himself at the head of the table.

Siggy, who was tall and thin and blond, hurried in, grinned in his eagerness as he came over and kissed his wife on the forehead. Dolf smiled shyly and nodded at Gisela as he sat at Dominyk's left side. He had a pleasant but craggy face, with brown hair and gentle brown eyes. He talked with his hands in gestures and signs that the other men seemed to understand perfectly.

Vincz, with droopy eyelids that belied his quick movements, broad shoulders, and work-hardened hands, sat beside Dolf. Heinric followed close behind. He was the tallest and broadest of the men, with wide eyes that followed Gisela's every move, and a bit of saliva that threatened to drip from each corner of his mouth. But at least he was smiling.

On the other side of the table sat Gotfrid. He scowled at Gisela, then scowled at the food, then crossed his arms and scowled some more. The large scar that covered one side of his head also seemed to scowl at Gisela, where it puckered the skin and prevented any hair from growing.

Bartel, the healer, came in next wearing a monk's coarse robe and a placid look on his handsome face. He walked as if on stilts, making her realize there was something wrong with his feet. He nodded to her solemnly, then sat down on the bench next to Gotfrid.

Valten and his men entered the room. Valten's hand was unbandaged and still looked horribly bruised and swollen. The men indicated that he should sit at the end of the table opposite Dominyk, in the place of honor, and Gisela should sit at his left. Roslind squeezed in next to her husband, and Bartel spoke to Valten.

"I can see your hand will need some special attention, brother knight. Would you like to wait until after we eat?"

"Yes, I thank you." Valten bowed to him respectfully. Bartel bowed back.

The two knights who had traveled with Valten and Gisela packed in with the rest of the men on the benches down the long sides of the table and began to eat, spearing venison with their knives and ladling gravy and cooked vegetables and fruits onto their trenchers with wooden serving spoons. Soon the only sound was the muted sounds of eating. Then Heinric belched … and smiled.

Gisela couldn't help smiling back. She caught Roslind's eye. The girl was also smiling at her, sitting shoulder to shoulder with her husband, who didn't seem to mind that she was crowding him.

Valten's knee brushed hers under the table. She glanced up at him and could have sworn he was blushing.

They all went back to eating, and Gisela sighed, feeling more content in this house full of misfit men than ever in her life.

"We are expecting the arrival of your brother, Lord Gabehart," Dominyk said, looking at Valten, "and Lady Sophie this evening. They are on their way from Hohendorf to Hagenheim for a visit."

Valten's eyes widened slightly. He didn't say anything right away, but continued to chew his food. "Will you have enough room for everyone? My men and I can sleep outside."

"If your men have no objection to sleeping in the stable, we shall have accommodations for all."

Valten's guards grunted their consent, saying a pile of hay was as good as a feather bed.

Gisela finished eating and sat waiting for the others to finish so she and Roslind could clear the table. She laid her hands in her lap. If Valten's hand wasn't broken, would he try to hold hers?

Everyone seemed to have finished eating and were taking

the last swills of their drink. Then three of the men stood and started clearing the table. Gisela looked at Roslind, but she sat still, talking quietly with Siggy. Was she letting the men do the menial task of clearing the table?

The other men stood and Dominyk herded the rest of them outside, with Roslind and Siggy the last to go, leaving Valten, Gisela, and Bartel still sitting at the table.

Bartel fixed Gisela with a dark brown eye. "I will look at your ankle now."

"But Valten's hand is in more urgent need of your care."

"He will not allow me to look at his hand until I've tended your ankle." Bartel spoke factually, his expression as calm and still as the small lake near her home.

Valten stared straight ahead in stubborn silence, his chin looking like it was carved from stone.

Gisela decided not to argue. A few more minutes wouldn't matter.

They moved to the adjoining room, with Valten helping to support her as she walked, and Bartel had her sit on a bench. Valten sat beside her and Bartel sat across from her on a stool. He lifted her foot and silently examined it, pressing lightly, looking at it from all sides.

"It isn't badly swollen, but you should not walk on it if it is painful to do so. Be sure to rest and keep it propped up whenever possible. And in a week or two it may be well."

"May be?" Valten asked.

Bartel shrugged. "I can't say for sure. It depends on whether she is careful or not. But I do not believe it is broken."

Bartel moved his stool closer, and Valten squeezed her hand with his right one as Bartel took his poor swollen left hand. Bartel turned it every which way and pressed his fingers on the back of Valten's hand, which seemed three times its normal size and was covered in dark shades of purple and green.

Valten's good hand tightened on Gisela's, and sweat appeared at his temple. Bartel bent Valten's fingers forward while pressing down on the broken bone in the back of his hand. Valten's face took on an ashen color as sweat ran down his cheek, but he kept his jaw clenched and did not make a sound or pull away.

What good did it do to press on the broken bone? Her heart constricted at the pain he was inflicting. But she kept quiet, hoping the healer knew what he was doing and that he was doing Valten more good than harm.

Bartel then grasped the knuckle of Valten's middle finger, held his wrist with his other hand, and yanked in opposite directions.

Valten let out a gasp, then he slumped forward, breathing hard. Perspiration coursed down his temple and cheek, beading on his forehead and upper lip.

Gisela glared at Bartel. Must he make Valten suffer so? She leaned forward and touched Valten's arm, wishing she could comfort him. His eyes were closed and he was still pale and breathing hard.

"Don't move," Bartel said. "I'll be right back with a splint and some cold water." The man stood and stumped out of the room.

Gisela moved her hand along his upper arm. "Are you all right?" she asked softly.

He grunted.

"Was it necessary to cause you so much pain? I don't think I like that man."

One corner of Valten's mouth went up, but she wasn't sure if it was a half smile or a grimace. "He had to reset the bone. If he didn't, it wouldn't grow back correctly."

That nasty Ruexner. This was all his fault. And to think he was her cousin!

"I'm so sorry," Gisela said, caressing his arm. "Can I get you something? I wish you could lie down."

"I am well." Valten's voice sounded gruff and irritable, but when he spoke again, his voice was softer, and he turned his head to look at her. "It is nothing, *liebchen*. I've had broken bones before."

Her heart missed a beat at his calling her *liebchen* again.

"You wouldn't want to marry a man with a crooked hand, would you?" There was a teasing light in his gray-green eyes.

A burst of honesty made her whisper, "I would want to marry you no matter what your hand looked like."

The teasing glint in Valten's eyes turned more serious, and he focused on her lips. She was about to lean forward and kiss him when Bartel came back into the room. He was carrying a bucket in one hand and some sticks and bandages in the other.

Valten reached for her hand again with his uninjured one and squeezed it, as if he knew what was coming wouldn't be pleasant.

Gisela squeezed back and held her breath as Bartel carefully took Valten's broken hand and placed the sticks on either side then wrapped a long strip of cloth around it a few times before tying it tightly in place.

"Now put your hand in this water—you will have to sit on the floor."

Valten got down on the floor beside her bench, where he could lean his back against the wall. Bartel placed the bucket beside him and Valten dipped his hand in. The only evidence of his pain was his closed eyes, the tightness in his jaw where a muscle flexed whenever he clenched his teeth, and the creases of tension in his forehead.

"I wish I had some snow or ice," Bartel said, "but the cold water will do almost as well. Leave it in until I come back." And he left the room again.

Gisela scooted back on her bench until she was leaning against the wall beside Valten. She drew his good hand up to her lips. After discreetly kissing his knuckles, she held his hand in her lap and compared his massive fingers to hers. Many scars—some long, some short, some mere dots—covered his skin. But she thought his hand beautiful. His nails were clean and short, his hand wide and calloused, and she caressed his fingers, wishing she could take away the pain in his other hand.

Valten was looking at her like he wanted to kiss her. But alas, he couldn't reach her lips sitting on the floor, and he was fairly immobile, with his hand in the bucket.

"Are you sure you want to marry me?" She wasn't sure what made her ask him.

He looked a bit confused. "Why would you ask?"

Do I dare say it? "You haven't said you love me. It may be silly, but I want you to marry me because you love me, not out of a sense of duty or propriety." She tried to look teasing and flippant, but she watched his face for his reaction.

A look came over his features—confusion or hurt, she wasn't sure. "Haven't I shown you I love you by my actions, by coming to rescue you? By kissing you and telling you that you were beautiful? Did I deal with you in any way that made you think I didn't love you?"

The tears that she couldn't seem to get rid of lately came rushing in. Her bottom lip trembled, and she clamped down on it with her teeth. She wasn't sure what she felt—anger, embarrassment, pain. Was it so terrible that she wanted him to say the words? Perhaps her stepmother's evil treatment had made it difficult for her to believe that anyone could love her. But hadn't Valten shown her that he did love her? He'd risked his life to save her multiple times. What could be more loving than that? She felt guilty for demanding that he say it. And yet, she still wanted him to.

She let go of his hand and turned away as a tear slipped down her cheek. She wiped it away with her fist, wondering if he would decide he didn't want to marry someone so teary-eyed and bothersome.

I am a dim-witted oaf. He had no sense when it came to talking to Gisela and telling her what she wanted to hear. And now he had made her cry by making her feel bad for wanting him to say he loved her. "You are right," he said. She didn't turn her head to look at him.

Of course she would wonder if he loved her. When she'd confessed in the church tower that she loved him, he hadn't told her he loved her in return. He'd been too intent on kissing her. He'd asked her to marry him, but he hadn't said he loved her.

"I should have told you I loved you. I'm sorry."

She was wiping her face, trying to hide her tears. "I understand if you don't," she said in a watery voice. "You don't have to marry me if you don't love me."

Was she not listening to him? He closed his eyes, then sighed. To get angry with her would not help. He knew that from experience with his sisters. If he grew annoyed with them for crying, they just cried harder. Besides, Gisela was worth a hundred confessions of love.

He reached out and ran his hand along her arm until he caught her hand in his. She continued to wipe her face with her other hand and still wouldn't look at him.

"Listen to me. I love you, Gisela." He leaned toward her, as far as he was able. "I was falling in love with you almost from the moment I saw you, and had nearly made up my mind to ask you to marry me the night of the banquet."

"Truly?" She turned her face to him, her mouth open and her eyes wide. Her lashes were wet with tears. "But why? I'm not a duke's daughter, or even a wealthy knight's daughter. I'm only an orphan, and one who's related to your worst enemy, at that."

"Why would I care if you were a duke's daughter, or wealthy?"

"I thought a duke's son would need to marry someone whose status was closer to his own."

Valten sighed as he looked into her deep blue eyes, made even bluer by her tears. "I don't need prestige or wealth," he said softly. "I need you, and I want you with me forever." He looked at her lips just above him, so sweet and tempting.

Her bottom lip quivered and she captured it with her teeth.

Valten went on. "I want to marry you. I haven't been able to think about anything but you, and I could barely keep my mind on the tournament because of it." He pulled her hand closer, placing it over his heart, forcing her to lean over him. "I love you and only you." He looked deeply into her lovely blue eyes. "I've always been a man of action. I'm not like my brother, Gabe, who seems to know the right thing to say. And if I didn't have my hand in a bucket of water, I'd come up there and show you how much I love you."

Her eyes went wide again. "What?"

He gave her a wicked smile, but when she looked alarmed, he said, "I only want to kiss you."

She climbed down off the bench.

"Be careful of your ankle," he said, as she knelt beside him and slipped her arms around his neck.

She stared at him in a way that made him glad he was alive ... *very* glad. Then she closed her eyes and the gap between them and pressed her lips to his so fervently it made him thank God again for protecting him so many times. He wrapped his arm around her waist and kissed her just as fervently, hoping she could hear "I love you" loud and clear in his actions. But if the words "I love you" had this kind of effect, he could imagine himself saying them quite a lot in the years to come.

She pulled away, holding his face in her hands. "I used to sit at my window, when I felt alone, and stare at the towers of Hagenheim Castle and wonder about you—where you were, what you were doing. I wondered what it would be like to see you again. It feels like a dream to hear you say you love me."

Touching her cheek with his fingertips, her skin was softer than silk. He slipped his hand behind her head and pulled her in for another kiss.

"I will always love you, and you will never be alone again." He touched his forehead to hers. "When my brother asked me to break my betrothal to Sophie, I was angry. But now I'm grateful. I know God planned all along for me to find you and marry you." Gisela was *his* damsel in distress, and she loved him. Even if he wasn't good at thinking of charming words, now that he knew how she felt about "I love you," he would say them every day. For the rest of their lives.

Chapter 31

She took a deep breath to keep the tears of joy from flowing. When had she become such a weepy person? Her stepmother had said horrible things to her, hurt her physically, and yet Gisela had rarely ever cried.

Gisela was grateful to Valten's brother too. "I shall have to remember to thank both Lord Gabehart and Lady Sophie."

Valten brushed his thumb over her cheek.

She sat on the floor beside him, letting him gather her to his side, and rested her head against his chest. She'd never felt happier, but thoughts of her stepmother invaded, and even though she'd rather just keep kissing Valten, Bartel would probably be back at any moment.

"What will become of my stepmother and stepsisters when we go back to Hagenheim?"

"What do you want to become of them?" He squeezed her tighter.

She thought for a moment. In spite of the fact that she had often hated them, especially her stepmother, she found she didn't really like imagining her in the dungeon. It must be a terrible place. But she did hope her stepmother and Irma and Contzel were thinking about how badly they had treated her and were wishing they had been kinder. She hoped they had trouble sleeping at night. She hoped they shuddered at the thought of

Gisela getting revenge on them, now that the duke's son loved her and was marrying her—now that *she* had power over *them*.

No, that was wrong. The priest had told her once, "Vengeance is mine, saith the Lord." It was wrong for her to hate her stepmother and stepsisters, no matter what they had done to her.

Gisela sighed. "I don't want to get revenge on them. And I want to forgive them, but I don't ever want to see them again." She rubbed her cheek against his shirt. The men must have brought supplies, because his tunic was new, and he smelled better now that he was clean. "My father's house rightfully belongs to my stepmother. But do you think it would be acceptable to move my father's horses to Hagenheim Castle's stables?"

He gave her another squeeze. "Yes, I think that will be the least your stepmother can do. The horses shall be her wedding gift to you."

"Whether she likes it or not." Gisela giggled. But she suppressed her delight in imagining Evfemia's discomfiture. *Don't be vengeful.* It was enough to know she would no longer be under her stepmother's control, that she was finally loved. It was what she'd always longed for.

Gisela was lying on the bench with her foot propped up per Bartel's orders that night. Valten sat beside her, in a chair this time, with his hand again in a bucket of cold water for the second time that day, sneaking kisses from her whenever no one was looking. Three of the seven men were playing musical instruments, while the others tapped their feet or clapped their hands. A more pleasant night Gisela could hardly imagine.

Bartel came toward them. He took Valten's hand out of the bucket of water and dried it carefully, then took off the splint. After his hand had fully dried, he put on another splint and wrapped it tightly.

"We shall repeat this twice a day while you are here."

As soon as Bartel left the room Roslind burst out, "Sophie and Gabe are here!"

Gisela took her foot down from the bench and sat up straight. Valten stood too and sat down beside her on the bench.

He whispered, "Now you'll get to meet my brother and Sophie."

Gisela was too nervous to reply. She looked down at her dress. Roslind had washed her beautiful ball gown, but it still looked the worse for wear, reflecting the rough days and nights spent sleeping on the ground, in a cave, and hurrying through forests. Perhaps she could explain and Lady Sophie wouldn't think too little of her. But she had heard that Valten's former betrothed, though she was a duke's daughter, had grown up with a cruel stepmother who made her work as a scullery maid—not so different from Gisela's life. She was excited to meet her.

The front door opened and two people swept in. The man was tall, although not as tall as Valten, and smiled as he took the cloak from the lady's shoulders. His hair was darker than Valten's, but from his profile, she did see a slight resemblance between them. His lady greeted the seven men, clasping the hands of each one and bidding them to rise, as they had all fallen to one knee in front of her. Her voice was high but pleasant, and she laughed good-naturedly. She stood with her back to Valten and Gisela. Valten rose and walked toward them. Gisela stood and waited.

When Gabe caught sight of him, his smile grew wider. They embraced for a moment and clapped each other on the back. Valten politely took Sophie's hand and bowed over it.

"We didn't expect to see you here." Sophie's voice was warm and kind, but without the least bit of flirtation. Her head was turned now so that Gisela could see her face. She was beautiful, with hair as black as night, and delicate but perfectly proportioned features. "Oh, what happened to you?" She pointed to Valten's splinted and bandaged hand.

"Just a minor tournament injury."

"How was the tournament?" Gabe asked.

"I won."

"Of course you did." Gabe clapped him on the back again and laughed.

"I have someone I want you both to meet." Valten turned and motioned Gisela forward with his hand.

She tried not to limp as she walked forward. Her cheeks heated as they all turned their attention to her. Sophie was elegant, beautifully dressed, so easy and graceful. Gisela felt like a servant in her presence. And since Sophie was the daughter of a duke, Gisela curtsied.

"This is Gisela Mueller, and she and I are to be married."

"Oh, how wonderful!" Sophie bent and clasped Gisela's hand, drawing her up, then embracing her.

"I am so happy for you." Sophie pressed her cheek to Gisela's, then pulled away and looked her in the eye. "You will be so happy, I am sure. Valten is a wonderful man, and you must be very special to have won his heart." Her sincerity fairly glowed from her eyes.

Gabe was congratulating Valten, saying something about how he didn't need any help finding a beautiful wife. Then he turned to her and squeezed her hand. "Welcome to the family."

"Thank you." Those unwelcome tears still weren't finished embarrassing her, as they stung her eyes again at the truly warm and sincere looks Valten's brother and his wife were giving her. "I am very happy to meet you both."

"And how wonderful that we have found you here!" Sophie was delightful in her enthusiasm. And Gisela now noticed that she also was looking a bit rounded in the middle; she was expecting a child. "Will you be able to accompany us to Hagenheim?"

Valten nodded. "If Gisela's ankle is well enough."

Sophie exclaimed over Gisela, and she had to explain that it wasn't badly hurt, only a minor sprain. "Valten's hand is much more seriously injured than my ankle."

That led to questions about how he hurt his hand at the tournament. So while Gabe and Sophie sat down to eat some cold meat, cheese, and bread after their long journey, they begged Valten and Gisela to sit with them and tell them about the events of the last few days.

Had it only been a few days since Gisela was living at home with Evfemia, Irma, and Contzel, cleaning up after them and helping Wido tend to the horses? Valten was telling them about the jousts and battles, and of Gisela spying Ruexner's squire putting poison hemlock in Sieger's food.

"And then Valten saved me from Ruexner."

Valten looked her in the eye, and she found she didn't want to turn away.

"That is just as it should be," Sophie said.

Valten winked at her, and Gisela blushed.

Valten continued the story, telling of the kidnapping, and Gisela was relieved he didn't tell them of her stepmother locking her in her chamber and making a deal with Ruexner to force Gisela to marry him. A stab of shame went through her at the thought of this beautiful, elegant lady knowing that Gisela's family could treat her so despicably.

"What happened then?" Sophie asked. "Did Valten go after you and rescue you?"

Gisela nodded. "He gave himself up to Ruexner and his men to save me." She told the remainder of the story quickly.

Gabe stared at her, openmouthed, while she talked. When she had finished her tale, he looked at Valten and said, "I am impressed, as always, big brother."

"Gisela must hear your story of rescuing Sophie from an evil duchess and her archer."

"Oh yes," Sophie said, her face lively, as she reached over and squeezed Gisela's arm. "I shall tell you all about that, and you shall have to tell me more about your adventure with Valten."

Valten placed his hand on Gisela's back and stood. "But now I think the ladies need to get some sleep."

"I agree." Gabe looked at Sophie with such loving concern in his eyes that it made Gisela sigh.

Four weeks later, in Hagenheim Castle, Gisela stared into the looking glass Margaretha held up for her. *The most blessed girl in the world*, Gisela told her reflection. If her father and mother were here, would they be proud and happy for her? In her heart, she knew the answer was yes.

"You're so beautiful," Margaretha gushed. "Your hair is the prettiest shade of blonde, so full and bouncy. And your eyes shimmer like a moonlit lake. Valten is so blessed. You have the sweetest disposition, but you're not afraid to make my brother pay attention and talk to you. He's not much for talking, as I'm sure you know. He's just stubborn. But you are good for him. He won't get away with ignoring you, I have a feeling." She grinned. "I'd never before seen that look he gets on his face when he looks at you."

"He loves me." The wonder of it was breathtaking.

"Yes." Margaretha sighed dramatically. "Come. You mustn't be late." Margaretha gave her a little push to turn her toward the stairs. "They'll blame me and say I was talking too much."

Gisela hurried down the steps, her stomach quaking at facing all the people that had come to see the next duke of Hagenheim wed her, a little nobody with no claim to noble birth or wealth. What if everyone laughed at her? What if they were laughing at Valten even now, ridiculing him for not marrying at least a baron's daughter?

By the time she reached the bottom of the steps, her knees were shaking and she could barely stand. But when she looked up, Valten was holding his hand out to her. The fierce look on his face softened to the look he wore for no one but her.

Her stomach settled to normal and her legs felt strong again as she placed her hand in his. Without a word, he tucked her hand in the crook of his arm and started out the door.

As they walked from the castle and through the town square and Marktplatz, down the street toward the cathedral, she caught glimpses of Evfemia. Her stepmother had Gisela to thank for her freedom, since Gisela had spoken to Duke Wilhelm and asked him to free her from the dungeon. But Rainhilda, Evfemia, Irma, and Contzel were formally reprimanded by Duke Wilhelm, in Gisela's presence, for helping Ruexner to kidnap Gisela. The duke ordered them never to come near Gisela again without her expressed permission. Sir Edgar, Rainhilda's father, was so angry with her, when he heard what she had done, that he sent her to live with relatives in the north, the land of frozen lakes.

She had given her stepfamily permission to come to the wedding, but they were not allowed at the wedding feast afterward. Now as her stepsisters stood with the rest of the crowd, Irma scrunched her face into a sour grimace. Contzel poked out her tongue at her sister, then moved to the other side of her mother, away from Irma. Apparently, no one else wanted to be around Irma either, after what she and Evfemia had done to Gisela. It seemed wise to their former friends to distance themselves from the family that Duke Wilhelm had forbidden to go near the Earl of Hamlin's beloved bride.

Valten's parents, Duke Wilhelm and Lady Rose, in contrast, were smiling and looking content and happy. Valten's siblings—Margaretha, Kirstyn, Steffan, Wolfhart, Gabe with his wife, Sophie, and Adela—all smiled and waved from a few feet away. Valten gave them a half smile, but Gisela waved back. Gabe nodded and Sophie sent Gisela a tiny wave, then Sophie covered her mouth with her hand as her eyes filled with tears. Ava was always more prone to tears when she was pregnant too.

Gisela took a deep breath and hugged Valten's arm. He glanced down at her. She tilted her head up and he rewarded her with a brief kiss. He bent lower to whisper in her ear, "I love you, queen of beauty and love."

He smiled and faced forward again.

For a man of action and few words, the ones he did say were quite lovely.

~ THE END ~

[illegible]

THE END

Acknowledgments

*Once again, I want to thank all the wonder*ful people who make my books a reality, including everyone at Zondervan in all the various departments, many of whom I don't know but I deeply appreciate. Thanks to Gwen Hendrickson, Sara Merritt, Chriscynethia Floyd, and Marcus Drenth, who work behind the scenes to get my books noticed; to Jaime Krupp and all the wonderful people in the sales department who get my books in stores; and to my talented editor, Jacque Alberta, who is able to look at the big picture and point out plot holes, repetitions, and missed opportunities.

Thanks to Mike Heath of Magnus Creative for blessing me with another beautiful cover that I love. You always wow me!

I want to thank my horse expert, Cory Kohl, who is always willing to answer my questions. If there are equine mistakes in the book, it's solely my fault, because Cory knows horses.

I want to thank my wonderful beta readers who help me so much more than they realize: Grace Dickerson, Joe Dickerson, Faith Dickerson, Carol Moncado, Debbie Lynne Costello, Linore Burkard, Regina Carbulon, Caren Fullerton, Jamie Driggers, and Suzy Parish.

I also want to express my thanks to Sir Walter Scott for inventing the historical novel, and for writing *Ivanhoe*, which inspired the tournament scenes in *The Captive Maiden*.

And in case anyone doubts Dan Doty when he says the character of Friar Daniel was named after him, it is true.

Thanks to my family—Joe, Grace, and Faith—for being so supportive when I'm doing edits! I love you.

And thanks again to my readers, who keep me writing and motivated and striving to make my stories the best I can. Thank you so much for your encouraging notes! God bless you.

Want more? Check out this excerpt from

The Fairest Beauty

for a taste of Sophie's story, then buy the book, in stores now!

Prologue

Pinnosa passed through the town square and the cobblestone *Marktplatz*. Hagenheim Castle loomed straight ahead. Once she passed the guard at the gatehouse, she would need to find her way to the young lord.

A chill passed over her thin, old shoulders. This fever, brought on by rain and exhaustion, would probably kill her, but if she could only make it to the castle, could only tell them that Sophie was still alive, Pinnosa's life would not have been in vain. Perhaps God would forgive her for helping the duchess perpetuate so many lies.

She plodded forward, wanting to hurry, but she could only force her swollen feet to take slow, mincing steps. Sweat dripped from her eyebrows even as she shivered and fought the urge to drop to the ground, close her eyes, and sleep.

"Who goes there?"

Pinnosa stopped, then leaned her head back as far as she could. When she parted her cracked lips, no sound came out. The guard's face began to blur, her knees trembled, and the ground quickly came up to meet her. Strange how she didn't . . . even . . . feel it.

Chapter 1

Sophie kept her head bowed as she waited for the duchess to speak. She started to clasp her hands together but stopped. Clasped hands presented an image of idleness, the duchess often said, and the gesture sent her into a rage every time. Sophie let her arms hang limply at her sides.

Carefully, she peeked through her lashes at Duchess Ermengard. The woman's skin was unnaturally white, her hair dyed ebony using black hickory hulls. Her lips were stained red from berries, and her teeth were so white they made Sophie want to shade her eyes. Did the duchess ever think of anything besides beauty? The irony was that she was naturally beautiful and would look better without all the powder and dye.

The duchess stood unmoving, not making a sound. The silence began to crowd against Sophie's ears. Duchess Ermengard liked to draw out the waiting, knowing it only increased her victims' apprehension. Having to stand and wait to hear what her punishment would be was perhaps the worst part.

At long last, when the duchess addressed Sophie, her hoarse voice sent a chill down Sophie's spine.

"So this is how you repay my kindness to you? You, an orphan, and a girl at that. I could have let you starve by the roadside. Others would have done so in my place."

No one but you would be so cruel. Sophie's breaths came

faster—she was dangerously close to speaking—but she forced the words down.

"How could you be so audacious as to think ... when I rightfully punish one of my servants ... No. No, I want you to confess what you have done. You seem to enjoy prayer. Surely you enjoy confession as well. Now confess." Sophie's skin crawled as the duchess's voice lowered to a slow, quiet whisper. "What ... did ... you ... do?"

Sophie almost wished the duchess would scream instead. A dark feeling of oppression, of an evil presence in the room, came over her, as it often did when the duchess was interrogating her. *Jesus, help me. Take away my anger.*

The oppressive feeling subsided.

Following the rote formula required by the duchess, Sophie began, "Duchess Ermengard, your servant Sophie confesses to sneaking food to your servant Roslind while Roslind was being punished in the dungeon." Sophie curtsied humbly. *Oh, God, please, please, please let it be enough. Let my confession be enough to appease her. And let me appear meek before her.*

Silence. Again. With a churning stomach, Sophie waited for the duchess to speak. Her hands trembled but she dared not hide them behind her back. The duchess had a rule against that as well.

Sophie waited so long for the duchess's next words that her mind began to wander, imagining what her friends, the other servants, would be doing now. But she pulled herself back, bracing herself for what the duchess would say or do next.

"You confess as though you're not truly sorry for what you did."

"Please forgive me, Duchess Ermengard." Sophie suppressed a shudder. This was not going well. It was no longer a matter of if she'd be punished, but how severely. She bowed her head lower, hoping to appear truly repentant. Even though she wasn't.

"And there is more, isn't there?" Once again, the duchess let the silence linger.

What would the duchess accuse her of now? Sophie searched her mind for things she had done that the duchess may have uncovered. She had given food to some starving children who had come begging at the kitchen door, but that had been days ago. She searched her memory for something else ...

Then she remembered. Yesterday she had followed a guard into the woods, and after he'd heaved a sack of squirming puppies into the river, against her better judgment, Sophie had dived in after them. Dragging the heavy cloth bag from the bottom of the shallow river, she'd dumped out all five creatures on the riverbank, wet but alive. Someone must have seen her and told the duchess. She couldn't read minds, could she?

"Nothing to say? You know what you did. You defied me." The duchess's voice sounded like the hiss of a snake. "You followed the guard to the river in order to save those worthless, mongrel puppies. You are a disobedient, deceitful, horrible little wretch." She spat out the words as if they were venom.

Sophie's mouth went dry. Duchess Ermengard hated dogs, especially lap dogs. Anything small and helpless incited her hatred. And these puppies would never grow anywhere close to the size of hunting dogs, which the duchess gave to Lorencz the huntsman to use in his deer hunts.

"I expect my orders to be obeyed. I don't expect my scullery maid to defy them." She said the words *scullery maid* the way she always did, as though they were a curse.

Sophie thought about the tiny dogs she'd saved and remembered their soft fur and the way they'd whimpered and licked her hand. For a moment she could almost feel the little brown-and-white one snuggled against her cheek. The feel of his furry little face against her skin had made her feel loved, as if he knew she'd saved him.

"You are a wicked ..." The cold, hard edge of the duchess's voice tore Sophie out of her pleasant memory.

Sophie closed her eyes. *I will not listen. I will not listen . . .*

". . . rebellious, disrespectful girl. You will learn to respect me. You were nothing, a changeling orphan, an ugly child. You wouldn't even be alive if it weren't for me."

I am not wicked. I am not ugly.

The duchess was snarling now, her voice growing louder. "You will learn not to treat my rules with contempt. You will be disciplined."

Sophie didn't have to open her eyes to see the malicious glint in the duchess's eyes or to see her lips pressed into that tiny, pinched, cold smile, the smile she always wore when doling out punishment.

I am not wicked. I am not rebellious . . .

Sophie longed to touch the wooden cross that hung from her neck, to squeeze it and feel comforted by the thought of her Savior's suffering, his compassion and forgiveness. But she didn't dare. If the duchess found the cross that was hidden under her dress, she would tear it away from Sophie and destroy it.

"For your wickedness," the duchess went on, slowly, as though savoring each word, "you shall spend the next two days and nights in the dungeon with no food or water."

Two days and nights. Sophie's heart seemed to stop beating. But at least, maybe, the duchess was finished with her.

Sophie curtsied, keeping her head low. She focused on replying according to the duchess's rules. "Let it be as you say, Duchess Ermengard. I am your servant Sophie."

Two soldiers came forward and grabbed her by her arms.

Just as she relaxed slightly, Sophie heard, "Wait! Bring her here."

Sophie's stomach dropped. What would the duchess do now? Sophie determined not to show panic as the two guards dragged her forward. Any expression of fear would only make things worse.

"Look at me," the duchess ordered.

Sophie lifted her face, preparing herself for the black emptiness of the duchess's eyes.

As soon as their gaze met, the duchess lifted her hand and slapped Sophie across the face.

Stunned, Sophie closed her eyes against the sting, tasting blood on her teeth. Her eyes watered but she refused to cry. She took deep, slow breaths to drive away the tears as the duchess kept up her cold stare. *I mustn't show weakness.*

Time and silence hung heavy in the air. Then Duchess Ermengard ordered, "Take her away."

The guards pulled Sophie, stumbling, across the stone floor toward the dungeon.

Gabehart hurried down the corridor with his father, Duke Wilhelm. The slap of their boots on the flagstones echoed against the walls. An old woman had been brought in the day before, feverish and unconscious. Gabe had paid the visitor little mind until their healer, Frau Lena, sent for him and his father, saying the woman had awakened and was telling a tale they needed to hear firsthand to believe.

Of course, if his older brother Valten hadn't broken his leg a few days ago, keeping him confined to his chamber, she wouldn't have sent for Gabe at all.

Gabe and his father entered the healer's tower and strode across the room to the sickbed. The mysterious traveler lay still, her white hair plastered to her head, her wrinkled eyelids closed. Her lips were white and her cheeks gray. *Is she already dead?*

Frau Lena, their tall, red-haired healer, curtsied to Duke Wilhelm. "Your Grace"—a nod to Gabe—"my lord. Thank you for coming."

"Are we too late?" Gabe glanced from the healer to the old woman on the bed.

Frau Lena smiled. "She's only sleeping." The healer's expression grew thoughtful as she stared down at her. "She'd been mumbling since she was brought in, but her words made no sense—something about saving someone before the evil one kills her." Frau Lena shrugged. "She was so feverish I didn't pay attention. But this morning, she awoke. Her fever had lessened, and she begged me to send for 'the young lord who is betrothed to Duke Baldewin's daughter.'"

What? Gabe glanced at his father. Duke Wilhelm's forehead creased.

"Go on," Duke Wilhelm said.

"When I told her Duke Baldewin's daughter died as a small child many years ago, she said, 'No, it's a lie. She lives. Tell the young lord to go to her, posthaste, and save her from ...'" Frau Lena hesitated.

"From?" Gabe found himself leaning toward the healer.

Frau Lena let out a deep breath, then whispered, "From Duchess Ermengard."

Gabe sank back on his heels. Visiting merchants often told stories about the queenly duchess, claiming she never left her castle in Hohendorf, dabbled in black magic to the extent of placing curses on those who crossed her, and even poisoned people. But Gabe had never seen her. Rumors said she never left her castle.

If Duke Baldewin's daughter *were* still alive, it made sense that she could be in danger from the shadowy Ermengard; Duke Baldewin's daughter would be sixteen, maybe seventeen years old, making her a threat to the duchess's rule. Though surely someone would have corrected the erroneous report of her demise by now. The truth would surely have leaked out and spread to Hagenheim. Or so one would think.

And if Duke Baldewin's daughter were still alive, that would mean Valten was still betrothed. His brother was going to be awfully surprised to find out he had a bride.

A strangled croaking sound came from the bed. The old woman's faded blue eyes opened and locked on Gabe's face. She lifted an emaciated hand toward him, beckoning him closer with a crooked, skeletal finger.

"Come here."

He looked back at his father, who nodded, so Gabe stepped forward and dropped to one knee by her bedside.

He was handsome, though he looked quite young. There was something so pleasing in his features. Such gentleness, an earnest look in his eyes. If only he were strong enough, clever enough … *God, help him.*

Pinnosa's voice was weak, along with the rest of her, and she willed her words to reach the young man's ears. He was Sophie's only hope. "My lord, I am an old woman, soon to look my last on this earth." She paused to breathe. She was here. The one she had journeyed to find knelt before her, and she would soon impart her secret to him. If she weren't so feeble, she'd laugh with joy.

The man picked up her limp hand and pressed it gently. Such kindness to a poor, old woman on her deathbed.

"And you are Duke Wilhelm's son?"

"I am."

"The secret I have to tell you has cost the lives of more than one person." Pinnosa spoke haltingly, stopping frequently to draw in another shallow breath. "You must be brave, strong, and highly favored by God to escape the same fate. Are you willing to hear my tale?"

"Aye, frau. Proceed."

"I was a servant in Duke Baldewin's castle when his daughter was born. The poor mother died, and His Grace was heartbroken. His wife had been exceedingly fair—her skin, pure and perfect as new-fallen snow; her eyes, the bluest blue; and her hair, black as ebony and silky as a waterfall. The baby girl was the very image of her."

Pinnosa closed her eyes to rest for a moment. Her strength seemed to be ebbing away with every word she spoke. She must impart only the most pertinent information. After managing to take in a little air, she opened her eyes and continued.

"The duke remarried. His new wife was beautiful, but heartless and cold. I believe she killed the duke."

Shock flickered over the young lord's face. He was sheltered and seemed inexperienced, but at least the surprise was quickly replaced by anger. *Stoke that fire inside him, that sense of outraged justice I see in his eyes.*

"People would tell me I shouldn't say such things. But I am old. It doesn't matter what happens to me if I can save Sophie."

"Did you walk all the way from Hohendorf?"

Pinnosa tried to laugh, but all she could manage was a wheeze. "You can look at my feet and legs if you don't believe me." They were swollen to twice their normal size. "I would walk much farther for Sophie."

The only way she'd been able to get away without raising the duchess's suspicions was by faking her own death. She'd taken a bit of one of the duchess's sleeping potions, which slowed her heart and breathing until people thought she was dead. She had bribed the mute son of a farmer to dig her back up after dark. It had been risky and terrifying to be buried alive beneath the cold earth, but if Pinnosa had left the castle any other way, the duchess would have sent her men after her to kill her. Duchess Ermengard was too powerful, too clever. Pinnosa was one of only two people still alive who knew that Duchess Ermengard had faked the death of her stepdaughter. The duchess had long ago killed everyone else who could have revealed this secret.

"Who is Sophie?" the young lord asked.

"Sophie is a servant in Duchess Ermengard's service. A scullery maid. But the truth is she is the duke's daughter." Pinnosa managed to squeeze his hand. "I saw in a dream that the duchess will kill her soon if someone doesn't intercede. Please ... save her. If you don't hurry, Duchess Ermengard will destroy her. She delights in tormenting her. Sophie ... so kind and gentle ... may God ... watch ... over her."

It was done. Now she could sleep.

Chapter 2

The moment the woman stopped talking, her hand went limp in his. Gabe waited as Frau Lena examined her. After a few minutes, Frau Lena shook her head.

"Her heart has stopped. She's gone."

A chill passed over Gabe's shoulders and he shuddered. What if it were true? A beautiful girl, born to be a duchess but being used as a scullery maid, tormented by her own stepmother. How would he feel if such a thing happened to one of his sisters? His chest tightened at the cruel injustice.

He couldn't stop staring at the old woman's body, trying to divine the truth from her features. But what reason did she have to lie? Someone had to at least investigate the old woman's claims and attempt to help this Sophie.

Valten should save her. His brother Valten was the warrior, always excelling in tourneys, in jousting and sword fighting with the best knights of the Holy Roman Empire and beyond. But right now, Valten couldn't even walk without help.

"Gabe." His father touched his shoulder, pulling his gaze away from the face of the dead woman. "Come. We must discuss this with Valten."

Gabe followed his father through the castle corridor to Valten's chamber. What would his brother think of this woman's claim? Would he believe it? And who would their father send to uncover the truth in Hohendorf?

Gabe should go. His father had too many concerns and duties at home to go cantering off on a wild chase after a kitchen maid who may or may not be a dead duke's daughter. And Gabe couldn't imagine his father sending one of the knights out to handle something so intimately connected to their family.

He also had to admit that the thought of saving this girl himself was strangely appealing. No one thought of Gabe as a warrior. He was a rambler, a fun-loving friend, but certainly not a knight. He had never cared for fighting or jousting and left the tournaments to his older brother and his father's knights. As the second son, Gabe *should* have trained as a knight or applied himself to a trade such as a master mason or even joined the church. But none of those things appealed to him — a life of chastity least of all. He preferred roaming the countryside with his friends, sometimes drinking too much and doing other activities he was glad his parents knew nothing of. His few skills included flirting with fair maidens, playing the lute, and archery. In fact, archery was the only war sport in which he could best Valten.

If Gabe rescued his brother's betrothed while Valten lay helpless in bed with a broken leg, it would be perfectly ironic. Valten traveled the world entering tournaments and winning glory and gold. But Gabe could do one better — rescue a girl from a terrible fate, thwart an evil ruler, and complete a quest that should have been Valten's.

Perhaps Gabe wasn't as tall or as muscular as his brother, had not the sheer girth or physical power his brother possessed. But here was his opportunity to impress his parents, his brother, and even Brittola, the girl he was expected to marry.

Gabe followed close behind as his father entered Valten's bedchamber. The heir to the duchy of Hagenheim was propped up by pillows and reading a book.

"Thank God you've come." Valten closed the tome with a loud snap. "I was about to come out of my skin from boredom."

Valten was indeed pitiable in his forced confinement to his room. With all his purpose and energy and strength, the passivity of healing didn't fit him very well.

Gabe hung back as his father approached Valten's bed and began relating the story of the old woman who had just died in the healer's chambers and the tale she had told. Gabe watched closely as astonishment and something akin to disbelief clouded his brother's eyes.

Several moments passed while they waited for Valten to absorb the information. He seemed to be concentrating on the cover of the book in his lap, his eyebrows scrunched. Gabe had the strangest feeling that his future depended on what his brother would say.

When he finally spoke, Valten's voice was low. "Probably just an old woman's senile ramblings." He glanced up and met his father's eyes. "But we must find out."

Duchess Ermengard stared into her mirror. During the past year, tiny lines had appeared around her eyes. The white powder hid them. Mostly.

Sophie had no wrinkles or even a blemish. Ermengard's lip curled as she thought about the girl's pale, perfect skin and the natural red of her lips, her thick black eyelashes and brows. The way Lorencz the huntsman's eyes lingered on the girl made Ermengard's blood boil. Did he think the little chit was fairer than Ermengard? While two days in the dungeon should take some of that rosy glow out of the girl's cheeks, the duchess had started to question if she should keep that wretched child around. Ermengard enjoyed forcing her to work as a scullery maid, making her do her bidding. Inwardly she gloated over Duke Baldewin and imagined his pain; if he only knew what his only *beloved* daughter was suffering. But watching her capture the attention of Lorencz ... it was time to get rid of either her or Lorencz—or both.

She gazed into the mirror, studying her face more closely. Was her skin starting to sag beneath her chin? Perhaps if she cut off a fold of skin just below her jawline it would be tighter when it grew back together. She couldn't abide sagging jowls. She wouldn't allow them.

A knock sounded at the door. "Come in."

Lorencz entered and bowed low. She extended her hand and he kissed it, lingering long enough to make her smirk at him. *You'd* better *endear yourself to me ...*

"You wanted to see me?"

"Yes. I need you to do something."

"Anything, Your Grace."

Perhaps she should insist he call her something besides "Your Grace." That sounded too formal. Her husband had called Sophie "my precious," never noticing the seething rage it caused in her, his wife. He never called Ermengard sweet endearments like that. She could order Lorencz to call her that ... No. He wouldn't mean it.

What did everyone see in Sophie? It seemed as though her fellow servants couldn't do enough for her. They all flocked to her, wanting to help her. It was sickening.

"I want you to kill someone for me."

Lorencz did not look away from her direct gaze, a quality she admired in a man. "Did someone try to run away again? One of the servants?"

"No." But if they had, the penalty was death. The duchess couldn't afford to have anyone leaking her secrets. If the king knew of the people she had killed or of Sophie or of what had become of Duke Baldewin ... "I have just sent the scullery maid, Sophie, to the dungeon. I want you to gain her trust. Then, when she gets out, I want you to take her somewhere in the woods and kill her."

There, the look on his face ... was that disgust? Or merely distaste? Her huntsman wasn't going soft on her, was he?

"Take her some food or some wine, maybe. I want you to kill her without a struggle, without anyone knowing. No screams. I want her to simply ... disappear." She allowed a smile, imagining the girl's pain when Lorencz betrayed her, when he thrust his knife through her heart.

"You will have to bury her afterward. I don't want anyone finding her body. We'll say she ran away, and no one will be the wiser." *And no one will ever know who she truly is.*

Unless she was mistaken, Lorencz had turned a shade paler. "It shall be done as you say, Duchess Ermengard."

"Do not fail me. Now go."

Be sure to check out these additional award-winning fairy-tale reimagining's from Melanie Dickerson today!

The Healer's Apprentice

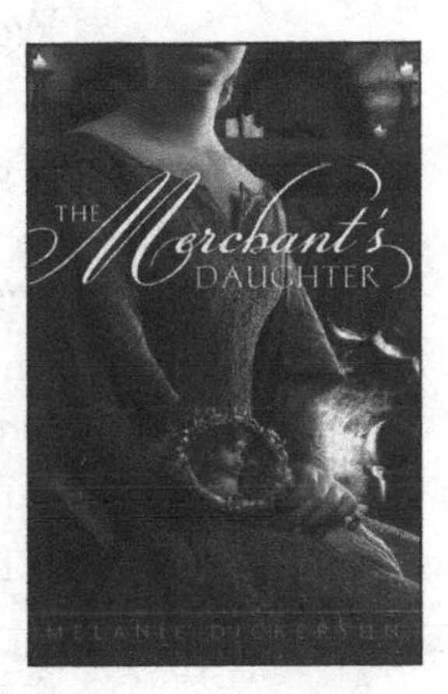

The Merchant's Daughter

The Fairest Beauty

Available in stores and online!